BORDERLANDS®
THE FALLEN

BORDERLANDS®
THE FALLEN

A NOVEL BY
JOHN SHIRLEY

Based on the video game from
Gearbox Software

GALLERY BOOKS
New York London Toronto Sydney New Delhi

Gallery Books
A Division of Simon & Schuster, Inc.
1230 Avenue of the Americas
New York, NY 10020

First Gallery Books trade paperback edition November 2011

GALLERY BOOKS and colophon are registered trademarks of Simon & Schuster, Inc.

For information about special discounts for bulk purchases, please contact Simon & Schuster Special Sales at 1-866-506-1949 or business@simonandschuster.com

The Simon & Schuster Speakers Bureau can bring authors to your live event. For more information or to book an event contact the Simon & Schuster Speakers Bureau at 1-866-248-3049 or visit our website at www.simonspeakers.com.

Manufactured in the United States of America

10 9 8 7 6 5 4 3 2 1

Library of Congress Cataloging-in-Publication Data is available.

ISBN 978-1-4391-9847-6
ISBN 978-1-4391-9851-3 (ebook)

Dedicated to the fans of Borderlands

I'm makin' monsters for my friends

—*The Ramones*

BORDERLANDS®
THE FALLEN

PROLOGUE

Riding in the bus from the spaceport to Fyrestone, looking out the dusty, louvered window at the craggy gray-blue landscape, the aluminum-blue sky, McNee can't believe he'd talked himself into coming back to this vicious planet.

It was all Roland's fault. Roland knows that McNee likes him. Took to him almost like a son—McNee is old enough to be Roland's old man. Takes advantage, that Roland, that's what he does, damn his eyes . . .

«McNee—easy pickings. Real juicy trove of Eridian weapons—just gotta take it from some oversized mutated cretins. No problem, right? Can't do it without you! Get your ass back here! We're burning daylight! —Roland.»

That's what the subspace message had said. But the real message was the "Can't do it without you" part. That's what McNee is a sucker for; that's what brings him to this hellworld on the outer edge of the galaxy. First time Roland had admitted he needs McNee's help. But of course, it's hard to find anyone you can really trust on Pandora.

2 | JOHN SHIRLEY

Speaking of which—there's that big chunk of a weapons dealer, Marcus Kincaid, chuckling to himself as he drives the creaky old hydrogen-cell-powered bus. They're alone on the bus, except for a Claptrap robot in the very back, muttering to itself. Kincaid, with his squat face and short black beard, isn't just the guy who drives the treasure hunters and prospectors in from the spaceport—he's the one who sells them weapons. Unauthorized weapons. Some good—some not so good. He brings you here, then sells a weapon to the guy who's likely to kill you in the next half hour. Or sells you the weapon to kill the guy trying to kill you. McNee doesn't have much use for Kincaid, but you have to put up with him.

From somewhere on the bus canned music plays, some group singing, *"Ain't no rest for the wicked, until we close our eyes for good . . ."*

They come to that old, decrepit billboard McNee sees every time he comes. *WELCOME TO PANDORA, Your Final Destination*—McNee wonders what wise guy came up with that slogan.

A skag runs across the road, the vicious four-legged, three-jawed predator leaping right into the bus's path. The bus doesn't slow and the skag becomes red mush on the windshield, before oozing off.

McNee shakes his head. Here he is, heading back into the Borderlands.

"Ha ha, time to wake up!" Kincaid says, glancing back at McNee. He speaks in a jovial, heavily accented growl. "It's a beautiful day, full of opportunity!" His accent sounds like one of the desert nomads of the homeworld, to McNee.

"Well, you got any new weapons in Fyrestone, Kincaid?"

"Got plenty new weapons always," Kincaid rumbles, chuckling. "Nice Eridian beauty, fry your enemy in ten seconds. If you can pay!"

McNee sighs. He'd blown most of his money from the last trip here—blew it on the Planet of Pleasure. But he didn't regret it. Good memories to get a man through a cold, lonely Pandora night. "Rumors of another Vault out on this dirtball somewhere, I heard . . ."

"Ah the Vault . . . So, you want to hear a story, eh?"

"Marcus—you really don't have to tell me that one again . . ." Kincaid tells the same story over and over to keep the Vault Hunters coming. So he could sell them weapons. Some story about the Vault he'd worked up talking to a nephew.

But once Marcus Kincaid gets started, it's hard to stop him. "What . . . about treasure hunters? Ha! Have I got a story for you!"

"I've actually heard it . . ."

"Pandora! This is our home! But make no mistake, this is not a planet of peace and love . . ."

"That's one hell of an understatement."

"They say that it's a waste planet, that it's dangerous. That only a fool would search for something of value here . . ."

"Thanks for that, Kincaid, always nice to hear that from you . . ."

"Many people tell it, the legend of the Vault—"

"That one's shut down, from what I heard," McNee says, leaning forward and asserting himself with jabs of his finger at Marcus Kincaid. "But what about that new Vault they're talking about—or some kind of crashed ship or something with a lot of artifacts, way out in the Borderlands . . ."

Marcus glances at him, scowling. "That is something maybe is not wise to talk about! Atlas, others . . . they don't like it when I ask . . . Best you not ask either. Just go after that weapons cache Roland wants you to find. Kill a few Psychos. Try to come back with all your fingers and toes."

"Wait—how'd you know what Roland said to me on subspace transmission?"

"Who you think he came to, to send the transmission? Me! And when you find the weapons cache—you sell it to me! I sell for profit! Everyone will be happy, ha ha." After a moment he adds: "If you live. Not so likely. Very dangerous out there where Roland has gone. Very dangerous . . ."

"Okay so it's dangerous."

"Very, very . . . very . . ."

"You *said* that, Kincaid."

". . . dangerous. So, back to my story—you're going to love this one, I promise . . ."

It was raining in the Arid Lands, on the planet Pandora.

"Some *arid* lands," Roland muttered to McNee, as they stared out the mouth of the cave, watching raindrops splash from rocks, flow in crevices. "Oughta be called the Wetlands."

"Don't happen but once or twice a year," McNee said, tinkering with an Anshin shield—Anshin was a not especially effective brand of force field armor.

Roland and McNee were a stark contrast. McNee was middle-aged, Roland was fairly young; McNee was as slender as Roland was bulky with muscle; as sunburnt and pink as Roland was dark-skinned.

"Rain'll spur some plant growth, mebbe," McNee went on, frowning over the device. "Wake up a Wyrm Squid to come out 'n' play."

"Don't care to meet any Wyrm Squids today," Roland declared. "I'm sure as hell not in the mood. Saw a big one eat a whole town once. It was hungrier than my fat aunt Matilda and that's going some. You gonna get that shield running or not?"

"I dunno, the rain seems to make the cheap ones short out and all we got's cheap ones. Need to get back to Fyrestone, get some decent gear. But you're all about, 'I *know* there's a big Atlas weapons cache out East in the Graves for the Brave, it'll be easy pickins!' Sure it will, Roland. And I think 'Why would I go any place called Graves for the Brave' anyway? But I just trail after Roland like a skag pup after a brain-damaged mama . . ."

"You *insisted* on coming along," Roland reminded him. But he was smiling to himself. For some reason he enjoyed McNee's eternal bitching.

"Who'd watch your back? A back a sniper couldn't miss, I might add, what with the size you are . . . Ow!" A small electric arc had jumped from the shield and he sucked his burnt finger. "The hell with this shield . . ." He tossed the tool and the broken shield aside. "I'll do without one today."

"Don't seem wise." Roland himself had a pretty strong Pangolin shield. "You oughta fix it."

"Don't seem wise to go without your Scorpio Turret either. And where the hell is it?"

"Not my fault that spiderant come outta the ground right under the Scorpio. I'll get it fixed up first chance. Looks like the rain's quitting . . . Speaking of skags, McNee, you did check this cave out all the way back, didn't you? Stinks of skag in here."

"I kilt a family of the buggers, in the back, while you were tucking the outrunner away. You want some skag meat, go back and skin 'em. The motherbuggers haven't been dead more'n twelve hours or so."

"I'll pass. Come on, we're burning daylight. Let's check the outrunner, see if it's swamped. Psycho Midgets might've messed with it."

Hefting his Tediore Defender—a shotgun he'd upgraded to vicious effectiveness—Roland ducked his head and led the way out of the low cave mouth, into the steaming afternoon. The clouds were parting; the sun was burning through, sucking streamers of mist from the wet ground. The red-stone canyon walls dripped water, but already the sandy ground had soaked up most of the rain. There was even a rainbow over the juttingly slanted butte.

"Another be-*yoot*-iful day!" McNee jeered. "On the most dangerous planet in the galaxy . . ."

Roland automatically scanned the ancient bed of the canyon for any movement. A little stream was running through the canyon; flowering bushes and purple thatch were poked up here and there.

He didn't see any of the local fauna. Almost all the animal life of Pandora was hostile. Anything you saw might attack you. It was a strange food chain—made up entirely of predators, as far as he could tell. Predators eating predators eating predators. But it was the humans, and the descendents of humans—the subhumans, really—who were the most troublesome creatures on the planet, to Roland's mind.

The rain released curious scents from the red and blue sands; some putrid, some spicy, some acrid, some earthy. A twisted, leafless growth, like branch coral, spiked on a nearby outcropping of clay—its tips seemed to be writhing. He paused and watched it warily. Some new threat?

"Hey now look there!" said McNee, admiring the writing bush. "That's gotta be a rare sight, some plant response to rain in the Arid Lands! Maybe something you see only a couple times a year . . . Could be no other humans saw it before . . ."

The plant's tubules extruded what looked like small tongues, the wet red organs "razzing" in every direction, fibrillating furiously, spitting some kind of seedlings.

Roland was more interested in scanning for enemies. There wasn't *too* much to worry about—just scythids, rakks, spiderants, bruisers, stalkers—

"I mean," McNee was saying, as they headed down the canyon, "I seen some pretty impressive critchers on this planet, but I tell you what, who knows what lives way underground? Besides the tunnel rats I mean. Now, in a cavern down in Freebottle, I saw somethin' like giant fleas—"

—bugmorphs, crystaliths, larva crab worms, tunnel rats, Nomads, goliaths—

"—fleas big as St. Bernards," McNee went on. "Turn a regular dog inside out with one slurp—"

—wyrm squids, drifters, skags, spitter skags, elder skags, alpha skags, corrosive skags, spiderants, gyro spiderants, Badass spiderant burners, Psychos, Midget Psychos, Burning Psychos, Badass Psychos, Roid Rage Psychos—

"—but I knew a guy tried to make a flea circus with 'em, hired a clown to get 'em to jump through hoops. The giant fleas ate the clown, though, first crack out of the box . . . Hey, looks like the outrunner's okay."

The open-air outrunner, hidden away between two boulders, looked untouched. It was even gleaming, a little cleaner from the rain. The outrunners were something like the old Desert Terrain Vehicles, with a big gun in the back. "I'll drive," Roland said. "You get on the turret."

"Okay—so we're going to find that weapons cache today?"

"Sure, sure," Roland said, climbing into the driver's seat. "We'll find the bandits, if they don't find us first, follow 'em back to the Graves of the Brave. It's hidden back there in the Hunter Lands. Somewhere. Anyway there's something going on back there—has to be. All kinds of mercs and bandits looking for something back there . . ."

"Yeah well—" McNee climbed up behind the turret in back, took hold of the big weapon, checking out the ammo feed. "I'm always hearing about something great right over the next sand dune. Usually don't turn up. I dunno why I came to this misbegotten planet."

"Same reason we all did," Roland said, fitting his shotgun into the gun rack. "Same reason the Dahl Corp. did, way back when. 'Cause it's wide open, there's treasure here, if you get lucky, and no one can tell you what to do."

"If you get lucky—that's the part I haven't worked out yet. You havin' some trouble startin' 'er up?"

Roland had to hit the ignition three times to get the engine to catch. Finally it roared to life. "There it is. Kind of slow starting. After we score the goods we gotta take it back to Scooter for servicing."

"If he's not dead! Every time I think I'm gonna see somebody back in the settlements, seems like half the time you hear, 'Oh so-and-so, the skags got him! Oh you mean her, the Psychos got 'em! Or the—'"

Roland gunned the engine, the noise drowning out

McNee's bellyaching. He rammed the vehicle into reverse so that McNee, cursing, had to clutch hard at the turret to keep from falling over.

"Why you son of a—"

Another roar of the engine muffled McNee as Roland screeched the outrunner around almost 360 degrees, then darted off to the east. He bumped the outrunner at a good clip across the rugged landscape, splashing through puddles, enjoying the wind in his face. The ground was shifting to the gray-blue that you saw so widely on Pandora. The pale blue sky was clearing, so that he could see the dark, wheeling shapes of rakks flying over the horizon. Not a threat at this distance.

Up ahead, the mist parted to show a narrowing of the canyon walls, a natural passageway just wide enough to get the outrunner through.

Roland slowed down to little more than walking speed, not knowing what was up ahead, not eager to run into an alpha skag head on, and not wanting to alert the bandits— or whoever else might be waiting for him. On Pandora, you never knew.

Maybe that's why he stayed on this misbegotten rock. Because you never knew. There was always another threat—which meant not much time to think. You didn't brood. You didn't think about the past. You just kept looking for that edge, for whatever it took to survive. It was one long adrenaline rush. Till you slammed into that final wall . . .

He eased through the twisty stone passageway, keeping the engine as quiet as possible. He listened for the screech of rakks, the burbling snarf of sniffling skags, the mad giggling of Psychos. But he heard only the wind keening through the narrow stone pass.

Then it widened, and a rolling plain opened ahead of them. Broken gray clouds admitted shafts of sunlight and mists swirled. He made out a group of skags far to the north—spots moving restlessly out there, near a stone burrow, still a good quarter kilometer off. Skags were relentless killers.

"Keep your eyes peeled, McNee," Roland growled.

"Peeled my eyes years ago and left 'em that way."

They drove over a rise, and on the low ground beyond a tumble of skeletal parts lay an old encampment. Human skeletons, mostly. Some from creatures he didn't recognize. Broken weapons rusted amid the bones. He drove around the bones, up onto gradually rising ground—then slowed up, seeing figures silhouetted against the sky on the next crest of stone. The strangers were about forty meters away, at least nine armed men standing side by side on the crest.

As Roland got closer he saw them more clearly: scarred, tattooed men, broad chests crisscrossed with bandoliers, their eyes opaqued by dusty goggles. Ex-military, he figured—he recognized the tattoo of the Crimson Lances on a forearm of the big one to the right. He didn't know the guy—though Roland had been with the Lances himself, back in the day. He'd rated Soldier, and fought his way through three campaigns on three planets, till he got to Pandora—and resigned in disgust with the corruption of . . .

. . . Of the tenth man, stepping into view on the crest. *Crannigan.*

Roland stopped the outrunner, angled up the slope toward the armed strangers. He let the vehicle idle, pondering his next move. "Them the bandits you were talking about?" McNee asked, his voice low. "I thought we were supposed to see them *first*?"

"This bunch ain't bandits," Roland whispered. "Look like mercenaries to me. Some of them are Crimson Lance. Or were. That big, broken-nosed, bald-headed thug in the middle—that's Scrap Crannigan. Used to work with him. He's a real backstabber."

"What, a backstabber on this planet? You're kiddin'."

"Stuff the sarcasm and keep quiet—lemme just see if I can get the prick to tell me what they're up to before they open fire."

Heavy-caliber weapons were already trained on the outrunner. Roland's expert eye picked out a Pearl Havoc combat rifle, two Cobras, a Stomper, a bunch of Atlas pistols, and a Helix rocket launcher. Crannigan himself toted an Eridian rifle—alien technology, recognizable by those curves in the rifle's organic lines, as if the weapon had grown like a plant instead of being manufactured.

Lots of ordnance on that crest. This could get ugly fast.

Very slowly, Roland raised his two hands over his head—not in surrender, which wasn't much use in Pandora anyway—but in a greeting that old Crimson Lance vets knew, hands open—then fisted—then open again. *Parley.*

Crannigan nodded, then took a few strides closer, down the slope, before stopping and calling out, "That's Roland isn't it?"

"That's who it is, Scrap!" Roland said, lowering his hands.

"You back with the Lances?"

"Not me. Don't look like you are either."

"Working for Atlas," Crannigan said. "New division. Acquisitions Department. You heard?"

"No, haven't heard of it. What are you 'acquiring' for Acquisitions?"

"That's our business! Course, it could be yours, if you're looking for work! You could hire on with us. Don't know about the little gnome you've got there."

"What did he call me?!" McNee fumed.

"Quiet!" Roland whispered. "If he didn't know me, we'd both be dead already! Just don't make any quick moves—but if they open fire, you hammer them hard with that turret!"

"You interested or not?" Crannigan bellowed. "Big pay!"

"I'll think on it!" Roland called. "Where do I find you after I decide?"

Crannigan shook his head. "Uh-uh. It's now or never, pal. Sign up with us—or . . ."

Roland gauged the shooting angle. Awkward. The shotgun wouldn't be much use from here. But he had a good Atlas Raptor pistol on his hip. He might be able to pull the Raptor and nail Crannigan in the forehead before the merc used the Eridian rifle—but the others would open up. Maybe McNee'd be able to machine-gun a few of them while the outrunner slammed right through the middle of them, run a couple of the bastards over. But that Helix rocket launcher with its multiplying blasts would probably bring the outrunner down.

Crannigan grinned—a nasty sight, showing green, crooked teeth. "I can see you trying to figure the odds, Roland!" He shook his head. "You'll never make it alive! Better choose joining up instead! Tell you what—shoot your little pal there to show your commitment! *Then* I'll cue you in on the mission . . ."

McNee snorted. "As if he'd . . ." He peered around his gun at Roland. "You wouldn't, would you?"

"Shut up and let me think," Roland muttered. After a moment he called out, "Crannigan! Lemme point something out—if this comes to gunfire, you'll be the first to go down. So I'll tell you what: I'm gonna put this in reverse, and back out of here, and think on your offer! And you can avoid a firefight."

"Oh—I don't have to get in a firefight!" Crannigan said, his corroded grin widening. "*They'll* take care of you for us!" He pointed past the outrunner.

Roland turned to see a sight that was bizarre even for Pandora—he'd heard of these creatures, but never seen them before.

"Primal Beasts!" McNee burst out, whistling.

There were three of the hulking semihuman creatures—and riding on each Primal was a Psycho Midget. The little jockey-like lunatic mutants, wearing goggles and finned helmets, sat in small saddles on the upper backs of the Primals. The Midgets were hooting and giggling and shrieking with murderous delight as they approached, flourishing their throwing hatchets.

The Primals were six-limbed creatures native to Pandora, reminding Roland of the enormous jungle anthropoids of the homeworld, in rough outline, but larger, far more savage, and each with four large forelimbs that sometimes acted as additional legs . . . and sometimes, when the creatures reared on their hind legs, became arms. Their clawed forelimbs had opposable thumbs; there was armor across their sides, catching the sunlight as the creatures splashed through puddles in the lowland. Metal embossments on their head indicated mind control devices.

Psycho Midgets were puzzling little muties. Encounter a screeching, sprinting Psycho Midget in the field and the little SOB seemed completely insane—muscular, rabid, unable to focus on anything but killing. Hard to imagine one working on electronic devices—but they seemed to have periods of relative rationality, and in those they'd mastered the Primal Beasts, using them as mounts and living catapults. The catapult analogy came to mind as swiftly as the boulder that was now hurtling through the air toward the outrunner, thrown by one of the rearing Primals.

Half a ton of boulder was flying directly at him.

Roland put the outrunner in gear, floored it, spinning the steering wheel, and the boulder smashed into the slope close behind them, spraying sand. The turret gun rattled as, cussing a blue streak, McNee brought it around to fire at the Primals and the Psycho Midgets riding them.

The repetitive high-pitched *zing-BOOM* of Crannigan's Eridian rifle projected a bubble of destructive energy in front of the outrunner. Roland veered hard left to keep from giving Crannigan a clean shot at him. He glanced over his shoulder—saw the mercenaries withdrawing over the crest, Crannigan sending him a final mocking salute.

"Bastard!" Roland muttered. "Mess with the bull and

you get the horns! And you'll get mine, Crannigan, right through your gut!" But how was he going to get at Crannigan any time soon? He might cut right, over the crest—draw the Psycho Midgets and the Primals that way and just maybe they'd attack the mercenaries.

An explosion to his right bucked the outrunner up on two wheels, almost overturning it. Twisting the wheel, he just managed to bring the vehicle down safely with a jarring crash. He looked over his shoulder at the Primals—saw one of them was throwing some kind of stubby metallic cylinder at them. He'd seen those explosive barrels before. Bad news.

"Where the hell they get that blasting barrel?" McNee yelled. "It's like the damn thing pulled it out of its ass!"

"Strapped low on their backs! Come on, McNee, time is bullets! Spray 'em and slay 'em!"

McNee let go another strafe with the outrunner turret as Roland tried an evasive maneuver, swerving left, right, and left again.

Another barrel came arcing through the air, thrown by the enormous Primal—a two-hundred-kilo object flung the way a man would throw a football—and it exploded just behind the racing outrunner. Roland's shield protected him, though it flashed with shrapnel impacts.

Roland heard a yell of pain, twisted in his seat to see McNee slumped over the turret gun, his head a mass of bloody shreds. Shrapnel had blown the top of McNee's skull off.

Should have got that shield fixed, McNee.

Seething inside, Roland turned away and jerked the outrunner to the right. Revenge would have to wait.

He blamed Crannigan for this—Crannigan had hemmed them in so the Primals would go after them.

But there was no hope of leading the Primals back toward Crannigan's mercs now. The Psycho Midgets had fixated on the outrunner—they hated outrunners, as settlers had used them to run the little killers down whenever they got a chance.

Roland veered hard left, sharply as he could without overturning the outrunner—just managing to avoid a flying boulder, he zagged right again, coming up on a low, rocky hilltop. He accelerated, jumped the hilltop, coming down on the other side with a jolt, holding on with all his strength. The outrunner almost flipped over again—then clunked back down on its wheels.

He spun the vehicle in a doughnut, brought it around facing the hilltop, came to a full stop, and clambered hastily up in the back.

At some point, McNee's body had fallen out. All that remained of him in the outrunner was blood, and brain matter, bits of bone near the turret.

Roland caught a movement at the corner of his eyes—he looked around, caught a glimpse of someone down the slope on his side of the hill, half-hidden behind an outcropping of rock. Someone watching and waiting. He knew the type—a big bulky figure in helmet, long coat, and slitted goggles. A Nomad. Another threat.

One thing at a time. The Primals were coming.

Roland ground his teeth, gripped the turret gun handles, and then the first Primal was there, poised on the hilltop not more than fifteen meters away, a shrieking Psycho Midget riding on its back. The Primal scooped up

a fifty-kilo boulder with the ease of a kid grabbing a snow-
ball, and threw it underhand. Roland ignored the stone
missile—taking the chance it'd miss—and fired a burst at
the Psycho Midget. The Primal was too heavily armored
to bring down at this angle. Its rider was just barely visible
from here, hunched down on the Primal's back, getting
ready to launch one of those vicious little hatchets.

Roland got lucky twice: the boulder missed him and
one of his turret rounds caught the Psycho in the forehead.
The mad Midget jerked in the saddle, shrieking in despair.
The Primal, psychically linked to its rider, went bounding
off in maddened confusion, tearing at its own head with a
forearm talon.

But the other two were coming. Roland doubted he
could get them both.

An idea suddenly came to him. He vaulted back into the
driver's seat, put the outrunner in gear, spun it around, and
started down the hill, close to the outcropping where the
Nomad was still watching.

He didn't head straight for the Nomad, but drove right
by him.

The mad giggling of Psycho Midgets came from close behind as he passed the Nomad—then came a snarling roar,
the thumping of feet. Bellows of rage, a spate of cursing.

He smiled. He knew his outlanders.

Nomads hated Psycho Midgets. *Hated* them. Never
missed a chance to kill them. One of their favorite methods
was binding them and holding them up as living shields to
catch gunfire meant for the Nomad.

He heard a grenade blast, another, a burst of gunfire,
and lunatic giggling that became shouts of pain.

The Nomad had gone for the targets, engaging both Psycho Midgets and their mounts. That'd keep them all busy for a while.

Roland gunned the outrunner, circling off to the right, heading back to try to intersect Crannigan.

He bounded the vehicle over ridges, low hills, around boulders—finally pulled up, seeing a flying vessel of some kind—hard to make out what exactly—taking off in the distance.

Chances were, Crannigan was in that orbital shuttle, heading off to conference with his handlers at the Atlas Corporation.

Okay. He'd catch up with Crannigan eventually. All he had to do was wait, and patrol the area. And meanwhile look for those bandits. That cache of salable goods.

He went back to the lowlands, looking for McNee's body.

There it was, about fifty meters off. It was already being torn apart by scavenging skags.

Roland pulled the outrunner up, and stared, thinking that McNee deserved better.

But that's what happened on Pandora. You made a friend—they got killed. Should've learned that lesson a long time ago.

Stay solitary as long as you stayed on this planet.

Because Pandora wasn't just a world. It was a planet-sized homicidal maniac.

Pandora glowed like a dying ember in the big rectangular viewport of the *Homeworld Bound*. Zac Finn stood in the ship's lounge with his arm around his wife's shoulders, the two of them looking at the viewport. Their son, Cal, his face in VR blinders, was playing mindtouch on a sofa nearby, the boy's fingers and shoulders twitching as he played. The artificial gravity was on, the ship at 80 percent gravity, still lighter than the homeworld, so Zac felt mildly buoyant.

A drunk, pudgy, middle-aged man with a bubbly green cocktail in his hand stepped wobblingly up, nodded at the viewport. "Lookitthat. Another goddamn planet. Sick of all these planet stops. Shoulda taken th' express ship. Tryin' a get to Xanthus." The drunk turned to Zac, pointed at him with the hand holding his drink, so he spilled some on the lounge carpet. He didn't seem to notice. "Where you folks headed?"

"Heading to Xanthus, too," Zac said shortly, not wanting to encourage the guy. "Settlers."

But Zac hoped he wouldn't have to be a hardscrabble settler on Xanthus, if things worked out here on Pandora. With luck, he could leave here with some real money, buy an estate on Xanthus for his family, and they'd all live there comfortably. He glanced at his wife, Marla, a compact, shapely woman in a traveler's clingsuit; she had copper-colored hair and bright green eyes. She seemed only mildly interested in Pandora, the third planet the *Homeworld Bound* had stopped at, on this zigzag trip across the galaxy, and he felt a twinge of guilt.

She didn't know he was going down there. Pandora had a reputation—a bad one. If Zac told her what he was planning she might take Cal and go back to the homeworld . . .

Zac glanced at the time under the viewport. 24:00— Rans would be arriving any minute.

There—was that a transport, that silvery oblong emerging from the upper atmosphere?

"Looks like the passengers from Pandora are coming," said Marla. "Maybe we'll be able to get out of orbit and on to Xanthus soon."

"Yeah. Keep an eye on Cal, huh? I'm going to go and . . . check with the bursar."

"Cal?" She shook her head, her green eyes flashing as she looked at her son. "He's been locked in that thing for hours. He's thirteen, he ought to show more interest in the real world. It's no way for a kid to grow up."

"Oh, he's not there all day. Just . . . part of it. Anyway, it's just a phase, hon. Wait'll he discovers girls. He'll take more interest in the real world."

"They mostly discover VR girls. It's a surprise people still manage to reproduce."

"Me and you had no trouble," he whispered, kissing her on the cheek. He turned and hurried off to the deck lift. But he wasn't going to the bursar.

Cal Finn was flying a bodysuit through a lightning storm, evading the blasts of enemy fighters, and calculating his counterattack—when someone knocked on the sky. *Thunk thunk thunk.*

It sounded like a door being hammered on in the distance. The hammering sound came right through the roar of his repulsors, the crack of lightning and the whining of machine gun rounds. *Knock knock knock . . . KNOCK.*

"*Cal!*"

"Awright *awright!*" Hissing to himself he pulled the VR helmet off, blinking in the transition to the peaceful lounge of the *Homeworld Bound*. There was something intimidating about the way the big golden-red planet hung there, filling the viewport. But his mom, hands on her hips, stepped into his line of sight, silhouetting herself against Pandora.

"Cal—you need to put that thing away."

"Why? It's just another orbit. We're going back into subspace, right? This trip is taking, like, *forever*—"

"No we'll be here awhile—they're delivering supplies down to Pandora."

"I thought there was no one on Pandora but a bunch of criminals and crazies."

"That's not true. Exactly. There are settlers. Towns. In fact—we said we were going to learn about the planets we saw on the trip . . ."

He rolled his eyes. "Seeing it from orbit isn't really seeing it."

". . . So we're going to learn about this one." She sat down next to him, took a uniceiver from her shoulder bag, and began tapping at the uni's screen for the *Identify* application. The universal receiver was also a powerful computer. She held the uni up so it looked at the planet hanging in space.

The uni took the image in and said, in a woman's friendly voice, "The planet Pandora."

"Text," Marla told the uni. "Pandora history."

"*Mo*-om. . . ."

"Quiet, Cal." She squinted at the text on the screen. "Okay, here we go, I'll just pick out some of the main points: 'Pandora has human-friendly conditions with respect to gravity and atmosphere. Its mineral deposits convinced the Dahl Corporation to set up colonization on Pandora, largely for mining purposes.' And—says they were also interested in the alien ruins."

Cal peered over her shoulder at the small image accompanying the text. "Alien ruins? I wish we could see that." Mostly he said it just to make his mom happy. Partly because he wanted her to lay off him—and also for a reason he wouldn't like to admit out loud: he loved his mom and wanted her to be happy.

"The alien ruins," his mom went on, paraphrasing the text, "were thought to belong to the same culture that left similar artifacts on the planet Promethia . . ."

"Promethia—that's where we got the new starship tech, everybody knows that."

"We got faster starships, anyway. Um—'a large sealed vault on Promethia discovered by the Atlas Corporation contained alien technology and weaponry.' The Dahl Corporation hoped to find a similar trove on Pandora. Says here that before they could really find it, they kind of gave up—"

"Gave up? Why?"

"Apparently some kind of cyclic change happened on Pandora, and all kinds of local creatures came out of hibernation and started . . . well, they attacked people, and destroyed a lot of the mining camps. Plus it turned out the best minerals had mostly been used by the aliens thousands of years ago, although there are 'useful deposits of specialized crystal.' Says it's 'not known if the extraterrestrials who left the artifacts were native to the planet, as none are known to have survived there.' So I guess they didn't find as much as they'd hoped for, and the planet was so dangerous the Dahl Corporation basically pulled out."

"But you said there were settlements."

"Some settlers stayed. There's New Haven, some other settlements—but it's tough down there. Especially because . . . if I understand what it's saying here . . . Dahl brought a lot of convict labor to the planet to do most of the mining work. When they left, they just unlocked the gates of the prison camps and abandoned the convicts. So the convicts are wandering around down there terrorizing the colonists. According to this, a lot of the convict laborers have gone psychotic, right out of their minds. There are still some working factories down there. Hyperion has a robot operation on Pandora—robots, and weapons. Especially weapons. There are more weapons of different types sold on Pandora than on any other known planet . . ."

"But—nobody ever found the Vault they were looking for?"

She scanned the univiewer, going on to the next page. "Seems like they found some stuff, but not the big discovery—not the Vault itself. Or anyway they couldn't get close to it . . . Says there're conflicting accounts of what happened to that."

He gazed at the enigmatic orb of Pandora. "So—the Vault *could* still be down there . . . somewhere."

She nodded. "But I wouldn't want to go and look for it! There are a few scientists—but mostly they stay on the Study Station."

"What's the Study Station?"

"It's the station the *Homeworld Bound*'s docked at right now—which you'd know if you didn't have your head in that helmet all day. I guess from up here they can look at Pandora from a safe distance. Even without the bandits from the prison camps and the . . . good Lord, look at that picture! Is that a human being? Must be some kind of mutation. Some of the bandits are cannibals, it says. Even without that, the animals that roam around down there are as savage as anywhere in the galaxy. Oh—here's a picture of a *rakk*. They're flying creatures—not like a bird, more like a pterodactyl. But they don't have beaks. Barbed mouth slits, barbed tails. 'They swoop down and strike without warning.' Some of them get huge . . . Oh! Apparently they're born in a rakk *hive* . . . which is a quadruped, bigger than a bus, that sort of spews the rakks out of its mouth. Oh and look at that creature—they call it a spider-ant. But it's a good two meters long, that one. . . ." Her voice trailed off. "Really quite interesting . . ."

Cal looked at his mom. She seemed a bit wistful. "You wanted to be an exobiologist. Sounds like you kind of wish you could go down there and study these creatures."

She sighed. "I was a year away from getting my degree when I quit to help your dad. These creatures are best studied from a distance—like from orbit. They're just too dangerous." She smiled wanly. "Believe me—I'm *glad* we're not going down there."

It took Zac a long moment to recognize Rans Veritas. His old patrol partner was standing in front of the wedge-shaped transport in the shuttle hangar of the *Homeworld Bound*. Rans had changed—gotten chunky, red-nosed, and balding. The layered, rugged, dirt-streaked outfit he wore, goggles pushed up on his head, seemed more suited for the dusty plain of the wasteland below than a spacecraft. Didn't they have a laundry on Pandora? "Rans!"

Hearing his name called, Rans seemed to cringe, then he looked nervously around the echoing, metal-walled hangar—and spotted Zac.

"Zac!" Rans came limping toward him, wide face split in a grin, and they shook hands warmly. "You haven't changed much."

"Oh, I'm an old married man now. I've slowed down a lot."

"Not too much I hope." Rans lowered his voice, eyes shifting around nervously. They were alone except for a self-operating forklift carrying supplies into the shuttle cargo bay and a single shuttle crewman hurrying toward the station's bar. "You'll need some guts, Zac—it's a great opportunity but it's going to take nerve." Rans's face twitched, and he gnawed a knuckle, as his eyes darted around again.

"There's a commissary for the crew—no one in it right now. Let's talk there."

"Good, good, lead the way . . ."

Zac noticed Rans limping again. "You okay there?"

"Yeah—yeah that's a big parta the reason I can't go after this myself. Don't get around as well as I used to. Skags jumped me, tore up my leg. Almost didn't get outta there alive. We got some good medical rebuilds planetside, from ol' Dr. Zed, but they ain't free. Can't afford it right now. Wouldn't've been able to get to orbit here, except I had a trip ticket left over." That facial tic twitched again.

They went through the glass doors and into the commissary. It was a low-ceilinged, overlit room filled with plain white plasteel tables and orange chairs, the farther wall inset with snack and drink dispensers.

"Have a seat," Rans said. "I'll—oh, uh, say, you got any cred? I'm busted."

"Oh—here, take this. We talked about the advance so you can have it now . . ." Zac passed him the smart voucher for a thousand dollars. It hadn't been easy to raise the money. He'd had to sell his late father's collection of computerized insects.

"Great, great!" Rans took the card, used a fraction of it to buy a chocolate bourbon at the dispenser, brought it back to the table. "I need a drink, bad . . . got the shakes again . . ."

Zac had heard about Pandora Syndrome. Lots of settlers on the planet suffered from a specialized PTSD. The constant fear of predation, Psychos, and bandits was traumatic.

They sat across from one another in the bright room, Rans sipping the booze and glancing at the door with twitching eyes. "So uh, let's get right to it. When we talked on the subspace gabber, I toldya maybe I'd found the Eridian Vault but I couldn't get it to it myself. Well—turns out, it's not Eridian. It's something else."

"Now wait a minute, Rans, you said—"

"I know, but hear me out. It's an old alien ship—an ET crash site. I saw it, I took pictures, and I found a xenotech who could analyze them for me. He confirms it! It's alien, pure offworld stuff—but it's *not* Eridian. Far as my guy can tell, it's from a civilization we've never seen before. I used up the last of my cred talking to this guy and I'm not sure I trust him. Now, Atlas has hired some mercs to find this thing. They know the general area within a hundred klicks—but not exactly *where* it is. Guy named Crannigan, ex–Crimson Lance, real pain in the ass—he's their man.

We gotta find this thing before he does, Zac. We'll take it to their competitors, you and me, we'll go right to Hyperion, they'll pay double to keep it away from Atlas! There's gotta be alien weaponry on that ship Hyperion could retro-engineer!"

"A crash site, huh?"

"You got it. Now it just happens the crash site is under a kind of overhang in an old volcanic cone—so the Study Station can't see it. Only me and you know where it is!"

"If you've got photos, that might be proof enough for Hyperion . . ."

"Could be faked! You've got to get in closer, retrieve an artifact out of there. Take the real goods to Hyperion! You and me, we'll split the take!"

"I don't know—you told me it was Eridian—"

"Stop obsessing about that, dammit! This is even better! Listen, all you gotta do is wait till the Study Station is over the area—less than an hour from now. Then you take a DropCraft, give it the coordinates, drop almost right on top of the thing. You'll hop out, grab a few artifacts, get back in the DropCraft, hit return, bing-bang-boom it'll bring you up here and you're on your way. We'll be rich! Now—I got all the info you'll need right here . . ."

"I dunno, Rans, sounds pretty risky. What can I expect to run into down there?"

"What? Oh-h-h—a rakk or two, or a skag whelp, little bitty spiderant maybe. There's a gun on every DropCraft, don't even worry about it."

The DropCraft bay was in the bottom level of the Study Station. Zac walked along the semiflexible transparent

corridor, thirty meters long, between the ship and the station, glancing up through the shield glass at the moon over
Pandora. He felt naked, exposed to space here, though a
filtering force field insulated him from damaging radiation. He heard a whirring sound, glanced over his shoulder—something was flickering in the air back there: a
small, disklike flying security drone. Was it following
him? No big deal—probably it routinely patrolled the
Study Station.

He entered the station proper, nodding to two scientists
at a scanning monitor, and crossed hastily to the elevator.
Theoretically, passengers on the *Homeworld Bound* had the
run of the station while it was docked here, but the scientists always seemed annoyed by tourists.

He took the elevator down, thinking he heard that
whirring again, this time coming from the elevator shaft
overhead. Probably some servo noise.

He found six shiny DropCrafts lined up on the lowest
level, in release bays. The little vessels, no bigger than a flying car, could be rented by the hour. His was craft number
one.

DropCraft One was an iridescent teardrop-shaped vehicle designed mostly for emergency escapes, but it could
be used for a quick visit to a narrow-gauge area. It carried
just enough fuel for one trip straight down and one back
up.

He would have to confess all to his wife—but only when
he had the goods. Once he'd succeeded, actually had the
money coming in, she'd be delighted. He hoped.

Zac hadn't succeeded at much in recent years. He was a
trained engineer, but he had a tendency to take shortcuts

in getting the work done, just so he could get the paycheck and move on to the next job. It'd worked until that portable bridge had gotten stuck halfway, stranding a dozen people between skyscrapers for three hours. The portable bridge had teetered in the air, might have crashed if he hadn't flown over there on a quickchopper and reprogrammed it.

Zac felt a sick gnawing doubt as he climbed into the DropCraft's cockpit, buckled himself into the seat, and read the coordinates into the navigator. Could Rans be setting him up? Was it all about the "advance" he'd given him for the landing coordinates? Rans had been a reliable guy in the old days, but he seemed different now. He stank of desperation.

Crazy chance he was taking, even if Rans was on the up-and-up. Zac was leaving his wife and son in orbit, and heading down to a hostile planet. True, he'd only be planetside for a few minutes. But there were risks—probably more than he could know. It was a planet of imponderables.

"Destination fixed and confirmed," said the craft's computer. *"Close heat shield hatch and press ignition."*

That whirring came overhead, unmistakable this time.

He looked up, spotted the small, spherical drone hovering nearby, angling itself as if about to dart down at him.

So it *had* been following him. The expert Rans had shown the pictures to must've shared them with someone else. Maybe he'd shown them to an operative of the Dahl Corporation, or Atlas. And they might not want this little expedition moving ahead.

"Uh, I *do* have ship-to-planet landing permit," Zac told

the drone. Which was true—he was legal to take a quick trip to the surface. "And I did a transfer rental for the DropCraft . . ."

The drone didn't respond. A red light started flashing on its top. Zac knew what that meant.

He had to get out of here. He fumbled at the console, found the tab marked *Hatch Close/Auto Ignition,* and thumbed it. The shield hatch hummed closed—but not before the drone zipped in. It hovered inside the DropCraft, whirring angrily to itself right in front of his eyes, the red light now flashing with furious rapidity.

"No, wait—!" Zac said as the airlock closed over the DropCraft—and the bottom dropped out of the Drop-Craft bay.

His stomach seemed to fly up to catch in his throat as the DropCraft plummeted out the lower hull of the Study Station and into orbital space. On autopilot, the craft veered down toward the atmosphere, as the security drone, now inside the cockpit with him, slipped to hover near the navigational unit on his left. He grabbed at the drone—but it fired a short, sharp laser into the craft's navigational unit.

A *crack*, and smoke drifted up from the blackened unit, choking the cockpit.

Zac coughed, turned in his seat, grabbed the whirring disk—it sparked, jolted him, punishing with electricity. He held on, raised it over his head, smashed it down into the bulkhead of the cockpit. It cracked, gave out a last, sad hum, its red light going out.

He tossed the drone aside and stared out through the transparent heat shield as the DropCraft plunged into the atmosphere—spiraling out of control. Red-and-blue-streaked vapors were swirling over the little vessel, flames guttered up around its prow . . . as it veered sharply down toward the planet's surface.

Marla and Cal were in the little stateroom, with its three sleeping snugs, its small table and chairs, its single view-screen showing a digital image of space outside with the planet they were orbiting—or in-flight entertainment. Cal was flicking through the entertainment guide as Marla went again to the door and opened it to look down the corridor.

No Zac. He hadn't gone to the bursar's office—she'd called there and they hadn't seen him. What was he up to?

"Looking down the hall's not gonna make Dad come back sooner, Mom. He'll be back. Anyway it's embarrassing, you doing that . . ."

"I know, Cal, I just . . ." A chime sounded from her handbag, sitting on a shelf by the door. She hurried to it, and answered the fone on the uni. "Zac?"

At first all she heard was static, and a kind of roaring. Then she heard Zac's voice, only half-audible. ". . . not on the ship . . . not on . . . I'm on a DropCraft."

"You're *what*?"

"I'm calling you on ship-to-ship but the signal's weak, technical problems, there was sabotage . . . Craft out of control . . ."

"Did you say *sabotage*? Of what?"

"The DropCraft was . . ." Static, roaring. ". . . I'm transmitting my landing coordinates to you so you can arrange for someone to pick me up . . . this thing's not going to make it back . . ."

"Landing coordinates for what? Zac—tell me you're not going down to Pandora!"

"No turning back now . . . there's a treasure there . . . crashed ship . . . ET site . . . going down to . . . Oh shit, this thing's on fire . . . Marla, maybe I shouldn't have sent you those coordinates. They might go after you on the . . ." Static. ". . . that I love you . . . I'm sorry I went behind your back and . . . just tell Cal that I . . ."

Static, roaring.

"Zac!"

The uni's polite digital voice said, *"Call ended."*

Marla tried calling him back—the fone couldn't find a return number.

"Mom? Did you say Dad was going down to . . ."

A blaring alarm interrupted him, the ululating siren breaking off for an announcement. *"Evacuate ship! All passengers to Study Station! Passengers take Airlock Three to the Study Station! Do not gather luggage! Go immediately! This is an emergency! Evacuate ship! All passengers to . . ."*

"Mom—what's going on?"

"Never mind, we're getting out of here—" She grabbed her shoulder bag and hustled Cal ahead of her, down the hallway.

"Wait, Mom! Stop pushing! I just want to get my mind-touch!"

Was he really worried about a VR helmet at a time like this? "Forget that thing and just *move*! Hurry!"

They rushed down the corridor, down a ramp to an elevator. They took the elevator to the main corridor, the two of them breathing hard, side by side, during the short ride. "Our room is a long ways from Airlock Three," she

said, putting one arm around her son. "It's the other side of
the ship. Hurry!"

The elevator doors opened and they hurried down another corridor, turned a corner, went down another ramp,
then a short flight of stairs. They reached the main corridor
down the center of the ship, and saw a panting ship's steward, a round-faced little man in purple coveralls, his popeyes
made even more so by panic as she rushed from a side hall.

"Go!" he gasped as he passed them. "Get to Airlock
Three!"

"What is it?" she asked, hastening after him. "What's
going on?"

"Those things behind me—those damn drones! Someone's overridden the security drones—they're sabotag-
ing the ship!" He pelted on ahead of them. She glanced
back—saw four disklike drone bots flying along, their tops
blinking, lasers licking out from a node on their under-
sides, the energy beams hitting power conduits along the
corridor. Wherever the beams struck, the lights went out,
section by section, so that the corridor was being consumed
by darkness, a bite at a time.

"Oh my *God*," she muttered, pushing Cal along ahead
of her.

They reached an intersection and saw the entrance to
Airlock Three off to the right. The airlock led to a flexible
tube, an umbilicus that extended from the ship to the main
body of the Study Station. Running up to the airlock, Cal
tugged at the door latch—it wouldn't turn. A small indica-
tor read: LOCKED DOWN. An oval viewport to the right of
the airlock showed the umbilicus extending through space
to the station.

Marla could see the popeyed steward running through the transparent passage, arms pumping up and down, passing a hastening group of passengers. There was no one else in the umbilicus . . . which was now detaching from the *Homeworld Bound*, as if the station were recoiling from the starship. Marla realized with a thrill of horror that they were simply too late.

"Mom—they left us!" Cal yelled. "*Now* what do we do?"

Behind them came the angry whir of the drones—and the *crump* of a distant explosion.

The ship shuddered from an internal shock wave. Marla and Cal staggered to keep their feet as the deck rollicked under them. "Mom!"

"Stay calm! There are lifeboats on the lower deck. Come on!"

Another thump, jarring through the starship, made them stagger as they hurried through the corridor. The way looked strangely foggy—smoke was thickening around them.

"There, Mom!" Cal shouted. He grabbed her hand, led her down a plasteel ramp, then down another, switching back in the other direction, till they emerged in the Emergency Hangar. Down the center of the deck was a row of shiny metal capsules, each big enough for one person—not much larger than coffins.

"Mom? They're one-person lifeboats!"

"Never mind, we'll go separately, it'll send us to the same place . . ." She hit the emergency release on the nearest capsule, and its hatch hissed open. She helped her son climb into it—the deck again rocking under their feet.

"Mom, wait!"

"I'll find you, Cal! I'll find you and we'll find Dad! I love you!"

Coughing in thickening smoke, she pushed him down into the recliner. Its cushioning arms automatically enfolded him, holding him in place. He looked frightened—though she could see he was trying to seem brave.

Marla made herself close the see-through hatch over him—just as another explosion shook the *Homeworld Bound* and she heard a high-pitched metallic squealing sound. Wind rushed past her, making her hair swish and slap around her head, suction roaring in her ears.

A hull breach, somewhere. Air was rushing out of the ship.

Marla forced herself to turn away from Cal, staggered on the shivering, pitching deck toward the next lifeboat. She slapped at the emergency latch, and it popped open—just as she felt herself tugged backward, away from the capsule, the increasing vacuum trying to drag her toward the breach in the hull. She grabbed at the rim of the lifeboat passenger hutch, held on to it, used all her strength to try to pull herself into its compartment, fighting agonizingly against the decompression. The breath was ripped from her lungs, and she felt that her trembling arms might be pulled from their sockets—then she grabbed a passenger strap, pulled herself down out of the stream of suction, managed to twist about onto her back, and hit the CLOSE button. The hatch hissed shut; the cushions enfolded her. She was surprised when she realized she still had her shoulder bag.

The Emergency Hangar seemed to tear apart around the lifeboat, debris flashed by the transparent hatch like trash in a tornado, and smoke darkened her view.

This is it, she thought. *I was too late. I'm going to die. And so is Cal.*

Then the hangar vanished entirely. There was a sickening feeling of plunging into nothingness . . .

Stars—blocked out when the planet rolled enormously into view. The sullen globe of Pandora rushed toward her.

Pulsers hummed to life on the underside of the lifeboat. An energy parachute bloomed around the little vessel . . .

Then the lifeboat began to spin, faster and faster . . .

Centrifugal force built up, pressing her deep into the cushions. She could barely draw a breath. Pressure threatened to crush her flat . . .

Marla screamed—and lost consciousness.

Z ac sat on the rim of the small impact crater in the late afternoon sunlight and watched the Drop-Craft burning. It was about ten meters from him, downslope, the fire crackling and spewing black smoke.

He ached. He'd been thumped around in the crash landing, but, to his surprise, he didn't seem seriously injured. An energy parachute had deployed about a kilometer from the ground, tilting the little vessel into this rugged landscape of rolling gray desert and purple plateaus. But there was no possibility of returning to orbit in the crumpled wreck of the DropCraft. He'd barely gotten out before it had burst into flame.

And maybe there was no starship to return to. He'd seen a white flash in the sky, just before hitting the ground. Was that the *Homeworld Bound*—blowing up?

If so, had Marla and Cal gotten to the Study Station? Or had someone sabotaged the station too? Was his family alive?

Zac shook his head miserably, muttering, "I'm an idiot." He should never have transmitted the coordinates to Marla. Whoever was trying to stop him from getting to the area of the alien craft wouldn't want Marla to have the coordinates either. He knew from experience how ruthless the corporate powers could be. If there was truly major profit to be had, they'd sacrifice a starship full of people. He could imagine the cover-up. *Interstellar Transport* Homeworld Bound *was destroyed in a tragic accident when malfunctioning security drones damaged its . . .*

A sob racked him and he thumped his own forehead with his fists. "Idiot!"

But, on the other hand . . . there was no proof the *Homeworld Bound* had been destroyed. Even if it had been, he had no idea if Marla and Cal were dead. His wife was a smart, resourceful woman. She'd get the two of them to safety in the Study Station. She'd make the station engineers look for him. Maybe the DropCraft had sent an automatic mayday. Maybe a landing craft was looking for him right now. Could be they'd spot the smoke of his burning craft . . .

He stood up, wincing with pain, and looked at the sky. He scanned the horizon, shading his eyes against the sun, turning all the way around.

He saw only rolling hills, a few crests of stony ground, indistinct scrub plants, swaths of clouds in the pale blue sky. But there—something *was* moving in the sky, quite a ways off. A rescue craft? He squinted at it, and watched closely.

He made out several spots moving in the sky. They swooped about randomly, it seemed to him—like vultures.

After a moment he was sure they were flying animals of some kind, not rescue craft.

Zac suddenly wondered if he had come down anywhere near the alien crash site. He looked around for a volcanic cone, and the terrain Rans had described. He saw nothing of that sort. No surprise—the DropCraft had gone out of control, had spun way off course. He might be thousands of klicks from his original destination.

He was lost on Pandora.

If only he could call someone. He reached into his pocket—and felt a surge of hope. His uni was there.

He tugged it out—and groaned. It was smashed. He'd been knocked around too much in the crash. He tried to activate it, but there was no response.

Zac sighed, tossed away the broken uniceiver, and looked back at the DropCraft. Rans—that son of a bitch!—had claimed there was a gun in the DropCraft, but Zac hadn't seen one. Now that the DropCraft was just a half-buried teardrop of flame and greasy smoke, it wasn't likely to render up usable weapons. He had no food, no water, no transportation, no working communicator. Nothing but his coveralls and a thin jacket.

"Come on," he muttered. "You're alive. You're okay. *Survive!*"

He had to assume his family was all right. He *had* to believe it.

He heard a distant snarfing sound, a growling that sent chills up his spine, and turned to see a four-legged beast, clearly a pack predator, coming toward him across a basin of sand about forty meters away—then another, and two more, trailing after it, sniffing the ground. Four of them, seeming intent on investigating the smoke from the crash. They had armored, scaly, bone-slabbed hides, and spiky ruffs. One of them opened its mouthparts in a shrieking roar—and he saw that the beasts weren't much like home-world pack predators: this thing's mouth split into three jaws, two that opened laterally, one from beneath. Each jaw with its own set of teeth.

He'd seen pictures. These were skags. Like the ones that had almost killed Rans. And they were coming his way. They'd seen him—were running at him, now, picking up speed.

Was this it? Was he to die within minutes of landing on Pandora, torn apart like a rabbit in the jaws of a coyote?

Not without a fight.

Zac turned and jumped down into the impact crater, ran toward the burning DropCraft, feeling its heat on his face as he got nearer. He dodged around behind the blazing wreck, coughing from the fumes, hoping to hide there, hidden by the smoke . . .

But the skags spread out around the rim of the small impact crater, roaring down at him. There was no hiding from them. He unzipped his coat, slung one end of it through the flames over the DropCraft, caught it on fire, kept swinging it so the flaming cloth met the skag charging at him down the crater's slope. The flames snapped like a whip into the animal's gaping maw—it squealed in pain and writhed back from the flame. Another skag came at him, roaring, slashing with its talons at his right hip, tearing fabric and skin—he whipped the burning jacket into its face, and it yipped, backed away, lowering its head. A third skag charged him and he jumped aside, so that it ran headlong into the burning wreckage, shrieking in pain, bounding off in confusion.

Then something struck Zac in the middle of the chest, making him stumble back. A tongue had struck from a skag's gullet—they could use their long, strong, leathery tongues as secondary weapons.

Zac fell on his back, close enough to the burning wreckage that it seared the side of his head—he kicked at the roaring, looming skag, caught it square in its trisected mouth and it squealed and took a step back. He jumped to his feet—but the skags were closing in on him.

Then two gunshots boomed, and the nearest skag fell on its side, writhing, blasted through the back of its head. Zac looked up with a sudden surge of hope to see three men standing on the rim of the crater. The heat near his head distorted his vision—he saw their forms rippling, twisted with smoke. Another gunshot banged, a third, and the skags turned and rushed the gunmen. A hail of shots, and the skags went down—one of them with its head on the boots of the biggest of the three men, as if it were an affectionate pet. The big man kicked the body out of the way and took a step down toward Zac.

The stranger was large as a bull, his eyes hidden in goggles, head shaved but for a fin of hair, his mouth covered with a dark surgical mask. In his hands was a combat rifle—and it was pointed down at Zac's head. He said something to the other two men—Zac couldn't it make it out through the muffling mask and the crackle of flames. The smaller men came down to Zac, each of them in identical leather jerkins, glowing red goggles, faces covered in dust-filter masks; they wore high leather boots, and there was a red stripe centered on their helmets. They pointed pistols at him, and dragged him up to the crater rim between them.

Zac stood wobblingly, coughing from the smoke drifting up onto the crater rim, as the three men looked mutely at him. Their weapons were directed at him from almost point-blank range. "Fellas," Zac said, between coughs, "I was never so glad to see anyone. Another thirty seconds and I'd have been skag chow."

They just stared at him, their goggles reflecting smoke and flames.

"Yeah, sooooo . . . thanks. I'm, uh, from . . . from a starship in orbit. I . . . was just . . . just, you know, sightseeing and uh . . ."

"You search for the Vault," said the big man in the surgical mask in a voice like a belt sander. "You search for what is to be ours one day."

"Actually—no!" It was true, anyway, that he wasn't looking for the Vault. "I just . . . you know, wondered if maybe there was some good land for . . . for settlement . . . see, we're on our way to, ah, Xanthus and . . . thinking maybe we'd, ah, stay here instead." And that was . . . untrue.

"Stay here? Why would anyone stay here? We, the condemned—we have no choice. But you . . ."

"Oh, well, there are lots of, um, business . . . opportunities, here . . ."

"Can we kill him now?" asked the smallest of the three men, in a whining tone. "I'm hungry!"

"We could cook him over that fire, down there in the pit," suggested the other helmeted man, helpfully.

"I don't like it when people come here, looking to take what is ours," rumbled the big man. "So, yeah—you can *begin* killing him now. But, kill him slowly. Piece by piece. Cut off a piece of his leg. Then let him watch as you eat it. Then another piece, perhaps his groin."

"Yes," said one of the smaller helmeted men.

"Oh yes," agreed the other, taking a step toward Zac.

Then the nearest man coming at Zac went rigid . . . and screamed, as he clawed at himself—his face was sizzling away, burning up in phosphorescent blue ooze, mask, goggles, nose, eyes, lips—and all. He fell, babbling with pain . . .

The other two turned toward the knoll overlooking the crater—where Zac saw a great gangly creature rear up over them, towering on four long, thin stalks, like a gigantic daddy longlegs, but with an oblong, blue-glowing body as big as a man's torso, its four jointed and fleshless legs each seven meters long, while long antennae curved high over its yellow-eyed head.

"Drifter!" yelled the shorter bandit.

The drifter spat out another glob of glowing blue projectile that struck the biggest bandit square in the chest. The big thug yelled in agony and fired a burst with his rifle at the creature—but he was shaking with pain and couldn't aim straight.

Zac saw his chance and sprinted away from the Drop-Craft wreckage, running for an outcropping of gray and purple stone. Someone in the darkness shouted, "You wanna eat, you eat some rockets, you Bruiser son of a whore!"

It sounded like it was coming from the drifter but that didn't seem possible.

Zac heard a *whuff* and a series of short sharp explosions rocked the ground. He reached the rocks, vaulted over a low boulder, and looked back to see a ragged little man with a smoking rocket launcher standing under the drifter. The bandits were blown to pieces that bubbled with glowing blue ooze. The little man had a crudely made hat, roughly conical, sewn together from pieces of skag hide; he wore a long, frayed dirty-brown overcoat. His craggy, white-bearded face squinted toward Zac. "You still alive over there?"

Zac said nothing but only crouched lower. He wasn't about to trust anybody on this planet.

The little man whistled through his teeth, and the drifter responded, bobbing once on its legs as if nodding with its whole body, then it turned and, with just three long strides, came to tower over Zac. He was suddenly in its shadow, looking up at its gnashing mandibles, its glowing pale-yellow eyes.

Remembering the blue ooze this thing spat, Zac was afraid to move.

"Bizzy won't hurtcha!" the stranger called, jogging over to Zac. "Nossir! He won't hurt ya at all! Less'n I tell him to!"

Zac swallowed. "Uh . . . Bizzy?"

"My friend the drifter here!" said the old man. "I found him out in the Parched Fathoms, brought him over here, made him my buddy!"

"And . . . how . . . did you do that?" Zac asked, afraid to look away from "Bizzy." He cleared his throat. "How'd you tame a creature like that?"

"Oh, I . . . well, that's none of your business, is what that isn't!" said the old man. "You're lucky to be alive, buster! Onliest reason you're alive is, I hate Bruisers!"

Zac looked at him. What a gnarled, sunburnt, dust-caked face the old man had. He was so weathered it was difficult to tell how old he was. He noticed an odd sort of collar, as if made out of metal scales, on thick coppery wires around his neck. It had the look of alien technology. He forced himself not to stare at it. "Bruisers?"

"Like that big fella that I blowed up just now! No sir, I don't care for 'em! They gimme the willies! Don't like their little bandit buddies, neither! But Bruisers—they're bone mean, and ugly as hell, and cruel as a pig that eats its own young! They're really a mutie like them Psychos! That radiation from the Headstone Mine, it made 'em what they are! They wear them masks so you won't see how ugly-mugged their ol' faces is after that!"

"I see," Zac said. "I do thank you and . . . and Bizzy . . . for your . . . your intervention. And now . . ." Zac started to back away.

"You going somewhere's, buster? I don't think so! No water, no weapons, no shelter! I seen that little spacetube of yours crash! I know what's up! You're prospecting— just like I was! And being as I haven't had anyone but murderers and drifters and skags to talk to for many a moon—I'll let you live so's you can gab with me! What's your name?"

"It's Zac, Zac Finn. I'm—"

"Fine, Zac, just fine. Mine's Berl and you already met Bizzy. Berl 'n' Bizzy, Bizzy 'n' Berl, that's us! Now come along, right this way! I'll take you to shelter! If we don't get killed first! Always a possibility! I started out with a partner, you know, had more'n one. But they always get killed—and wasn't me that killed 'em, neither, in case you were wonderin' . . ."

"No, no, I wasn't wondering that . . ."

Berl turned and started immediately toward the bluffs in the distance, whistling in that odd way—and Bizzy turned cumbersomely about, making the ground tremble with the placement of its pole-like hooked legs, and followed.

Zac glanced around the vast, dust-swirling desert around him. He heard the grunt and snarl of skags in the distance.

He sighed, and hurried to follow after Berl and Bizzy.

Marla woke in the lifeboat—and was surprised to find that she was alive, and the lifeboat was still moving. It was warm in here, stuffy. She smelled her own sweat, heard a throaty machine rumble from outside.

She could see blue sky through the transparent hatch, and gaunt flying creatures soaring and dipping, high in the sky—rakks.

She was being carried along, somehow, inside the lifeboat. She had just room enough to get up on one elbow and peer over the edge of the compartment, through the curving pane of the hatch. She saw helmeted heads, each with its red stripe, jogging beside her.

Up front was the back of a truck of some kind. They were jogging along behind the slow-moving vehicle, their goggled heads turning this way and that. She saw rifle muzzles lift into view from time to time.

Armed men. Probably the notorious bandits of Pandora's arid outlands.

They'd found her lifeboat crash landed and had taken her, and the emergency craft, as a single prize. Judging by their discussion it seemed they were so far unable to get it open.

"I don't see why we can't just blast it open!" growled one of the bandits. "So what if she loses an eye or some such, the useful parts'll still be there!"

"Because Grunj says *no*, that's why!" piped up another bandit. "Vance called, gave us Grunj's orders clear as day! He intends to get a good price for her! Fine slaver you'd be if you blew off a girly-slave's face and hands! Price goes way down!"

"But if we got her out of there she could walk on her own and we could ride on the truck!"

"Stop your carpin'! We're almost to the Coast! Look—there's the Big Wetty, not more'n half a klick!"

The Coast? Slavers? Was she being taken to sea?

Marla lay back and hugged herself, biting her lip because she didn't want to give the bandits the satisfaction of hearing her sob. Then she thought of her shoulder bag.

She found it, jammed into a corner of the lifeboat, the strap broken. She looked through the bag—it contained only a holo ID, some brochures for Xanthus, a smartcard explaining about the *Homeworld Bound*, a few tampons, and the uni. Would it transmit far enough from here?

She flicked the uni on and tried *Local Emergency Services*. The signal roamed—and found nothing. Working transmission towers were few and far between on Pandora.

She tried calling Zac, in case he was near enough for direct transmission. She watched the screen, and chewed a knuckle as she waited.

Call failed. But that didn't mean he was dead.

Cal. Was her son alive? The bandits hadn't mentioned another lifeboat. In the explosion of the *Homeworld Bound,* they must both have been blown way off course. They could be thousands of kilometers from each other.

And if these bandits sold her into slavery, she might never know what had happened to her family. . . .

THREE

Cal was afraid he was going to burn to death right here in his lifeboat.

Through the transparent hatch he could see a furrow of stony dirt to his right; to his left, flames curled up over the lifeboat. Its pulsers had probably burned up with the friction of the long skid after impact. He'd seen the energy parachute flicker out not long before he'd crashed. The parachute had gotten the space capsule tilted to hit the ground at a shallow angle. He must've skidded at least a hundred meters before sliding to a stop.

But the hatch didn't seem to want to open. And it was getting hot in here.

Trying not to panic, Cal fumbled around the inside of the capsule, looking for an emergency hatch release. Nothing.

"Dammit!" he yelled. "Mom! Are you out there? Is anyone out there? I'm stuck in here!"

"Could you state your needs more specifically?" said a calm voice at his ear.

"What?" After a moment he realized it was the lifeboat's computer. "I need to get out! Hatch release!"

"Hatch release initiated."

The hatch whined, shivered—then hummed open. Cooler air, and smoke, wafted in.

Cal scrambled up, and out, away from the lifeboat . . . just as flames closed over it.

But *now* what?

He looked around, feeling numb. It looked to be near sunset. The lifeboat had come down in a surprisingly pleasant little canyon. Water from some recent rain puddled in the outcroppings, reflecting a blue sky streaked with orange. Bushes growing from stony crevices were bright with violet and blue blossoms. A thin stream ran through the middle of the gulch. Behind him, flames burnt up his lifeboat, with any resources it contained. Ahead, a little stream chuckled.

The big question was, where was his mom? He couldn't see the other lifeboat. Shouldn't they have come down together?

And his dad might be anywhere on Pandora. Might have crashed into an ocean. Might be drowned and dead; might have burned alive. And his mom . . .

He couldn't think about what might have happened to his mom.

Still, there was a chance she had come down somewhere around here. A chance she was alive.

"Mom!" he called. His voice echoed mockingly back to him. He opened his mouth to call her again, but thought that the sound might attract someone or something unsavory.

He decided to go in search of her. Shouldn't stray far from the crash site. The lifeboat might have sent out a mayday. Someone could come down from the Study Station to rescue him. Or maybe they'd fly over from one of the settlements.

Cal climbed an incline to a low ridge, and scanned the sky, seeing nothing but clouds and a few distant flying creatures. He saw no sign of his mother's lifeboat; no other smoke, no human habitation. The lowering sun cast long shadows, from plants that were something like barrel cactus, across the desert landscape. He walked over to one of the plants and stared at it. It wasn't a cactus—there were what looked like big, crude gemstones set in the side. For all he knew, it might be an animal that only looked like a plant. He stepped back from it and shaded his hand to look toward the lowering sun.

Maybe forty minutes till darkness, if that long. If no one came for him—what then? Could he find a cave to hide in?

Better stay close to the gulch—at least there was water there, and that's where the lifeboat had come down . . .

He set off along the low ridge edging the gulch, following the stream. He walked another forty meters and then stopped, listening. Sure was quiet out here. Should he call to his mom again?

The ground was shaking, every so slightly, under his feet. He looked down—and the ridge crumbled under him, so that he went down it on his rump like a small child on a slide, landing in the gulch.

"Shit." He got to his feet and felt the ground shaking again. Then he could *see* it shaking.

And see it erupting—with a man-sized, chitinous creature rearing up from beneath it, shaking off a cloak of dirt and sand. Cal recognized the thing instantly from the picture his mom had showed him. He remembered a caption: *Spiderant, vicious predator of Pandora.*

Emerging from hidden tunnels, the spiderant seemed a fusion of bug and scorpion. Unlike a scorpion, the creature had only four legs, its front legs shaped like down-cutting pickaxes. Its shiny, gray-black carapace, seeming eyeless, swept back to a spiky crest. Even if Cal had a weapon, it would be hard to kill something that fully armored.

The thing was at least as big as he was—it was armored and coming fast. Cal knew just what to do.

He turned and ran like hell.

Cal sprinted down the gulch alongside the thin little stream. He heard clattering, shrilling noises behind him, looked back to see now three of them in pursuit, the nearest almost in reach. It struck out with its pickaxe forelimb, slashing down into the soil just behind him. He felt the wind of it on the back of his neck and the ground shuddered under him. If that stabbing forelimb had connected, it would have punched right through his spine and out his front . . .

That thought gave his legs new energy. He sprinted faster, gasping for air, heart pounding in his ears, looking desperately for escape.

There, to the right—a low boulder, and another above it, almost like a stairs out of the gulch. His only hope.

He leapt onto the lower boulder and, without hesitation,

up onto the next one, bounding up the stairlike stones.

The creatures behind him shrieked and hissed and clattered up after him. They were only slowed a little by the rocky stairs.

Cal ran onward, dodging between boulders, and around the pole-like green plants, hoping to lose the spiderants. His breathing was a wheeze now, his eyes blurry with effort. Should have taken track in Phys Training. Instead he'd spent PT sneaking off with his VR helmet.

Maybe this wasn't real. Maybe he was lost in a VR game. He jumped onto a rock, turned, gasping—and saw the spiderants just four meters away, smashing through a clump of intervening pole-plants, knocking them to flinders with no effort at all.

This was real.

He turned at a roar behind him—and saw three skags clustered near an opening in the side of a low hill of layered gray stone, about five meters away. One of the skags screamed, its mouth splitting into its three jaws, trumpeting like an obscene toothy blossom. And then it charged—

While the spiderants closed in from the opposite direction.

One chance. A rock, no bigger than his fist, under his shoe.

Cal reached down, grabbed the rock, threw it hard at the skag, to make sure it came after him—then turned and jumped right at the carapace of the spiderant just as it rushed him.

He timed it right—jumping past the spiderant's slashing forelimbs, he came down on its head, used the carapace as a springboard, leapt past the creature's middle parts—landed in the dirt. Another spiderant was climbing a rock to loom up right in front of him.

Cal dodged to the right, sprinting toward an outcropping, where he ducked down under an overhanging shelf of stone—crouching, he turned to see the skag pack leaping headfirst into the spiderants, the spiderants cutting at them with their pickaxe forelimbs, skags lashing with their claws, blood flying . . .

Cal turned and crawled away under the overhang, slipped around another rock, ran to the rim of the gulch, dropped down, and ran upstream.

Panting, wiping sweat from his eyes, he stopped after about a hundred meters, and looked back—to see no pursuit. There was a distant squealing of beastly combat.

It worked. He'd turned one group of predators against another. He stood there, breathing hard, his heart still thudding, swept with a feeling of giddy triumph.

But what about the next attack? And it was getting dark out . . . The long shadows had joined one another, had multiplied into pools of darkness, and the sky had grown indigo and purple, red at the horizon. Night was coming.

What chance did he have to survive it?

"Sure I saw it," said the old man. Berl ran a filthy hand under his beaked nose, wiping it on his knuckles, and went on. "A white flash in the sky, it was. Not so long after you come down. I've seen it before. We've had other vehicles explode in orbit . . ."

Zac felt his heart shrivel in his chest. "You really think that was a big enough flash—it could've been a starship?"

"Hell yeah it was a starship," Berl sniffed.

They were sitting across from one another at a campfire, in a loop of corrugated metal slats tucked into a high narrow notch cut by nature into a butte. Flames painted the old man's face ghastly yellow and made shadows dance like devils on the rusty walls.

This was Berl's camp. The ring of metal was what was left of an old mining expedition's outpost. A spring bubbled up nearby from the ground, and a thick encircling copse of plants offered coolness in the heat of the day. Metal boxes, rusting weapons, odds and ends were piled up, scavenged by the old man from the wastelands.

"Ought to know a starship burning up when I see one," Berl went on. "I served on 'em. I was crystal feeder for one of the old wormhole jumpers. Mighty hairy, going through them wormholes. You had to take a strong drug, make your mind all hypnotized, to get through it. You didn't take the drug, why, the wormhole showed you the guts of the universe, and you went crazy mad outta your gourd for real and true. Once we come outta the travel trance and find a couple guys gibbering, and lickin' the walls. These new starships, with that alien tech, why, you got it easy . . . Sure I know a spaceship when I see it . . ."

Old Berl had been alone out here for a while, except for Bizzy, and he'd built up a lot of talk. It was hard to get a word in edgewise. Zac didn't want to talk about that spacecraft blowing up in orbit anymore. He was going to believe that what the old geezer had seen blowing up wasn't the *Homeworld Bound* or, if it was, his family had gotten out in time. If he thought anything else he'd go "gibbering" like those early starship travelers. "You didn't see any other vehicles come down?"

"Naw—well, I 'spec I saw a streak but it could've been burning debris."

"Whereabouts?"

"Off to the west at least a hunnerd klicks or so."

"Hmm. You don't have a radio I could use, at all, do you?"

"Don't have any such thing. Have something like that, people use it to find you. Steal from you. And worse!"

They were quiet for a while as Berl took a spitted skag flank out of the fire and bit into it while the meat sizzled and popped.

Berl chewed ruminatively, his mouth open, his small reddened eyes never straying long from Zac. He swallowed a big mouthful of meat, drank from a plastic jug, then lifted his head, whistled questioningly to Bizzy, who was crouched at the entrance to the old outpost. Bizzy made a reassuring clicking noise back. "Bizzy says we're all clear. I was afraid some shit-heel of a bandit spotted us, followed us back. They'd love to cut our throats in our sleep. Anyhow, Bizzy'll keep watch."

"You know me well enough yet to tell me how you tamed that Drifter thing?" Zac asked.

"Oh . . ." The old man touched the strange, alien-tech metal collar around his neck. "Not yet. Tell you someday maybe. If'n I decide I trust you. Which ain't likely."

He controlled the beast through that alien collar somehow, Zac guessed . . .

"You want some more skag meat, boy?" Berl asked.

"No. No that was enough, thanks."

"Skags're as much lizard as anything else. Tamed me a skag pup once. But it got hungry and bit off one of my fingers." He held the maimed hand up for Zac to see—the index finger was just a stump. "So I shot him."

He patted the shotgun by his side. Behind him, within reach, was the rocket launcher.

Seeing Zac look at the guns, Berl scowled. "Wonder how'm I gonna sleep with you around . . ."

Zac shrugged. "I don't snore much."

"Not what I meant. You might slip over here and choke me dead, so's you can take what's mine. I don't know you. Took a big chance takin' you in."

Zac tossed a stick onto the fire. "Berl, I'm a family man. I'm an engineer. I'm not a bandit. You saw what I came down in. I'm an offworlder."

"And that's supposed to make me feel better? Most of these sons of bitches was offworlders once. Some of the worst I met are offworlders. That bastard Crannigan—he's an offworlder. He'd feed a baby to a skag if it made him a nickel."

"Who's Crannigan?"

"Skunk mercenary got a job from the Atlas bunch to locate a . . . well, *somethin'* out here. He ain't found it yet. He'll murder to get there too, mark my words." He grinned, showing gapped teeth. "But he'll find more than he bargained for. Oh yes. Something'll be laughin' at him as it chews him up an' spits him out . . ."

Lying on her back in the sealed lifeboat, Marla decided that they'd camped for the night. The bandits were sitting around campfires, laughing, talking, cursing one another, drinking, arguing, giggling, jeering—just out of her line of sight. She could see the enormous rapacious moon of this hungry world hanging over them, as if it were waiting for a meal. Flamelight fluttered to the right; to the left was darkness broken by patches of moonlight.

It was difficult to see much more from here, with the lifeboat's hatch shut. It was like a coffin with a transparent lid. The lifeboat was giving her air, somehow; it had given her water from a tube, and another device allowed her to eliminate urine. She'd found a compartment close to her right hand, with several packets of food mash. She'd found a mayday beacon too, in the same compartment—but it appeared to be dead.

Still, she ought to be able to get out of this space tomb. There was a computer that would let her out if she asked it to. But she didn't want to leave with these thugs surrounding her. The only thing that had kept them from raping her, maybe killing her, was that they couldn't get in.

Sooner or later, though, they'd sell the lifeboat, and her with it, to someone who'd force it open somehow. And that would be the beginning of the end . . .

She turned on her side, lifted up on her arms, pressed an ear to the cool transparent hatch, listening. The gruff voices came through now. Some of the men seemed to be singing:

Oh I've got a very good friend, a very good friend he'll be
He's my best friend now for I've run out of meat
He's got strong legs, does he, and fine strong arms too:
Got fine good meat upon him, go real fine in a stew!
For I've run right out of food and he's
Looking good, awfully good, mighty good . . . to . . .
    eeeeeeat!

Much hooting and hilarity at that. "Sing another one!"

But an argument sprang up instead of a song.

"I told ya, you gamble, you lose, you pay, Snotty! Now cut off that fucking testicle or pay me the fucking money!"

"That wasn't no way a fair one! You rolled the bones, you cheated on it!"

"You gonna pay up or not?"

"I ain't paying no skagbuggerin' cheater!"

"What'd you call me?!"

There was the *boom* of a gun then, and a scream; the chatter of an automatic weapon returning fire. Another scream. Quiet. Then a burst of laughter.

"Lookit that—they done killed each other! Ha!"

"Well, who gets their stuff? Let's roll the bones for it!"

She shuddered and lay back down. Amazing they could even speak, these men, form something like sentences. They were animals in human form.

She waited, making up her mind. *Tonight.*

She thought about Zac, and Cal. She pictured them finding one another somehow. She imagined Zac taking care of Cal, getting their son to the nearest settlement. Then he'd organize a search party—a heavily armed search party—to bring her to safety.

But she couldn't wait for that. It would take too long, if it happened at all. And it wasn't all that likely. Zac wasn't a terribly efficient guy.

She counted off seconds, minutes, to keep her mind busy. She ate a little of the salty, barely palatable puree in the food tubes; she drank a little water.

She'd need her strength . . .

• • •

Sometime close to dawn, the men quieted down. Marla pressed her ear to the hatch, heard someone snoring. They were asleep. Maybe there was a bandit standing sentry but chances were the guard would be looking outward from the bandit camp, watching for wild beasts or enemies.

Time to take the risk.

She took the uni and a few other items from her bag, stuffed them in her pockets with the remaining food tubes and a little plastic packet of water. She had no idea what the weather was like—probably cold at night, as in most desert places. She had only her tight traveler's coveralls but they were designed to be insulated for anything but extreme temperatures.

She whispered, "Computer! Can you hear me? Please respond softly."

"I hear," came the soft, artificial voice.

"Computer—are you in touch with the Study Station? With anyone who can assist?"

"I am unable to establish contact. Mayday signaler is in the right-hand compartment. However it is likely nonoperational since it has not been recharged for three years. My own operational charge is nearly used up."

"Okay, computer—open the hatch. If you can open it slowly, do so."

"Opening hatch."

The hatch of the lifeboat hummed slowly open. Cool night air, freighted with campfire smoke, drifted in to her. She took a deep breath, then got to her knees on the compartment cushion, looked furtively around.

She saw two campfires, one on either side of the low, flatbed truck a few strides away. Men were sprawled beside the guttering fires. She saw only one sentry, his back to her, about ten meters away, leaning on a large, pipe-like weapon.

She stretched a little, then climbed as slowly as she could out of the lifeboat compartment, feeling the truck bed with her feet.

She got her feet under her, crouched beside the lifeboat, waiting for her eyes to adjust. The moon seemed to glare down at her. She had the odd idea that it was watching her; that it might call out a warning to the bandits.

She took a long slow breath and then climbed off the truck, onto the sandy ground—and paused, wondering if she could get into its cab, start it up, drive it off into the darkness. Escape that way. But the sentry would fire that big weapon at the truck—probably some kind of rocket launcher—and he'd blow her up before she got far. Anyway, she had no idea if she could get the vehicle started. No, she had to go afoot, and quickly.

She crouched, hunched over, making her way to the deeper shadow away from the fires. She could smell the bandits—rank, rotten. She saw the shapes of cactus-like plants silhouetted against the gray background of the desert. She heard a sound, beyond the snoring of the men— breakers. An ocean. Beach somewhere nearby. It was like places back on the homeworld, where sometimes the desert reached the sea.

She hesitated. Right in her way was a big man sprawled on his back, sleeping in his helmet and goggles, mouth wide open. The stench of him almost made her gag. She held her breath and stepped over him with one foot, very carefully, wincing when her feet made a crunching sound in the sand. She was straddling him now.

She stepped over him with her other foot, teetering. Then she caught her balance, biting her lip with the tension. The man she'd almost fallen on stopped snoring and muttered to himself in his sleep. "Whuh bassud took muh . . . took muh fuggin' . . ."

Marla waited. After an interminable time he resumed snoring.

She stepped over another man, who was curled up like a fetus—and then she was in the inky shadow beyond the firelight.

She headed toward the beach, thinking to follow it to some habitation along the sea.

In another three minutes she stumbled over a rock, fell headfirst . . . and slid down a sandy slope on her stomach. She came to a stop on the edge of a beach. She could see the moonlit wavecrests silver against blue-black, glimmering beyond the dark swath of sand.

She got to her feet and looked around—which way now? The bandits were roughly behind and to her right, so she went left.

She got a hundred meters down the beach—then stopped when a light struck her full in the face, dazzling her eyes. She stood there, frozen, terrified, not sure which way to run.

The light beamed from a flashlight held in a man's hand. The light angled down, so she was able to make him out.

The man holding the flashlight was brawny, with long black hair flowing over his broad shoulders and a lantern jaw. He wore loose pantaloons, and an open vest over his bare chest. He was just getting out of a longboat pulled up in the surf. Beside him stood two other dark, rugged men. All three of them were heavily armed.

One of the men, bearded and scarred, pointed at her and said, "Vance—look! It's the woman! It must be! Grunj ain't gonna be happy! The idjits have lost her!"

"So they have," said Vance. "But *we've* found her!"

C al Finn had a choice. Hide in one of the dark crevices that might end up being dens for skags—or
move toward that twinkling red light he saw in
the distance.

After what Mom had read in the uni about the bandits,
he figured the light might well belong to one of those
bloodthirsty gangs.

Some of the bandits are cannibals, she'd said.

But suppose the light was someone looking for him—
maybe his mom, lighting a fire to attract his attention?

Even if it was a bandit—it was late, and dark, and he
was hungry. If they were asleep, just one or two bandits,
they might not wake were he to slip into their camp and
steal some food canisters, say, even a weapon . . .

The gnawing feeling in his belly made the decision. He
had to take a look.

Cal crept from one pool of darkness to the next, guided

by moonlight. He froze in place more than once when he heard the rustling of something moving out on the plain, expecting that unidentified *something* to leap out at him, tear his limbs from his body. He kept envisioning the skag's three-jawed toothy maw trumpeting in rage.

But half an hour later, he'd made his way to the base of a hill of boulders, about thirty meters high. Firelight flickered red and yellow near the top. He couldn't see anyone up there.

A narrow path wound between boulders, and up the steep, sandy incline. It was mostly in shadow, picked out by moonlight here and there. Anything could be waiting on that path.

Cal plucked up his courage and pressed on, climbing the hill, hands stretched out in front of him to feel his way as quietly as he could.

Soon he could hear a campfire crackling; could see sparks wending their way up to extinguish in the night sky. He got down on his hands and knees and crept close to a boulder on all fours, feeling strangely like one of the desert's wild animals.

Creeping closer to the firelight, Cal peeked around the edge of the boulder and saw the camp just a step or two away. On the other side of a campfire, a big, dark-skinned man lay on his back, his head propped up on a folded coat, goggles pushed back on his forehead, a rifle of some kind in his hands. He was snoring softly, mouth slightly open. Cal couldn't see the rest of his face because of the shadows in the way. A random tumble of old bones lay to one side, including a skull. Not good. Maybe this guy *was* a cannibal.

Still—it was just one guy to sneak by. Cal noticed an open metal box on the far side of the fire from the sleeping gunman. Looked like the kind of thing someone might store food in. He could swipe the box. Maybe it'd contain a communicator of some kind, something he could use to call for help. But he had to do it silently . . .

Heart hammering, Cal crept forward on hands and knees, wincing when his stomach growled. He kept moving, hoping the crackle of the fire would cover any little noises he made.

He got closer to the box, closer still . . . then heard a clatter, loud as a fire alarm in his ears.

Cal looked down, realized he'd stumbled into a piece of string stretched tautly over the ground between two half-buried sticks. And strung on one of the sticks a cluster of empty tin cans was dancing, jangling together.

He jumped up, turned to run—and stopped in his tracks as a big, rough hand closed around his throat. He found himself looking up into the grim face of a scowling black man—the one who'd been sound asleep a minute ago.

The man's grip tightened around Cal's throat, and he demanded in a rumbling voice, "*Who* the hell are *you?*"

"How much you think we can sell 'er for, Vance?" asked Dimmle, as he leered at Marla. Sitting across from her in the boat, Dimmle was the bearded, scarred one, his face crisscrossed with old, blue-ink prison tattoos, mostly words, phrases like: *Rip Up & Rip Off . . . Die Slow, Die Fast, But Die . . . Call Me 4 QuickFux . . . Mama, May I? . . .* and . . . *First the Knife.*

"That I don't know," Vance said, rubbing his big jaw as

he eyed Marla. He had his hand on the engine tiller of the open boat, steering without having to look where he was going.

There were six of them, five sea thugs and Marla, riding a ten-meter inflatable boat out toward an island—a dark blotch on the horizon picked out by a few lights. Vance was at the stern of the boat, to Marla's left, where a glowing purple cylinder hummingly propelled them through the smooth sea. At the prow of the boat was an electric lantern.

Marla was thinking of throwing herself into the sea. She might drown, or be killed by some vicious aquatic predator. Better than dying slowly in the hands of human predators. Her hope of coming out of this intact had shriveled when they took her uni from her. Vance had it. *"Won't have you checking for signals, lady,"* he'd said.

She leaned over a little, trying to reposition herself to dive in the water . . .

Vance shook his head. "Forget it, lady, you try to jump overboard I'll grab you by the hair. And I'll drag your pretty behind inboard—none too gently!" He grinned at her, his smile broad and gleaming white. Despite the threat, there was something boyish about this brawny man. Maybe this Vance could be manipulated, tricked into giving her a chance to escape, if she waited for her moment.

"You wouldn't let me kinda rent her for a night, would you, boss?" Dimmle asked. "I'd pay ya good. Wouldn't leave her the worse for wear. Mostly."

Marla shuddered.

"Not a chance, Dimmle," Vance said, his growl surprisingly affable as he went on: "You and the others'll keep your hands off her or I'll lop your fingers off and feed 'em to the Cruncher."

Dimmle scratched his crotch meditatively. "Don't do no harm to ask. We don't see women away from the settlements much."

The other men in the boat, gawking at Marla, nodded and sighed sadly at that.

"True, true, we don't see 'em much," Vance said. "Might be the raping, killing, dying thing that keeps them in the settlements. Of course, there's always Broomy."

Now it was the men's turn to shudder. "Don't talk about Broomy," Dimmle said. "I've still got the scars on my thighs."

"Looks like we're almost home," Vance observed.

Marla turned and saw the island looming up close to them. It wasn't very big, for an island, maybe a couple of football fields' worth of junk, spiky growths, steel barrels chained together, shacks, dirty sand, and hulking shapes she couldn't identify in the dimness. Boats of various sizes, including a large, shabby houseboat, were tied up at a pier, and in a moment so was the inflatable craft.

"Okay, girlie," Dimmle said, leering, pointing a pistol at her. "Climb out and don't make a run for it—you'd run into worse on this island than you'd be running from."

Marla climbed onto the pier, Vance, Dimmle, and the others close behind her. She walked ahead of them, the rising wind fluttering her hair.

Then they got to the place where the pier joined the island, and she stopped, confused. The island seemed to be rippling. Moving.

"Is there an earthquake?" she asked.

Vance stepped up beside her, chuckling. "You've a good eye, woman! Grunj's Island isn't solid land—it's a vessel, several of them, chained and netted together, most of them hidden under all the camouflage we've laid down over them! We move it around at night, use it as a kind of Trojan horse to get to other vessels . . . Sometimes their crews just walk onto the island and we get 'em that way . . . Works dandy!"

"Oh, well, that's . . ."

"Creative and resourceful!" Vance laughed. "I know! When we need a hideout—we just move the island. Come on, down this way . . ."

He led her along a "beach" covered with sand—as they walked along she could feel wooden planks under a thin layer of grit. Faces peered out at her from the shacks nearby . . . she saw tongues flickering, eyes gleaming, gun barrels catching light. There were footsteps behind them . . .

Vance turned to see Dimmle and two other men following. He hefted his assault rifle. "And where do you think you're going?"

Dimmle cleared his throat. "If we could just, you know, share her around, for an hour or two, we promise not to leave any marks, boss!"

"I told you—no! I've got the woman under control—she's staying in my den and I'm going to sell her first chance! We'll end up fighting over her! Use your money, and buy some women at the slave market on the Coast if you want some!"

Dimmle snorted. "Those women! Precious few—and what there are is all used up and ugly! And some aren't even women, some is just painted men! But this one . . ." He stuck out his tongue at Marla and wiggled it. "I'd like to taste 'er little—"

"Dimmle—back off!" Vance barked, cocking his rifle.

Dimmle's mouth curved downward in a perfect inverted U, almost a cartoon of a frown. "Vance—you like to play boss. But you're only second in command. Might be that Grunj'll want to decide this."

"Then let him—when he gets back from the land raid. Till then, I call the shots. Now go on to Hell Hut—there's a case of whiskey behind the bar you can share with the boys! Knock yerself out!"

Grumbling, Dimmle led the other men away. Vance glared after them, muttering, "They're getting uppity. Going to need a lesson, and soon!" He gestured at Marla with his gun. "And I'm in no mood for nonsense from you either, woman! Head on up the beach! I'll be a step behind you."

She shook her head, holding her ground. " 'Woman' is my gender, not my name. My name's Marla Finn. And if you want a good ransom for me, you'd better see to it no one molests me—no one at all."

Vance raised his eyebrows in surprise. "Ransom? What makes you worth a ransom, woman? We listen real damn close to all the orbital chatter. Far as I've heard, ain't one's looking for you. If you're the kind to be ransomed, there'd be a damn search party out already."

Her heart sank at that but she lifted her chin defiantly. "My family is wealthy. They may believe I was killed when the ship exploded. But if we let them know I'm safe . . . they'll pay to get me back."

All lies, of course. Her family wasn't wealthy—her parents weren't even alive, and she wasn't sure her husband and son were either. Zac had barely scraped together the money to make the trip. But she figured if she could convince Vance that a ransom might be coming, she could stall him from selling her off to slavers.

"*Marla*, hey?" Vance flashed his bright grin at her. "I like it! I'm Vance Sletch, and proud of it! Wanted on seven planets! I kill only when I have to, lady, and I'm no rapist. Don't enjoy it the way the others might. I like a woman to open her legs to me because she wants to. So you can stop fretting for right now—only, if Grunj decides to sell you to the slavers, why, no way to know how you'll be treated. Some owners might treat you decent—some might treat you like a skag pup treats a bone, and it could go harsh with you."

"But if you ransom me . . ."

"Ah yes. Just how much you think we could get for ya?"

She shrugged, tried to lie as casually and convincingly as possible. "A million or so."

"Is that right?" He rubbed his prominent chin. "Well well well. You might be overvaluing yourself, Marla m'dear. But we'll just see. Come along to the den, and we'll get something to eat, and talk it over . . ."

Marla went along quietly—and gloomily. She was fairly sure that he hadn't believed a word she'd said.

"What the devil am I gonna do with you?" the big black man asked, slapping a pistol in the palm of one hand as he glowered at Cal.

Cal was sitting on a low boulder at the stranger's camp.

The stranger holstered his gun—a relief to Cal until he saw the man crack his knuckles. Big knuckles in big hands—made a big sound.

Cal gulped. "You could let me go. Then I'd just . . . be outta your hair. Gone. *Noooooo* problem." He stood up. "In fact—now that I've apologized for sneaking around in your camp, I'll just go . . ."

That powerful hand clamped down on Cal's shoulder, spun him easily around, and sat him down on the rock again. "Nah. You're staying here. I don't like X factors, mysteries, or riddles. I need to know who you are and what you're up to. You say you crash landed in a lifeboat near here?"

"Sure. Down the gulch there, a kilometer or so." Cal pointed.

"That way? Yeah right. That's a hangout for spiderants and skags. You'd have been eaten alive."

"I almost was! I tricked the spiderants and the skags into fighting so I could get away! Got one bunch to follow me to another."

"Did you now." The big man put a hand over his mouth to cover a smile. "Pretty smart. Or lucky. Did the same thing myself not long ago with some Psycho Midgets and a Nomad." He frowned. "What's that noise? That your stomach?"

"Probably," Cal admitted.

"So you were after food, huh? Why didn't you ask for it?"

"I uh . . . didn't want to disturb you."

"More likely you thought I was a bandit. Might mean you are pretty smart at that. I'm not a bandit—but that's

mostly the kinda people you find out here. A few mercenaries, armed scavengers like me, take the occasional job.
There's a fair number of murderin' lunatics too. The bandits, now, they belong to outfits, gangs, and they got certain
styles about 'em—take fanatical pride in their crazy clas-
sifications. Bruisers, Badasses, what have you. You'll learn
to recognize 'em."

This encouraged Cal. It didn't sound like he was about
to be killed. "My name's Cal—Cal Finn. You hear of anyone else with that last name around? Other people coming
down from orbit, out here?"

"Cal, huh? You can call me Roland. Naw, I haven't
heard of anyone else lately. I did see an explosion in the
sky, if that's what it was. Meteors—debris coming down.
You get separated from your folks?"

Cal nodded. "My dad came down ahead of us. In a
DropCraft. My mom was in another lifeboat. We got separated . . ."

Roland nodded. "Well kid, if I hear about 'em, I'll tell
you. But I wouldn't want to give you false hope. They
made it down alive, chances are . . ." He shrugged. "This
is a mighty rough old planet. You know? My own partner
got himself killed recently. And he was tough. McNee—
the damn fool . . ." He turned around, hunkered, rooted
through a box. Cal thought of taking the chance to run.
But he was too tired, too hungry, and he was afraid to leave
the firelight. Anyway, maybe it was true—maybe the guy
wasn't a bandit.

On the other hand, he could be a psycho-killer, just
playing cat and mouse. Planning to murder Cal later and
do something horrible with his body. With the reputation
this planet had—you never knew.

Roland turned around, tossed Cal a package. "Eat that. When you expose the stuff inside to air, it'll suck up some moisture. Turn into something like bread and ham. Synthetic protein mostly, and vitamins, but it'll do you good . . ."

Hands shaking, Cal tore the package open, and immediately the little rectangle, no bigger than a candy bar, expanded to the size of a poorboy sandwich in his hands. "Never saw one of these. Camp food, huh?"

"Beats skag meat. But you can eat most of the local four-legged critters in a pinch. Chow down, I'll get you some water."

Cal chowed down, and though the food varied from tasteless to mildly disgusting, he felt better right away. He hadn't realized how shaky, how empty, how scared he'd been, till he was able to sit by a fire and eat something.

Roland sat near him, watching, elbows on his knees, clasped hands covering his mouth. Roland didn't like to show when he was smiling, but Cal could tell he was.

"You some kind of professional soldier?" Cal asked, when he'd eaten.

Roland passed him a canteen. "Yeah, I guess. I hire out to people when I feel like it. Take a mission here or there. Scavenge what I can. Used to work for one of the corporation armies. For Atlas—Crimson Lances." He shook his head. "Don't care for that anymore. They're not much better than the bandits."

Cal drank deeply from the canteen, amazed at how much flavor there was to water when you were really thirsty. "Wow. I needed that."

"You think your people are looking for you?"

"If they're alive—they're looking for me. That's why

you gotta get me to civilization—if you want the reward."
Cal assumed there was a reward for finding him. There
should be. How could there not be?

"A reward? For a scrawny little kid like you?"

"Hey, I'm not scrawny! Anyhow, even if I were—what's
that got to do with it?"

"Yeah, I guess you're right. Living here, we value people
for how they can survive. Scrawny doesn't usually live
long—though those crazy Psycho Midgets can surprise
you. They don't give up easy . . ."

"But I am a survivor!" Cal insisted. Now that he was no
longer scared of Roland, he didn't like getting ribbed by
him. "I beat those skags and spiderants today!"

Roland tossed a stick on the fire. It flared up a little,
adding yellow highlights to his face, and to the goggles on
his head. "Kid—you lie down, get some rest. We'll check
out your story tomorrow. But chances are, I'm gonna take
you to Fyrestone. Little settlement a ways from here. I've
gotta pick up a Scorpio Turret there anyhow. And send a
message to McNee's woman . . ." He shook his head sadly.
"Anyhow, it'll take a while, getting there. I'm gonna give
you my shield, help protect you on the trip."

"A shield? You don't have to do that."

"I know. I'm a damn fool like that, sometimes. But
McNee . . ." He tossed another stick on the fire and
scowled. "Never mind. You'll wear the shield. 'Cause
there's no way we won't run into trouble. Death comes
regular as milestones out here. It's gonna be us, or them.
I'd rather it was them."

"Who? The bandits?"

"Could be. Or spiderants, rakks, skags—ones you ran

into were the small, easy variety. Rumors have a *drifter* out in this desert somewhere's. Haven't seen it myself. Weird critters. Then there's Crannigan, and his bunch of killers. I'm trying to avoid that rat-bastard till I get the timing right. But you can't really avoid a fight on this planet, kid. Not for long. We got to be ready for it. And on the way to Fyrestone, we're gonna make a little stop."

"What for?"

"Gonna swipe some weapons from a bunch of bandits, is what. I just found out today exactly where they're holed up. We might even get you a weapon. But you're gonna have to do your part, kid. Now get some rest."

Cal sighed, and stretched out by the fire, exhausted. He was going to have to trust Roland. No choice.

He closed his eyes, and wondered, before dropping into a deep black abyss of sleep, whether his mom and dad were alive.

Dad had come down first—he should be alive, if he took a DropCraft . . . shouldn't he?

FIVE

Zac froze, hardly daring to breathe, when someone shoved a cold shotgun muzzle against the back of his neck.

"That's right," Berl said, jabbing him with the shotgun muzzle. "Don't you move, not a muscle."

Zac was on his knees, blinking in the morning light, his hands in an old backpack. "Take it easy, Berl, I was just looking for a bite to eat. I woke up so damn hungry . . . and I can't seem to choke down any of that rotting skag meat . . ."

Berl grunted and removed the gun muzzle. "It ain't rotten yet. Skag meat *always* smells like that. Who said you could muck around in my goods?"

Zac turned slowly around, sat on the dirt, giving Berl his best look of injured innocence. "I thought we were partners, Berl."

"Partners? Who said anything about partners?"

"Well you saved my life, you trusted me to stay in your camp . . ."

"Don't mean you can rob me! Next you'll be trying to find my stash of shock crystals!"

"I don't even know what those are."

"I sells 'em to settlement folks—sell 'em through them little Claptrap robots of theirs—and them New Haven types, they use the crystals to customize their fightin' for electricity. Some will pay big money for it—so keep your damn hands off!"

What did he spend the money *on*? Zac wondered, looking around the shabby camp. Probably saved it up in some account somewhere. "Berl, I was just hoping for some old can of beans not too far past its eat-by date."

Berl glared at him—then grunted, and pointed at a grungy cardboard box nearby. "There—packaged food. Scrounged it from a dead man's camp. Might be edible. I'm gonna check on . . . my goods. And I do mean *my* goods."

Berl shuffled off and Zac busied himself inspecting the contents of the cardboard box. Some of it was just edible. There was a package of something more or less like dried green beans, and another that *might* be synthetic chicken meat.

Zac ate hungrily, and waited to see if he'd get sick. It occurred to him he might perish right here, on this spot, writhing in the gray-blue dirt of this alien world—dead from food poisoning. That would be an ignominious death, but maybe it was what he deserved. He'd thrown away the last of his family's money on Rans's crackpot scheme. The whole plan seemed to have brought down the lightning on them—and in fact, on the *Homeworld Bound*, from what Berl was saying.

Zac had an intuition—or was it just denial?—that his family had escaped the ship. But had everyone aboard gotten out? Was he indirectly responsible for killing the crew of that vessel?

And—why had the flying security bot sabotaged his DropCraft? Who'd sent it? What exactly *had* happened to the *Homeworld Bound*?

Be good to talk to Rans. Talk to him or, better yet, shake the truth out of him. Guesswork suggested that Rans had told someone else about the crashed vessel—someone who didn't want Zac finding it. Or maybe any craft scheduled to go to those coordinates would be attacked.

And what had Zac done? Just sent the landing coordinates to his wife, that's all. Meaning that whoever targeted Zac—also targeted *her*. And Cal.

Yeah. He deserved food poisoning.

But it didn't come. Just a little nausea. And with it, the thought that even if his wife was alive—she might never forgive him. He'd felt her drawing quietly away from him, long before all this had happened. He'd been reckless, irresponsible more than once. She wasn't sure about the emigration to Xanthus. Now this . . .

Zac got up, and stretched, thinking he should check on Berl. He had to come to some kind of understanding with the old man, try to win his trust.

Blinking in the slanting beams of the rising sun, Zac looked around at the rusty sheet metal mess of Berl's camp. Spears of light pierced the rust holes in the walls of corrugated metal. He caught a movement from the corner of his eye, turned to see Bizzy rearing up in the distance, about forty meters away, looking down from its perch on its stilt-like legs, at something else. Probably listening to Berl.

He remembered the alien artifact the old man wore around his neck. Could be, in his fit of paranoia, Berl was off checking more than just his shock crystals. Maybe he had more alien artifacts over there.

Maybe that old man *did* know where the crashed ship was—the very thing that Zac had come here for.

Zac shook his head. He shouldn't get distracted trying to find that damned ship. Not without the DropCraft to get back in. He should try to find his family. *A hunnerd klicks to the west.*

A hundred kilometers to the west, something had fallen from the sky. Maybe just burning debris. Or maybe a life-boat. Not that far from where he'd come down. Was it his wife, his son?

He should go there and see. If he could even get there alive. He shouldn't look for that crashed spacecraft . . .

But suppose he found it? He'd make a fortune. Then Marla would *have* to forgive him.

Anyway, it couldn't hurt just to find out if the ship was nearby.

He hurried down the slope, crossed laterally on a sandy shelf of rock, heading toward Bizzy.

Rounding a great wedge of blue stone he spotted Bizzy first, the drifter with its back to him. It was poised on its four teetering legs high over the old man, who was crouched in the mouth of a cave about thirty meters away. The old man was looking at something that glinted in the sun. The shock crystals?

Zac crept closer, in the shelter of intervening boulders, feeling guilty—the old man had saved his life and now Zac was skulking about, spying on him. But he kept slipping closer, on tiptoes, until he was crouched behind a jut of rock just a few meters from the cave mouth. He could see Berl, between Bizzy's long, pipelike legs. The old hermit was crouching over a small pit dug in the soil under the cave mouth, lifting something into view. Not a crystal.

It was an artifact—and not Eridian. Zac had seen plenty of Eridian extraterrestrial artifacts in holograms.

This was something very different from the Eridian style. It was translucent, glimmering with inner power—a restless shape he'd never seen before, a spiral that *changed* shape, twisting like a snake as Berl switched it from hand to hand. It seemed almost alive.

Berl held it up to the sun—in his open palm—and it spun about, seemed to point itself, off across the desert.

Berl gazed that way himself. "Don't wanta go back to that ship, less'n I have to, Bizzy," Berl said. "But I might just have to . . ."

Zac drew back and slipped away, keeping the rocks between him and Berl, returning to the camp. The whole time, he kept hearing Berl's words echoing in his mind: *Don't wanta go back to that ship . . .*

Berl knew where the crashed ship was, and where a fortune in alien artifacts could be found. And the son of a bitch was keeping it all to himself.

Marla woke up, sitting bolt upright, staring around blearily in the unfamiliar surroundings. She hadn't expected to sleep—and certainly not without being attacked. But that's the way it had been. Had they drugged her? It didn't feel that way. She'd simply been exhausted. She was in a snug cabin of wood and metal, undecorated, with a white-painted metal door.

It was a houseboat, judging from the view out the window. A small swell from the breeze rocked it in the water.

Through the window she could see the pier, and bright sunlight on metal shacks, rusting junk piles scavenged from ships, small wooden shelters, walkways, rope bridges. Here and there was a tree, but she could see that it was faked up, somehow. Part of the island's camouflage.

She got up, slipped her shoes on, and tried the door to the passage—and no surprises there. It was locked.

She went back to the window. Suppose she got it open, squeezed out, swam away. To where?

The lock turned and she spun on her heel. Vance was grinning at her from the door. "Right this way. I'll show you where you can wash up, and we'll get some food. Then we'll talk about what's on this uni of yours."

He stepped into the narrow hall and she reluctantly followed. He gestured with a pistol—she walked ahead of him to a bathroom, of sorts. A spigot jutted high in the wall over a hole in the floor, a cake of soap that looked like it had never been used, a scrap of towel.

"Clean up in there," he said. "Water ain't potable but it's filtered enough to wash in. No window. Lock the door. But don't take your sweet time. Grunj wants a good look at you. He's come back early."

As it happened, Grunj didn't wait long to take a look at her. She was just toweling off after taking a shower when the door unlocked, and he entered, spinning a key ring on his finger, staring frankly at her naked body. A stocky, barrel-chested man, whose face was hard to see—it seemed mostly beard at first. The immediate effect was of someone who had an inverted, elaborately coiffed wig slipped over the lower part of his face. Grunj's great brown beard was curled and braided into an elaborate pelt sculpture. It grew up onto his cheekbones, nearly to his eye sockets; the hair on his head was cut into curlicues that rose like exotic plants from his scalp, long as a man's forearm. He had tiny brown eyes, and from his projecting ears dangled scrounged oddments of glass and copper. His stubby nose was beringed in gold. He wore a shiny brown leather coat that hung to his knees, large black boots, military green trousers, and a red silk shirt that strained with his bulging belly. The smell coming thickly off him suggested he rarely bathed. If ever.

Grunj chuckled, looking her over, rubbing his thick-fingered, hairy hands. "You'll do fine," he rumbled, as she tried to cover her nakedness. "I'll get a brimmin' bucket o' bucks for you, missy ho."

"Don't call me—"

Casually as a man smacking at a mosquito, he backhanded her, so that she stumbled backward and struck the wall, stunned. He turned and spoke to someone in the passage. "Missy ho has to be brushed up pretty, and then we'll take her to the slavers. Maybe in a day or two, after I've had my rest."

As she cringed into a corner of the shower, she heard Vance's voice from the hall. "If'n you say so. But suppose *I* want to bid for her?"

"I don't want none of you men buying her. If she's

'round here long, she'll cause trouble." All the time Grunj was still ogling her, though it seemed the look a man would give a horse he had bought, more than lust. "Already had some men kill each other over a bet. Don't have time to recruit men all the damn day. Hard to get. Going to have to hang another for insubordination. Waste of manpower. Just do what I said about missy ho, there."

"Sure thing, Grunj," Vance said. "How about a drink?"

"Naw, I've got a new guest in my cabin, I'm gonna go check on the dwarfish little bugger . . ."

Grunj lumbered off, closing the door behind him, and Marla quickly got dressed. Her clothes were self-cleaning, once taken off, and they were reasonably fresh now. What had he meant by 'dwarfish little bugger'? Could he have been referring to a child? He didn't have Cal in his cabin, did he?

She was just pulling on her shoes when the door opened—she drew back, but relaxed a little when she saw it was Vance.

He looked at her ruefully. "Enjoy meeting Grunj, did you? Decided he wanted to see everything there was to see, and quick."

"He mentioned someone small, a 'guest' in his cabin . . . it's not a boy, is it? I mean . . . an offworld boy . . ."

"Naw. Grunj, he sometimes will buy a boy from a slaver. Keeps 'em awhile, sells 'em, or feeds 'em to Skraggy if they piss him off."

"Who's Skraggy?"

"Skraggy the skag. Keeps it in his place onshore. Biggest skag this side of Skagzilla. Bred it himself, someway.

I mean—bred it with other skags . . . but then, anything's possible with him." Vance grinned, glancing down the hall to see if anyone was listening. He lowered his voice. "He's developed a taste for Psycho Midgets lately. He gags 'em, ties 'em up, plays with 'em for a while, then feeds 'em to Skraggy. One of them midgets—that's the 'guest' he's talkin' about." He drew her uni from his pocket. "Now you tell me about this—these coordinates on here. . . . not more than ninety-five clicks from the place we found you. I could get there in a day or two, depending. Says 'crashed ship' and there's the coordinates. Now Missy . . . Marla . . . what's all this about a crashed ship?"

She shook her head. "I don't know. My husband was going to . . . to investigate it."

"I heard a rumor there's a corporation hireling, a certain son of a bitch named Crannigan, doing a grid search out in that area. He's lookin' for something too." He rubbed his big jaw. It seemed that he'd recently shaved. "And there's also talk of an old man out that way, got some alien tech. Some say it ain't Eridian. So put that together, and I think we may have us something here . . ."

It occurred to her that those coordinates might be exactly where Zac was, if he was alive. Or close by there. Time for some old-fashioned feminine wiles. She took Vance by the hand and drew him into the room. He grinned and closed the door behind him.

"Listen," she whispered, "my husband mentioned a treasure—maybe he meant that crashed ship. We could slip away from this bunch, and head out to those coordinates ourselves, Vance! We could share in it!"

He snorted. "Now why would I need you for that?"

"For one thing, because . . . because that way you'd know I wouldn't tell anyone else about it. You know, if I'm sold or whatever. And—I can be of help. I really can. I can prove it, if you'll let me. I might remember something else Zac said, in time . . ."

"Maybe you would be of some use, at that. But as for telling people things I don't want them told— if I wanted to shut you up, there's a quicker way than bringing you with me."

She tried to hide the fear she felt, at that. "I know. But . . . you'd cost Grunj the price of me. And he'd hunt you down for sure, if you stole anything from him."

"But if I slip off with you, he'll still hunt me down. . . ."

She took a deep breath. Time for a really good lie. "There's something I haven't told you. My husband, right before he died"—best that everyone thought that—"gave me some details about where this thing is. Just knowing the location isn't enough—it's hidden. You have to know what to look for. And if you torture me to get that information . . ." She shrugged. "Grunj would find out. I'd be damaged goods. Besides . . ." She placed a hand on his bare skin, between the strips of vest. And was surprised at how something inside her responded to the way his taut skin, his firm muscle felt under her palm. "You wouldn't want to do that. There aren't a lot of women on this planet." She looked into his eyes, and then dropped her gaze shyly, hoping the ploy worked. "You might need one. Yourself. I'm no beauty but . . ."

He put his hand over hers. "I believe you're trying to get around me, darlin'. And by the blood in the sands, I think it's working."

He took her small shoulders in his big, rough hands, drew her close, and pressed a kiss to her lips.

She was startled—as much by her own passivity as by the kiss. She was letting it happen, and after a moment, she was no longer passive. She was returning it.

What's wrong with me? Am I just playacting? This is insane . . .

But she didn't push Vance away.

SIX

Almost midday, Cal and Roland were bumping along an old, barely visible road on a sandy plain, raising a rooster tail of dust. Cal had to hold on to the dashboard to keep from getting bounced out onto the sparse road. Between them was a gun rack with two big weapons upright in it: the Tediore Defender and a combat rifle. The wind of their passage eased the heat from the sun, which had been increasing steadily since early that morning.

Riding shotgun next to Roland, Cal watched the big soldier's motions as he drove. The outrunner was simple, user-friendly, like most tech.

"I bet I could drive this thing," Cal said, hoping Roland would take the hint.

Roland glanced at him and almost smiled. "Maybe—*if* we're out in the open, and *if* it looks safe, no bad guys on the horizon . . . I *might* let you learn how. But this ain't a toy, kid. Valuable machine. Takes maintenance."

"Oh I know." Cal looked over his shoulder at the turret gun. "Maybe it'd be better if I was on the turret gun, instead . . ."

"On the . . . Yeah, right, kid, you'd sneeze and blow my head off!"

Cal felt himself shrink inwardly at that. Made him bitter to hear it. "I've fired plenty of weapons!"

"Sure you have, kid. In a VR game."

"No, I . . ." But he couldn't quite utter the lie. Game weapons were all he'd fired. "Anyway—you could teach me."

"Maybe . . ."

"I know. If it's in a safe place, if there's no enemies on the horizon. *If* . . ."

Roland laughed. "You got it, kid."

They'd reached the welcome shade of a bluff overhang, and Roland turned a sharp right to follow the edge of the bluff, another quarter kilometer. He slowed when they came to an opening in the cliff face, taking the outrunner down to a crawl as he rounded the corner. They were driving through a defile, a narrow valley of red-streaked blue stone. Up ahead it widened out a bit, then narrowed again. At the narrows, he stopped the outrunner and spoke to Cal in an undertone. "Just stay close behind me, and keep your trap shut. We gotta scope out the situation. There's a little trail up here, goes up into the rocks. We can see the bastards from up there. Better if they don't see us . . . Unless we want 'em to." He pulled his battle rifle from the rack between them. "Come on!"

"What about me? *I* need a gun!"

"Like I said, you'd sneeze and . . . oh, hell." Seeing the

look on Cal's face Roland sighed and rolled his eyes. "Tell you what . . ." He reached under the dashboard, came out with a small orange pistol. It seemed made of plasteel. "Start with this. This is a BLR Hornet. Twelve shots. Here's the safety—on, and off. On again. Leave that safety on unless I tell you different! And if you shoot me, it better be on purpose, kid! If you shoot me by accident, I'll feed you to the rakks!"

He handed Cal the weapon, butt first. Cal thrilled to the heft of it, the masculinity, the intentionality in its design. It was a tool intended to kill, designed for that and nothing else.

Roland looked at him skeptically. "Hope I don't regret this."

"You won't, I'll be careful."

"It's not a big gun, oughta just fit in your pocket. Leave it there unless it's a case of life and death. Now come on, dammit."

They climbed out of the outrunner, Cal reluctantly stowing the gun in his right-hand pocket. It barely fit.

Feeling the weight of it as he walked, Cal followed Roland into the narrow passage, and up a side passage carved into the stone to his left. It rose like a ramp, switching back at intervals, a trail climbing the cliff.

Twenty minutes of climbing, with Cal breathing hard and growing hot and sweaty, despite the shade, and they reached a natural balcony of rock overlooking a gulley. As they emerged into the sunlight, Roland hunkered down, putting a finger to his lips for silence. He stretched out on his belly and crawled up to the edge of the stone balcony. Cal crawled up beside him. About thirty meters below them, a group of five men, standing within a ring of huts, were gathered around a wooden stake propped in a mound of stones. Smoke swirled up around the stake and a few small flames. And tied to the stake . . .

Cal's mouth went dry. "Is that a *man* they're . . . they're cooking there?"

"Yeah. Most bandits aren't really cannibals, kid, but out here, in this territory—some of them are."

Cal watched as an enormous, bare-chested bandit—a fin jutting from his helmet and a surgical mask covering his face—used a big knife to slice a chunk of thigh off the dead man slumped on the pole.

"The big guy's a 'Bruiser,'" Roland muttered. "One of the bandit castes. Usually in charge of the others."

The Bruiser tugged up his face mask with a thumb and jammed a slice of seared human flesh into his mouth.

Cal's stomach squirmed at the sight and he had to look away. "And you want us to go *down* there?"

Lying beside him on the rock, Roland shrugged. "Kid, I'm not going back to Fyrestone till I can get what I came here for. I lost a partner. I don't want that to be for nothing. Help me and you're gonna make it more likely you get that ride to Fyrestone. Could be your folks are there."

Cal looked at him. "You got something in mind—involving *me*? Maybe trade me for the stuff you want from them?"

"What? Trade you? Hell no, I'm not going to . . . give me some credit, for crying out loud. Naw. I'm not gonna let 'em kill you. Less one of them gets a lucky shot off. Probably wouldn't happen."

Cal snorted. "Real reassuring."

"Keep your voice down. We're burning daylight here, so let's get to it. Here's what I'm thinking . . . Now, you see that big boulder there, just inside the passage to the gulley? Well, I'm gonna go move the outrunner and you're gonna go to that boulder, and . . ."

About thirty minutes later, Cal emerged furtively from the passage through the cliff and paused, looking around, hoping he had enough cover from the big boulder. It was the size and shape of a haystack between him and the bandit camp. He saw smoke rising past the boulder, and he could catch the nauseous smell of charred human flesh. But he saw none of the bandits from here.

Then he heard footsteps crunching in the sand and turned to see a short bandit sentry carrying a pistol, rounding the big boulder. Head in a red-striped helmet, the compact little bandit's face was covered with goggles and a breathing mask; he wore a leather jerkin, sleeveless, and thigh-high leather boots.

The bandit spotted him—"Look what the skag dragged in!" the bandit cackled, his voice muffled by the breathing mask.

The metallic taste of fear in his mouth, Cal darted back into the stone passage. Gasping, he sprinted at full speed through the narrow pass, half expecting to be shot in the back. The pistol cracked—and Cal *was* shot in the back. But a crackling flash came as the bullet struck the armoring field—the energy shield Roland had given him. It wouldn't take too many hits before running through its charge. Maybe one or two more and the shield would fail.

"Come back here, boy!" the bandit shouted at him. "You

gonna squeal when I cook ya?" The bandit fired again, this time the bullet whistling past Cal's right ear.

Then Cal reached the end of the narrow pass between cliffs, and ran to the right—just as Roland had told him to. He pressed himself against the wall of stone, outside the defile. The bandit rushed out into view—to be met by Roland, who'd been waiting there for him on the other side of the opening, with the biggest knife Cal had ever seen, almost a machete. He swung it hard; the bandit's head was severed from his neck and spun away to bounce along the ground, some distance off, trailing blood. The bandit's headless body staggered, went to its knees, then flopped forward, the stump of its neck spouting scarlet from the surgically neat cut.

Cal turned away, retching. Only a little food came up.

Roland came over, handed him a canteen. "Good job, kid. But there's more to do. Have some water. Then we're gonna do a costume change."

The Bruiser watched as the two Psycho bandits with him carried a shiny chrome metal chest of weapons out from the hut. This stuff was worth good money—rare Eridian weapons in that chest. Might use the weapons himself. Might sell them in Jaynistown—if there was anyone left to sell them to. Last time he was there, they were all busy killing each other. But that was okay too. If they were all dead, he could loot the bodies.

"Put it down there, Vultch," he told the taller of the two Psychos.

The Psychos giggled and dropped the silver case.

"I didn't say drop it, goddamn it. Ya gonna bust something in there!"

Vultch pulled his buzz axe from the strap that held it to his back and waved the wicked cutting weapon in the air. "Lemme bust it open! I wanta bust something open!"

"Yeah, we been waiting a week to open this thing!" said Gunch, the other Psycho. Their faces were identically masked, their goggled eyes glowing yellow, their shirtless bodies *nearly* identical, except for the scars—but with long acquaintance, the Bruiser knew which was which. Gunch was the shorter, more heavily scarred one who sometimes spontaneously fell to the ground and started licking rocks. The Bruiser usually had to kick him in the head to get him to stop doing that.

"I've been waiting because that goddamn buncha mercenaries been around, we hadda either kill 'em or wait till they moved on. If they spied on us when we opened it, we'd have to fight 'em for it and the shitbuggers outnumber us. Now, I'll open it myself. Get outta the way before I jump on you and squeeze your guts outta your mouth."

"Hey!" someone yelled from the entrance to the gulley. "I got somethin' for ya!"

The Bruiser turned toward the sound and spotted what looked like his perimeter sentry, Mulch, up on the boulder that bulked in front of the passage to the gulley. He was poised up there with a prisoner who was lying on his belly, maybe unconscious, hands tied behind his back. The prisoner lying across the boulder was a big black guy, looked like that ex–Crimson Lance Roland, who'd been hanging out in the area. The guy was twice Mulch's size and dangerous as a gasoline can on fire—Mulch must've gotten lucky to bring him down.

"I got Roland here! He's all tied up!" His voice seemed

higher than usual. Shrill. Excited maybe. Catching Roland—who wouldn't be?

"Good catch, Mulch! Tied up like a skag pup waiting for the roaster!" He pointed at Vultch and Gunch. "Why can't you bums be useful like that! Come on!"

The Bruiser ran toward the boulder, catching up his shotgun as he went, the two Psychos coming along after him, hooting gleefully. "Another prisoner! Let's slice him up and . . ."

The sentry yelled, "Come 'n' get him!" He rolled the big prisoner off the boulder, so he fell on his side on the ground, with a grunt. Groaning, Roland got to his knees, managed to get to his feet, just as the three bandits got to him—then Roland's arms came from behind him, and the Bruiser saw that they hadn't been tied at all, the strips of cloth back there just window dressing. And in each of Roland's hands was a pistol: Vladolf Rage automatic pistols already barking out their five-round bursts.

Another shot came from the top of the boulder—but that's the last thing the Bruiser knew. Because Roland's auto pistol sent its burst up under his chin, the bullets passed through his palate, rocketed up through his skull—and darkness closed over him . . .

Cal fired, aiming downward with the pistol Roland had given him—he was still on the boulder, just a meter above the nearest of the Psycho bandits. The man was swinging his axe at Roland but one of Cal's bullets cracked into the axe-wielding Psycho's head so that he staggered back. Cal expected the Psycho to fall but the masked lunatic kept his feet and came stumbling back toward Roland, raising his axe.

Roland was blasting away at the other Psycho, hammering him with the automatic pistols, emptying the clip. As the bandit spun and fell, Roland dropped one of the pistols, turned, and caught the first Psycho's axe handle in his left fist, lifted the howling bandit off the ground with it, then smashed down—crushing the Psycho's skull with his own axe.

Cal watched in horror and fascination as the Psycho went limp, falling back across the legs of his fellow—the other Psycho who was somehow still barely alive, lying facedown, clawing off his own mask . . . and licking the rocks on the ground just once, before dying.

Cal tore his own mask off and threw it down, slid off the boulder after it. He was grateful to get that mask off. The thing stank, and there was something wet and sticky around the bottom of it—blood from the decapitation. He was wearing the bandit's jerkin, still. It fit him pretty well . . .

But this planet wasn't a great fit at all. It was making him sick.

"Kid—you throwing up again?" Roland asked, coming around the boulder to him. "You know, you keep vomiting, it's a waste of food. Food's scarce out here. One reason these scum turn to cannibalism. Me, I'd sooner starve than eat human flesh—there you go, barfing again . . . Never mind, I'm gonna get the Eridian goodies."

Ten minutes later, outside the passageway through the cliffs, Roland was just loading the metal case into the back of the idling outrunner, strapping the case down. They were in the shade of a conical outcropping, where Roland had parked the outrunner.

"What are you complaining about now, kid?" Roland asked gruffly.

"I mean, jeez, Roland," Cal was saying, "on a civilized planet, a respectable type guy, he'd, ya know, take a person like me, lost in the wilderness, right back to a town—without making him put on a mask and a costume and pretend to be a bandit and watch as he blows people's heads off . . ."

"First off, you already know the answer to that, kid," Roland said, tightening the straps. "It's not a civilized planet. Not since Dahl abandoned it. Anyhow, you wanted a gun, talked like a tough guy about how to use it. Acted like you wanted the action."

"I shot one of those guys. He just didn't . . . *stop*."

"Takes a lot of stopping power to put a Psycho down. That's why I nailed 'em up close with the auto pistols. Slam five rounds in the head point blank, you're on your way. Bam-bam-buh-lam-bam, critical hit."

"I knew it was a tough planet. I guess I just didn't think it'd be *this* bad. People cooking other people alive—and eating them. You cutting off a guy's head like you were cutting a . . . a melon off a vine."

Roland chuckled, pushing the case back a little more so it snugged against the base of the turret.

"I just think we should've avoided those guys, not gone sneaking up to their camp, and . . . and just . . ." Cal's voice trailed off.

What he really wanted to say was, *I want my mom and dad, I want to be back home.* But he couldn't say that to Roland.

He was still in shock, after what he'd seen. He'd carried out the deception easily enough—he'd always fallen into playacting with ease—but watching Roland execute those three . . .

Roland looked at him, his expression hardening. "Anyhow, kid—don't make sense to sugarcoat the truth, not out here. My guess is . . . you're gonna have to learn to survive right here on the planet Pandora—maybe for longer than you expect. No settlement's really safe, they're always getting raided—you got to be ready to defend yourself anytime."

"But I'll be able to go up to the Study Station from Fyrestone—won't I?"

"Will you? Who knows when the next starship'll be stopping by—besides, a supply ship wouldn't take you on. Got to be one that takes passengers. And orbit personnel, kid, *never* come down here. They only watch from the safety of *up there*. From what I saw at that lifeboat site of yours, no one's been there looking for you. And from what you told me—that starship is burned up and gone. So no help there. The corporations only send help if you pay 'em good money in advance. A lotta money neither of us has. Look—I'm gonna tell you straight up: there's a good chance your folks didn't make it. Which means you're gonna have to learn how to make it down here on your own. I can't be babysitting you all the time. If there's no one looking for you at Fyrestone, no sign of your folks, why, I'll get you to New Haven. The boss lady of the town—Helena Pierce is her name—she's a good sort. Seems to give a damn. I figure she'd take care of you. But even in New Haven—it's never really safe . . ."

There's a good chance your folks didn't make it.

Those words rang in Cal's mind, over and over. They

burned in his belly. They made him want to crawl under the outrunner and hide, and he felt his eyes stinging with tears. "You . . . you don't have a right to say that . . . what you said about my parents. That they didn't make it. You don't *know* that! They'll find me! If they're alive they'll never give up looking for me."

Roland sighed. "Yeah, if they're alive. But chances are . . . And kid, we don't have grief counselors around here, okay?"

That's when they heard engines revving and tires screeching.

They looked up to see two outriders driving out of the passage, right toward them, about thirty-five meters away. The bandit vehicles were similar to the outrunner but sleeker, lower to the ground, a dull dusty blue color. Skag skulls had been attached in place of fenders over the wheels. The driver seemed hidden in a tanklike turret under the machine guns.

"Uh-oh—looks like the buddies of the Bruiser we took down. I thought there was a couple others around here . . . that's what we get for gabbing when we should be moving."

"What'll we do? They're coming fast!"

Scrambling up to the outrunner's turret gun, Roland yelled, "Kid—you really think you could drive this thing? Then you need to do it!"

Impelled by sheer terror—as the outriders bore down on them, strafing bullets already whistling through the air overhead—Cal ran for the driver's seat, jumped in, and put the vehicle in gear. He slammed his foot on the accelerator—and the outrunner roared into action, wheels squealing, heading randomly out into the desert. He was jerked back by the acceleration, and had trouble holding on to the steering wheel, as if it were trying to spin out of his grip, vibrating with the jolting of the outrunner across the rugged ground.

"Hold on to that wheel, kid!" Roland shouted. "You want to roll this thing over? You'll kill us both! Keep it steady!"

"I'm trying but—"

He almost jumped out of his seat then, startled by the noise as Roland fired the big machine gun in the turret.

A long burst from the turret, then Roland shouted, "Ha! Nailed him! *Uh*-oh . . ."

One outrider had gone down but the other was coming up right beside the outrunner, engine roaring, close on their left. Roland was firing at it but the angle was awkward, the outrider was too close, the turret gun couldn't slant down that low. The wheels of the outrider were almost touching the outrunner's and the bandit's turret gun was swiveling toward Cal, ready to blast him . . .

Then up ahead, on the right, a sharp projection of blue stone reared from the plain. On a sudden impulse, Cal turned the wheel sharply toward the projection, accelerated as if he were deliberately planning to crash into it, the outrider following closely on his left. A burst from the outrider's machine gun sent bullets slashing just over Cal's head.

"What the hell, kid!" Roland yelled. "You're gonna crash us into that goddamn rock!"

The outcropping loomed up—then Cal cut as sharp a right as he could without overturning the outrunner. He veered past the big spike of rock—and the outrider, as he'd hoped, with the driver focusing on Cal, didn't see it . . . and smashed glancingly into it, spinning out of control, flipping, rolling . . .

Cal hit the brakes, so that the outrunner skidded, and Roland was launched from the turret with the inertia. "Shit!" Roland yelled, as he was flung out of the vehicle. He landed facedown, sliding over the dirt, ending in a cloud of dust.

Oh no, Cal thought. *I've killed him.*

Cal jumped out of the idling outrunner. "Roland!"

But Roland was getting up, coughing, brushing himself off. "I'm all right. Just scraped the skin off my belly."

He came stalking back to Cal, stood over him, glaring— then let out a short bark of laughter. "Damn, kid, you got good instincts! You lured those bastards right into that rock!" He looked toward the wreck of the outrider. "Except . . . they don't go down easy, just like I told you . . ."

Cal turned and saw a bloody Psycho, left arm hanging broken, right arm holding up a threatening buzz axe as he came pelting toward them. Teeth bared, the maimed Psycho was running full bore from the burning wreck of his outrider. Howling at them as he came: *"I'm gonna skin ya, put on your face, and say hi to your momma!"*

Roland vaulted into the back of the outrunner, spun the turret around, and fired, blowing the Psycho in half from two paces away.

"Don't be talking about my mama," Roland said.

SEVEN

Zac and Berl were on a sunny hilltop, about a quarter klick from Berl's camp, waiting for Bizzy to come back from hunting. It was late afternoon, and Berl was staring into the distance. Zac thought he was in some kind of crazy fugue state.

"What you got to learn about this here desert," Berl said, at last, never ceasing to stare into the distance, "is that most of the time it ain't what you see that's gonna kill you. It's what you cain't see. Lotta times, what's right under your feet—or right over your head. See there, that's what I mean—here they come, some of the toughest rakks around here! Whip out your shotgun, Zac!"

"I haven't *got* a shotgun!"

But Berl had one, a big rusty red shotgun that didn't look very reliable. When the dusty blue rakks, looking like decapitated pterodactyls, dived down at them, Berl had the shotgun butt wedged to his shoulder, squinting as he tracked it. The rakks shrieked triumphantly as they dive-bombed.

"Shoot it!" Zac yelled. "Hurry! It's going to—"

The nearest rakk flattened its trajectory and struck, slashing at them with its barbed forejaws. It didn't seem to have a full head, or eyes—just a wedge-shaped snout, mostly mouth, jutting out in front. It raked at them with talons as it went—and Zac was knocked off his feet. He fell onto his back, the air knocked out of him when he hit the stony hilltop. He gasped, smelled the sickly reptilian reek of the thing; his ears ached with the shrillness of its scream.

At the same moment there was the *boom* of the shotgun firing and he saw one of the rakks explode into bloody rags in midair, just three meters up—the one who'd knocked him down, though, was climbing back up into the sky on strong wing-sweeps, preparing to come around for another attack. The rakks squealed and shrieked angrily, working up to another slashing dive . . .

Zac sat up, gasping for air, clutching at the wound on his right shoulder. It wasn't deep, but blood seeped between his fingers.

"Well one of the bastuds got past me but I got the second one, boy!" Berl cackled. "Now if you just had your shotgun ready!"

"I told you I haven't *got* a shotgun—"

"Should never have come to this planet without a good shotgun, young fella!" Berl chambered another round.

Three rakks were flying overhead, their blue almost the same as the sky, sweeping tightly back and forth like kites in a crosswind. Then two of them dived directly at them . . .

The shotgun thundered again and one of the rakks burst apart, raining reeking blood and animal parts on the two men—the other, injured by the pellet spread, flapped away, followed by the other surviving rakk.

"Ha! I discouraged 'em! They're gone for now!" Berl crowed.

He lowered the shotgun and twitched his shoulders. "Ouch. Arthritis acting up. Harder to shoot upwards nowadays. Slower too. Was a time I'd have gotten all of the bastuds."

"You got any of that Dr. Zed medicine I heard about?" Zac asked, kicking rakk guts off his foot.

"I might have a shot or two. But you'll owe me for it. Hard to come by out here! I don't see that Claptrap very often."

They returned to the camp—they'd gone to the hilltop to see if bandits were moving in on them and spotted only rakks. To get to the camp, Zac had to follow the old man down a winding path between boulders, then right past Bizzy. Yellow eyes glowing, the creature seemed to watch him suspiciously as he walked by. It was only a meter away, sitting on a fat rock like a daddy longlegs on a toadstool, stiltlike legs half-folded to either side of the boulder, turning its whole body to watch Zac as he passed. Any moment it might decide to spit corrosive venom at him—and his face would burn away, like what happened to that bandit, screaming and dying . . .

Why the hell had he ever come here?

He had to make a move, soon, at least try to get back to the Study Station, find out what became of his family. But the lure of that crashed alien ship was still strong.

Sometimes he thought he could *feel* that treasure out there, in the wastelands, throbbing; hear it calling to him . . .

Zac shook his head, and entered the camp, sat on an old crate as Berl administered the med syringe. The infusion began its work immediately—he felt strengthened, restored. His injuries closed up, the bleeding stopped. Wondrous stuff: nano-nodes that rebuilt the cells from within.

"Like I say, you owe me for that, boy."

"Sure, Berl. How about we go to a settlement, so I can get some money wired down to pay you with?"

"Hm?" Berl's face creased in a scowl. "Settlement—*me?* I don't go there less'n I have to. I meet the Claptrap, I give him the goods, he gives me what I need. *It*, I should say, speaking of a robot. I guess he ain't no he."

"Well, uh—you could *direct* me there."

"I could. But you'd never make it. Hell I'd-a been dead a long time ago if not for Bizzy . . ."

Berl squinted over at the Drifter and unconsciously touched the collar-like necklace. Looking at the necklace up close, Zac realized that the scaly, iridescent segments strung together on the copper had been wired there by Berl. Those pearly scales, each one only half the size of the palm of his hand, were the extraterrestrial artifacts. Berl had put them together for some reason and it seemed to give him a psychic contact with Bizzy.

"What you looking at, young feller?" Berl demanded, glaring.

Zac decided it would just make the old guy more paranoid if he wasn't straight with him. "Just—that necklace, Berl. Seems like there's some connection between you and Bizzy through that thing."

"What about it?"

"Look, I came out here looking for that crashed ship. Seems likely you know where it is, Berl. Now, why can't we partner up for real? You want to stay out here, hell, then stay here—I can act as your agent for the find. We can split it. I don't even need a big share. I'll sign a contract, whatever you want."

The old man was fairly trembling with suppressed rage.

Zac cleared his throat and went nervously on. "Berl, come on, man, take it easy—I am not trying to take anything that's yours. I am grateful that you saved my life. Wasn't for you, why—"

"Wasn't for me, some cannibal bandit'd be crapping you out in his turds right about now, mister!" Berl snarled.

Zac winced. "Well I wouldn't've put it that way but yeah. I'm grateful. I'm not out to rip you off. But just imagine—if you want to stay out here, why not do it right? If you were rich, you could send for a construction bot, dig a hole in this hill, make yourself a real bunker—a whole fortress out here, if you wanted to! You could set up robot sentries. You could defend yourself from anything—a rich man could . . . Berl?"

Berl had the shotgun pointed at Zac's middle.

Zac licked his lips, suddenly very dry. *"Berl?"*

"Boy," Berl said, his voice almost inaudibly low, "I'm thinking the best way I can defend myself . . . is to cut you in half right here and now. 'Cause otherwise you're gonna bring hellfire down on me from up there . . ." He glanced at the sky, then looked quickly back at Zac. "Outworlders flat cannot be trusted! And I was a fool to trust you at all."

"Can I . . . have a drink of water instead? I'm really parched, Berl."

Berl glowered at him—then pointed with the shotgun

muzzle at a canteen lying on the ground nearby. "Go on and get you a drink. While I think on if I should kill you."

Heart thudding, Zac got up, picked up the canteen by its strap, desperate to stall, thinking to swing it around, maybe hit the old man in the head with it before he could fire that gun—Berl had said he was slowing down some.

But then a shadow fell over him. He looked up to see two yellow eyes glowing down. Bizzy the Drifter was towering over him, on its pole legs, quivering, opening its maw. Seeming ready to spit burning spume down at him . . .

Checkmate. Zac had a choice of sizzling to death or being shot. He preferred being shot. He drank deep from the canteen, put it aside, turned to Berl—and was struck hard in the forehead by the butt of Berl's shotgun.

He fell, spinning into a sucking pit, wondering if he'd ever wake up again. If he'd ever see his wife or son, if he'd ever find his way out of . . .

Darkness.

Sunset blazed in Marla's eyes. Her wrists were pinioned behind her back, and they ached as she was marched along the wooden false beach to the group of slavers standing by a battered flat-bottomed motorboat. Slavers—waiting to purchase her.

Dimmle was behind her, Grunj stalked along to her left. Another sea thug she couldn't see was off on the right, a step or two back. She hadn't seen Vance today, though he'd seemed ready to help her escape. She'd thought he'd gone for her scheme. But all he'd gone for was her body. Then he'd locked her up, made himself scarce. Now Vance was nowhere to be seen, and Dimmle had shown up, taken him to Grunj—who'd received her while standing over the smashed corpse of a midget, grinning. "Your time has come, missy ho," he'd said.

And here she was.

So she was to be sold to slavers. What would happen to her then? A series of degradations—living death?

There was nothing reassuring about the slavers. They were hairy, sunburnt men in layered clothing and hip boots, bits and pieces of armor, holsters and scabbards, a rifle in each pair of hands. Their leader, standing with his hands on his hips, was almost a giant, a one-eyed man with a dent in his forehead and patches of hair on his scarred scalp. It appeared he'd been shot in the forehead, and the skin had grown over the hole—and somehow he'd survived. The side of his face missing the eye was half crumpled in. The other side had once been handsome, she supposed. He wore a sleeveless jerkin; his arms were twined with strings of tattooed sayings, something like Dimmle's. *Take em make em have em use em sell em take em make em use em sell em kill em . . .*

It seemed Dimmle knew him, hence the tattoo connection. "Mash!" Dimmle called. "Good to see ya!"

Mash's voice was like a bone slowly breaking. It came grating out the intact side of his mouth. "Good? Not good. You shouldn'a come here to work for this son of a bitch. I don't like it when my men leave without asking me."

"I paid you for the privilege, Mash," Dimmle said.

"Hmph, after the fact!"

"Never mind all that," Grunj rumbled. "We making a deal for the missy ho or not?"

Mash grunted, looking Marla over. "So this is the woman, yeah? Not bad! Possibilities. Not terribly young but . . . we can make a profit on her. I got some special customers on the Trash Coast pay good for that."

She listened in stunned astonishment as they negotiated her price. Apparently Mash was buying her "wholesale." She looked around, wondering where she could run to. Nowhere—you can't outrun a bullet. There was the boat—a flat-bottomed electric boat Grunj used to ferry people to his "island." One of Grunj's men waited at the tiller of the idling boat, a heavily armored man with a full-face breathing mask. Why did they wear the breathing masks? The air seemed fine. Were they hideous under there?

The negotiation was over after two minutes and a handshake. Mash gave Grunj a bag of money, and after he counted it, he gave Marla a shove toward the boat. "Go on, my man'll take you and them to the Coast. Do what they tell you or it'll go hard."

Dazed, she let herself be herded into the boat. She sat near the big man at the tiller. Mash got in, just in front of her, then his men piled in. The boat was laden to the brim, sat low in the water as the man at the tiller put the engine in reverse and they backed away from the false beach of Grunj's Island. They left Grunj, Dimmle, and their men behind. Still no sign of Vance . . .

The feeling of hopelessness that had been creeping up on Marla seemed to lunge for her throat. She felt crushed by the jaws of despair. She'd never see Cal again, never see Zac, she'd die in some bloody bed, probably . . .

The boat was turning around, heading away from the

artificial island toward a headland. The setting sun was off to her right. The darkening, craggy outline of the Trash Coast, a quarter kilometer away, was waiting for her . . .

"Who you figure to sell the bitch to?" one of the men asked.

Mash scratched at his ruined forehead. "Maybe that bastard Greeb. He might pay double for her—he uses 'em up quick and this one looks strong. Like she might last a year or two . . ."

"If he don't take a fancy to kill her quick."

"Marla," the man at the tiller whispered. "Soon as you hear the explosions, lie down as flat in the boat as you can."

"What?" Then she recognized the voice of the man in the mask. Vance.

They were only about a hundred meters out from Grunj's Island when two things happened—Vance cut the engines, and the explosions. Five fiery blasts went off from one end of the island to the other within seconds. Each one threw chunks of phony island in the air, pieces of shack and metal slats and spikes of wood and metal crates and bodies, some bodies in pieces and some living and screaming and some already dead—burning bodies, burning chunks of wood, lifted on pillars of fire. The multiple roar of the explosions made the men in the boat turn and gawk. The flames lit up the evening sky. Then the shock wave hit them and the boat jolted, lifted on a wave and almost overturned.

"Motherbuggerin' son of a *whore*!" exclaimed Mash, as he clutched at the sides of the rollicking boat.

Pieces of the island were raining down in the water; its sections, held together by chain and rope, separated and

sloshed in the sea, some of them overturning. Men shouted
and their shouts were lost in gurgles. The water around
the shattered remains of Grunj's Island seethed and
churned and steamed, as pieces of the island vanished . . .

Then silence settled over the sea—except for the sound
of the men in the boat, swearing and muttering.

Only then did Marla remember to flatten herself in the
boat. She lay down, curled up in the small space between
the men—and the shooting began immediately. Before the
staring men turned around Vance shot them. His rifle fired
electrical charges that took out their personal shields, along
with the rounds that cut them down. The bullets jerked
the slavers around in the boat. A few rounds were fired in
return, to no effect.

There were three splashes as dead and wounded men
fell overboard—and again the boat almost overturned.
Mash snarled and stepped over Marla, tried to grapple
with Vance—she reached up and tugged hard on the
man's knee so he tilted off balance and pitched overboard.

"Ha!" Vance said. "Good work, Marla!" He pulled off
his mask and grinned at her.

The engine started again, and the boat continued toward
the Trash Coast. Marla sat up and looked around. Only two
men remained in the boat. Both clearly dead—both missing their heads. She turned away, stomach flip-flopping.

Someone thrashed in the sea to aft. It was Mash, still
alive, face bloody, trying to swim after them.

"Stop that boat and fight me, you scummy coward!"
Mash howled.

"Here, shoot the bastard," Vance said, handing her a
pistol.

She numbly took the gun—she knew how to use one, she'd been a security guard for two years, right out of school—and she aimed it at Mash's face. She could see his face only dimly, tinged by sunset and blood, four meters back. A wave lifted him up, seemed to roll him closer to the retreating boat.

It was the ideal moment to shoot him . . .

She had never killed anyone before. The man was a beast; he had talked of selling her to someone who *uses 'em up quick*. But she had to close her eyes before she could pull the trigger.

The gun banged and jumped in her hand, twice. She opened her eyes and looked. She didn't see him any-more . . .

"You get him?" Vance asked.

"I . . . I think so."

Vance sighed. "Hell. Wish I could be sure. Tried to time it so Grunj would get blown up, too. I need 'em both dead. Grunj woulda figured out I took most of his cash when I left. Lotta money. I got it in this pack I'm sittin' on here. And Mash'd never get over my killing his men—taking his prize. Need both of them dead."

"I don't see how anybody could have survived those explosions. You did that?"

Vance's toothy grin was bright in the twilight. "What you think I was doing all day? Had to kill Grunj's ferry-man, take his mask. Put the bombs where nobody'd see 'em—but where they'd do the most good. I hadda make sure nobody'd follow us." He paused to squint at the tossing waves behind the boat. "I don't see Mash . . . I just hope you got the bastard."

EIGHT

It was a bright morning in Fyrestone—a good time to despair.

"Nope, nobody been around here lookin' for no kid," said the leathery shopkeeper. He claimed to be "mayor" of Fyrestone "on account of the last one just got his face blowed off by the bandits down the road and nobody else'd take the job."

Nozz was his name, and his eyes were hidden in dusty sunglasses, his hands in bulky gloves as he handled a cluster of glowing green crystals on the workbench. "I did hear a starship blew up. But I also heard most of the passengers got out in time. They was at the Study Station—they already left orbit on a freighter bound for Xanthus. Crowded in pretty bad. Charlie was up there, picking up some ordnance, saw 'em sleeping in the cargo hold. Normally them ships won't take passengers but—"

"And *nobody*'s looking for the boy here?" Roland interrupted. "You sure? His name's Finn, Calvin Finn . . ."

"Nope. Not a soul. And I'll tell you something else—there's a blockade going on right now—Atlas says it ain't safe for starships to come to this damn planet now! That one freighter got through and not a one after that. Atlas has their own ship up there, somewhere, and some mercs down here up to no good, way I hear it. And they're not lettin' anybody go up to orbit or come down, not for a while, unless it's from their ship! So nobody's comin' from the Study Station to look for no kid! Looks like you're adoptin', there, Roland! Haw! Put him to work scrapin' skag hides for his dinner . . ."

Cal turned away, sickened by the shopkeeper's indifference.

He walked away, alone, down the middle of the dusty Fyrestone street, past Dr. Zed's clinic and the shop that sold weapons, heading for nowhere in particular.

He was startled by a chattering coming from a small metallic creature in the shadow of a building to his left. It was a small orange and white robot, shaped like an inverted trapezoid, with a single camera eye and skeletal metal arms. It rolled back and forth, chattering, bouncing on its wheel, almost dancing. "Hey, check me out everybody, I'm dancin', I'm dancin'!" It created a kind of beatbox rhythm with popping and jug-huffing noises as it bounced back and forth. "Ohhh come on, get down! I'm dannnnncin'!"

Cal stopped, staring, and it seemed to notice him, ceasing to dance to turn its camera eye at him. "Wow! You're not dead?"

"Why should I be dead?" Cal asked, frowning.

"Because you're not heavily armed! Don't forget to check out Marcus's store!"

"I saw the weapons store. I've got a weapon."

"You're not going to shoot me, are you?"

"No reason to. You seen Zac Finn, robot? Or Marla Finn? Anybody from the Study Station or the *Homeworld Bound*, down here, lately?"

"Sorry, traveler! But there are new bounties available in Fyrestone!"

"No thanks, I've got my own worries. Roland told me about you—said you're a model C . . . L . . . I forget. A *Claptrap*, that's what I remember."

"You're a craptrap, you shitbag flesh bundle!"

"What'd you say?"

"I said you're a crackin' shooter boy, boy-o!"

"I don't think that's what you said."

"My servos are seizing! I could be leaking. Could you check me for leaks?" Cal stepped toward the robot and it immediately spun around and trundled away. "No, no, don't shoot me!"

"Crazy-ass robot . . ." Cal snorted. He turned away. The encounter had irritated him. He was abandoned, he was alone, and he was getting crap from Claptraps.

Maybe he'd go sit out at the cemetery on the edge of town. Might be peaceful there.

His parents were probably dead. If he couldn't be at their graves . . . someone else's would have to do.

Wrapped in gloom, he strolled out to the boneyard. It suited his mood.

Cal was sitting on a grave, leaning back on an old

wooden cross, when a shadow fell across him. He looked up to see Roland blocking the sun, a dark silhouette. "You a damn fool, kid?"

"What I do now?"

"You're sitting near the gate to the road, that's all. That's a wide-open gate too. About three hundred meters from a skag burrow. Pretty much any time a skag or a Psycho might get it in his head to take a run at the settlement and you're the first piece of warm meat they're gonna see."

"They oughta put up a locked gate, set up some sentries," Cal said, not really caring if they did or not.

"Yeah. They oughta. They'd be better off with you as mayor instead of that old bastard Nozz. Come on, kid, I got my Scorpio Turret, and I'm ready to head out. I heard a little something interesting just now, at the gun shop . . ."

"What?"

"Fella there says a guy in an outrunner saw a crashed DropCraft . . ." He pointed out into the desert. "Out that way. Says he looked it over, didn't see any bones in it. Or nearby either. No sign of whoever came down in it. Said it looked kinda recent. . . ."

So his dad might be alive. "You know that area, Roland?"

"Kinda. People say that part of the wasteland—it's haunted by some old ghost who rides a drifter—"

"A ghost? Really?"

"Probably a myth. This planet's got a lot of myths going on. Some of 'em turn out to be true, in a way. Anyhow— I figure . . . your dad, he'd reward me, if I deliver you to him. Right? I mean—if he's alive. I don't want to raise any hopes now. Most likely your folks are—"

"I understand, Roland. But there's a chance they're alive—or at least my dad. Yeah—he'd reward you."

Cal felt bad, telling that lie—knowing his dad didn't have much to offer as a reward, if anything.

Roland reached down, offered his hand. Cal took it and Roland pulled him to his feet. "Come on, let's get some supplies. Need some food—and ammo. We got to be ready to kick ass out there." They walked toward the town. Roland suddenly halted, turned to him, and stopped him with a finger poked in his sternum. "You did okay out there, with those bandits. I got some money from that Eridian stash. I'll give you a share. And I got a nice Eridian weapon I kept from it too. But kid—you're gonna have to grow up fast, where we're going. You know what I mean? You take orders from me—and you carry your own weight. I don't wanna hear any complaining."

"Anything you say, Roland. I'll do my part—all the way." But as he said the words, he wondered if he could live up to them. He was going to need Roland a lot more than Roland would ever need him.

He had to do whatever it took to get to his parents. Because it seemed they weren't able to come to him. Maybe his father, at least, was still alive . . .

Zac was fed up with being tied to a wooden fence. It was not his idea of a good time. He'd been here overnight and most of the morning, since waking up with a banging headache.

The sun was getting hot, and a warm wind was blowing dust in his face, parching his lips. He was glad to see the elongated shadow of Bizzy, like a living bird cage, stretching out over the ground in front of him. That meant that Berl was close at hand.

"Well how you doing there, you treasonous bastud," Berl said, coming to look him over. Bizzy, towering over them, looked him over too. The seam-faced old man squinted at Zac, pausing to spit on the ground nearby. He was chewing something, like gum or tobacco. "I see them nylon ropes held you good. You're lucky no skags wandered into the camp. Might've eaten your face before it kilt you. I've seen it happen."

"Berl . . ." Zac had to pause, to cough up dust. "Berl, first off, if you're gonna kill me, just do it. But this is no fit way for a man to die."

"Haven't decided yet what I'm a-gonna do with you."

"I don't deserve this and you know it. You could give me a drink of water, anyhow."

"Again with the water. Water's precious. Maybe you deserve a drink, maybe you don't. You were trying to boondoggle me outta what's mine."

"I was offering you a perfectly fair deal, dammit!" Zac coughed, and spat dust.

"Sure you were. You were interested in making me show you where that spacebug starship crashed so's you could stab me in the back, take it all, and leave my bones bleachin' in the dust!"

"Bullshit. You giving me the water or not?"

Berl stared at him, then shrugged and unlimbered a canteen from a strap over his shoulder. He held it up so Zac could drink from it. The water had a metallic tang from being in the canteen but he could have happily drunk it dry.

"Thanks . . . thanks . . . that's better."

Berl corked the canteen. "Hell, I got a treat for you here." Berl took something that looked like a gnarled, dried-out chestnut from his shirt pocket. "Little food for ya! Chew this up!"

Zac stared at it and decided he'd better accept. He never knew when the old man might feed him again. Better not ask what it was. "If it's not poison."

"It ain't." Berl shoved the gnarled little sphere in Zac's mouth, and Zac chewed, half expecting it to burst with burning acid.

But it was kind of sweet, and cinnamon-like and a bit musty too, almost like an oyster. He managed to swallow most of it, then found he was chewing the hull like gum— so that's what Berl had been chewing.

Berl chuckled. "Nothing like candied Primal testicles to give a man a good outlook on life."

"Candied . . ." Zac remembered what he'd read about Pandora. The big semianthropoid four-armed creatures ridden by some of the Psycho Midgets. Primal Beasts. "You're not serious . . ."

"The hell I'm not! I get 'em from that Claptrap robot, along with my other supplies. Yeah, there's a feller in New Haven makes 'em. Gettin' to be a real popular treat there. Good for what ails you . . ."

Zac spat out the Primal's testicle. "God. Wait—did you say you saw that Claptrap robot? You went to New Haven?"

"No, I never go real close to it. Always under siege, that place. There's bandits and Psychos camped all around it. No, I got a spot I meet him, certain times. Out in the

Rust Commons. You got to know the safe ways to go . . .
There're ways through ain't no one but me knows . . ."

"But—did you send a message, tell someone I was here?"

"Course not! You're in my secret camp!"

"Dammit, Berl, my family's out there, somewhere,
they've got to be looking for me!"

Berl snorted derisively. "Man, get yourself a big dose of
reality! If your wife and boy came down on this planet,
why, even if they made it to the ground alive— they're
likely dead now. This world chews folks up"—he hocked
the Primal's testicle onto the ground—"and spits 'em out!
Only reason you ain't dead is 'cause I happened on you and
I did what no one else would likely do. Mostly out of bore-
dom. So forget about 'em. Now, I'm gonna put a little bit
of a shelter up over you here, and give you a couple more
candied balls, and we'll have us a good talk. I can tell you
all about the time I was lost in the old Dahl mines, and I
come upon that crazy woman, Broomy, that lives out with
the sea thugs—why, she nearly tore me in half and I don't
mean with a weapon. I'll tell you what that woman uses
for a weapon . . ."

The old man chattered on, as he built a rough shelter for
Zac. The shade was some relief but Berl refused to con-
sider letting him go, refused to even loosen his bonds.

There was nothing else to eat, so Zac chewed up the
candied testicles Berl fed him. The flavor wasn't bad—and
as it happened, they seemed to hold a kind of biological
charge. He felt stimulated, encouraged, strengthened by
them. When the old man started drinking from a liquor
flask—something else the robot had brought for him—
Zac thought to himself, *Maybe if he gets himself dead drunk,*

I can break out of this . . . But how do I get past Bizzy? Wait and watch . . .

So Zac waited, and Berl got steadily more drunk. He sat on a rock nearby, drinking, spitting in the sand, and nattering. "Lost my dang-buggered tolerance for this here whiskey . . . Don't get it often . . . Don't dare keep a stash up here or I'd just drink all day . . . That's another reason I'm out here. Stay away from that stuff. And that ol' Trank'n'Crank. I was terrible addicted to Trank'n'Crank! You ever had that stuff, boy? Stay away from it, make you crazy! Lord, lord. Had to leave Trelwether Four because of that. Why, they had a manhunt on across the planet for me. I kilt the colonial governor's son over a woman. Long ago it was. Before they had these fast stardrives we got now. Say now did I ever tell you about . . ."

All the time, Zac was quietly stretching out his bonds, pulling them a little more, and a little more, till he felt blood trickling down his wrists. He wasn't trying to break free yet. Just stretch them out, and wait.

"I was a miner for many a year you know," Berl was saying. "One time on Elvis . . . What is it, Bizzy?"

The drifter reared up and clicked at Berl.

"Oh yeah? Sure, go ahead on, do a patrol, find yourself somebody to eat, but don't be long." He whistled his instructions at the stilt-legged creature, and watched as it walked off like a giant four-legged stork, picking its way delicately between the boulders and down the hill.

Good, Bizzy was gone. The chances of escape were increasing a bit . . .

"Where was I? Oh, that time on Elvis. Well sir, I was there when the tunnels collapsed on Elvis Presley . . . that's a planet you don't hear about anymore, named after some old-time singer . . . well the reason you don't hear about the planet Elvis is, a fella went all crazy claustrophobic and set off the whole supply o' mining blasters at once, and it's all underground there, you see, Dahl built it and built it cheap, and the whole thing come down on top of us, *crash boom bang*, more'n three thousand mining colonists killed, boy, and I was one of only six fools who got out of there alive—and two of 'em nearly kilt me trying to get my water jug before it was over, but then, one of 'em became my partner here, best man I ever worked with, even if he did try'n kill me, he was a fine gent, why one time . . ."

Two hours later, in the hottest part of the day, the old man went to lie down in the shade of one of his crude sheet metal shelters, and was snoring loud enough to make the sheet metal rattle as Zac set himself to breaking free in earnest. The ropes were looser, now, in some places, and the blood was actually helping, lubricating his wrists and hands, helping him pull from the loops. Five minutes of painful, grating work—and he got one hand free. He was able to turn around enough to use the free hand to untie the other, then he unbound his feet, keeping watch on old Berl all the time.

At last Zac stood up—slowly, carefully—and stepped out of the ropes, wincing at the pain in his wrists and ankles. He found the canteen, slung that over his shoulder, then took the old man's shotgun. He looked at Berl and thought about taking the necklace—but that would probably wake the old hermit and then he'd have to kill him.

Zac shook his head—and turned away.

Berl went on blissfully snoring as Zac put a few supplies in an old rucksack. Food, ammo, medical dressing. He slung it over a shoulder, put on a floppy old sunhat that'd belonged to Berl's partner, got a good grip on the shotgun, and set off down the hill, walking quietly as he could. The old man's snoring receded into the distance.

Maybe a real native of Pandora would have killed the old bastard and taken everything. It had crossed Zac's mind. For one thing, when Berl woke, the old curmudgeon might send Bizzy after him. But he just couldn't do it.

He watched for the drifter, didn't see it, and worked his way laterally through the boulders to the shallow cave in the hillside. The cave entrance was actually a filled-in skag den, judging by the smell, where he'd seen Berl poring over his stash of alien artifacts.

He paused in the shade of a big rock to drink from the canteen, and to shore up his nerve. The old man might not trouble to come after him just for a shotgun and a bag of supplies. He hadn't taken the rocket launcher, nor most of the food. But this . . . if he took the alien artifacts . . .

Chances were, Berl would want to hunt him down.

Feeling strung out between certainty and utter confusion, Zac groaned softly to himself. Finally, he thought, *If I don't do this, it's all been for nothing.*

Zac screwed the canteen shut, slung it over his shoulder, and took a deep breath. Then he went to the cave, and began digging with his bare hands.

The box was only shallowly buried. He dug it up and found there were two artifacts in it. And he had no idea what they were, or how to use them. One was the contorted, squirming, tubelike glassy spiral, like a twist of a neon light, that Berl had pointed across the desert. The other was a kind of hoop, about the size of a bracelet, made of the same translucent semimetallic material as Berl's necklace.

He held the spiral tube up—and immediately it twisted about in his hands, startling him so that he almost dropped it. It was like a snake with arthritis. At last it fixed itself in a new shape—and he had the definite impression it was pointing, like the needle of a compass.

His working theory was, it pointed toward the crashed spaceship it had come from.

Zac tucked the artifacts in his rucksack, reburied the empty box, and hurried away, down the hill and into the ravenous wasteland.

NINE

Could she really trust him? Probably not.

But she was stuck with Vance, for now, Marla figured, as they trudged along the Trash Coast in moonlight so bright it was almost daylight. Despite having apparently eliminated his old shipmates, Vance seemed apprehensive, glancing to the right and left, keeping up a punishing pace on the cracked road.

Marla was still stunned by what she'd seen: Grunj's Island exploding. Men tossed in pieces, high into the air. Scores of men floundered, drowning. Others, in the boat with her, shot to pieces by Vance.

What were Zac and Cal going through, if they were alive? Perhaps if she'd stuck with Mash she'd have seen them in the "slave pens."

Long mooncast shadows crisscrossed the road in front of them from the angular outcroppings of rough stone; from the heaps of old debris from mining camps, and wrecked vehicles. She was aware of a bone-deep weariness sweeping over her. Where was Vance taking her?

"Are we going someplace . . . secure?" she asked.

"Yeah. We gotta get past some scumbags first. But I've got a little place that's pretty well hidden and protected; we can stay there till tomorrow. Then we look for that crashed alien ship of yours."

"What, um, scumbags are we going to have to get past?"

"You'll see. You still got that gun?" Vance asked her.

"I do. Right here."

"Be ready to use it. We might have trouble up ahead . . . And I need you to be ready to use your weapons. The more of us use 'em right, the better our chances. I figure you're gonna need some practice. And you're gonna have your chance pretty quick. We're getting near a hangout for Psychos . . . I got to go through there to get where I'm going . . ."

That gave her a little energy. The energy of being on edge. She seemed to see the deep shadows moving, twisting, giving birth to shapes in the debris piles edging the road . . .

But the shadows to the sides never took real form. When the attack came it was from straight ahead.

She heard the Psycho before she saw him. She heard a high-pitched, but definitely human, *"Eeeeeeeeeeeeeeeeeeeeeee!"* coming from the darkness down the road. Then she saw the man who was making the shrill war whoop as he ran toward them, about fifty meters away, an axe upraised in his right hand: one of the Psychos, this one of medium height. Helmeted, hockey-masked, eyes glowing like orange embers, bare-chested, muscular, high boots, orange pants—his body straining toward them, muscles rigid, shrieking wordlessly as he came . . . everything about him said: *I'm here to kill you.*

"Shoot him!" Vance urged her. "Let's see what you can do!"

The Psycho was closer, running through a strip of moonlight. "*Eeeeeeeeeeeeeeeeee!*"

"Go on, shoot him!"

"*Eeeeeeeeeeeeeeeeeeeeeeeeee!*" Closer yet.

She could see a sheen of sweat on the lunatic's chest . . .

Closer. She raised the pistol. Shoot him in the head? The chest?

"*Eeeeeeeeeeeeeeeeeeeeeeeeeee!*"

"Shoot him, woman!"

The Psycho was picking up speed, shrieking, mouth open wide, a few paces away—

She fired, shot him in the middle of the chest.

He kept coming.

She fired again. And again. And . . .

She shot the Psycho again as the axe came swinging down at her head—Vance stepped in, caught the axe as the Psycho fell forward, axe hand outstretched . . . dead.

Vance tossed the axe to one side. "You're lucky he didn't have a shield." He frowned at her. "And you cut that pretty fine, lady! Trying to test my nerve?"

"No." She lowered the gun. "I saw what you did in the boat. I don't have any doubts about your nerve. I just . . . never killed anyone before."

"In the case of one of these"—he nudged the Psycho's body with his boot—"I wouldn't say *anyone*. I'd say any*thing*."

She stepped back from the pool of blood spreading around the Psycho. She saw the moon reflected in the dead Psycho's blood. "How did they *get* this way?"

"Some say they went crazy looking for the Vault. But that doesn't explain everything. What I heard, there's something in the Headstone Mine—where all these bastards used to work. What it is I don't know, but a guy named Sledge found it. Used it on them, that made them crazy dangerous. Something to do with the iridium there maybe. All I know is, they started to go nuts . . . and mutate."

"You can't mutate after you're already born."

"You can on this planet. Anyhow—if you're exposed to certain things, here, you change in a way that—if it's not mutation, it's the next best thing. Like that one coming at us now . . . a prime example . . . and chances are he's got a shield . . ."

"Eeeeeeeeeeeeeeeeee!"

This one was glowing in the night—when he ran through a strip of light he looked like the other Psycho but when he ran through shadow he glowed against the backdrop, with a nimbus of fiery red.

"Better reload that gun," Vance said, giving Marla another clip. She fumbled with it in the dimness, but managed to load the gun.

"Now—aim for that shield. See where the gear is, on him? Aim right at it . . . use every bullet . . ."

She aimed the gun, licking her dry lips, wanting to just run from the thing coming at her, and knowing she'd never make it. "Why is he glowing like that?"

"'Cause he's a Burning Psycho."

As the Burning Psycho got closer she saw his mask was like a bird's face, beaky, crested in feathers; his arms were covered with feathered sheaths, and flames flickered from him like the feathers of some diabolic god.

She was frozen at the sight . . . the Psycho was getting closer . . .

"Eeeeeeeeeeeeeeeeee!"

"Marla—!"

She fired, again and again, and saw the Psycho's shield sparking with the impacts of the bullets. They seemed to barely slow him.

She fired again and the shield flickered, went out—just as she ran out of bullets. He cackled with glee and raised a hand over his head, to go with the uplifted axe—

"He's got a grenade!" Vance shouted, stepping in front of her. "Suicide attack!"

Vance fired his combat rifle from the hip, spraying the Burning Psycho with bullets. The Psycho went down, the grenade bounced from his hand . . .

Vance turned and grabbed her, threw her to the ground, and flung himself down beside her—and the grenade went off.

Fire plumed, fragments of road rained, shrapnel screamed over them.

She lay there, afraid to move. But at last, coughing with the dust, she got to her knees and looked around. Her ears rang with the sound of the explosion.

Now two dead men lay on the road, in two puddles of blood. And there was another figure running down the road toward them. "Why do they *do* that?" she asked dazedly. "I mean, come one at a time like that, head-on?"

Vance helped her to her feet. "They sometimes attack in groups. But asking why they do something—hey, they're *psychos*, aren't they?"

"This one's big . . . but . . . lopsided. And it's like he only has one arm . . ."

"Yeah." He was loading his rifle. "One big arm. And one stubby one. It's a deformity. Carries the axe with the big one . . ."

"*Eeeeeeeeeeeeeeeeeee!*"

He handed her the rifle. "Let's see you try this gun . . ."

"But I've never fired one of these!"

Vance grinned. "Better learn quick—here he comes! A Badass Psycho! Looks like he's got a shield—it's kinda flickering. Must be low on power. Put that rifle butt against your shoulder there . . ."

"*Eeeeeeeeeeeeeeeeeee!*"

"Hold it up like that . . . right, now line up the sights and squeeze the trigger easy, send him some bursts . . ."

The combat rifle bucked in her hands, rudely banged into her shoulder, made her stagger a step back with its recoil. The big, deformed, masked man rushing toward them caught rounds in the force field of his cheap shield—sparking blue and red—and came pounding onward, howling out actual words now: "Time to play . . . time to play . . . *time to play-pla-play ya meat puppets*!"

Vance stepped up close behind Marla, put his arms around her, helped her aim. She couldn't deny the sexual exhilaration she felt as he did it.

"Strip the flesh, salt the wound! Hahahaha *haaaaaaaaa*!" shrieked the Badass Psycho.

She fired—squeezing out the rest of her clip. The shield

BORDERLANDS: THE FALLEN | 137

fell, the big man staggered as bullets splashed his blood from a half-dozen geysering wounds.

He swung the axe as he took the last few steps—and it chunked down in the dirt at her feet, as he fell facedown in the dusty road.

The Badass Psycho lay there quivering, muttering as he died. Vance took a pistol from his belt and shot the Psycho in the back of his head, three times quickly, to finish him off.

Marla looked away.

But Vance took her head in his hands, and roughly turned it so she was looking at the gray and red splash of brains in the moonlight.

"Don't look away! You want to survive out here, you gotta look right at death, girl! You got to stare it in the face! You got to *want* to blow out their damn brains! You got to be almost as psycho as they are! If you're not . . . they'll get us both! You understand me?"

"Yes," she said, retching, pulling away from him. "Yes, yes, yes . . ."

He took the gun from her and pointed up the road. "Let's head on—I think that'll be all we hear outta these fuckers if we don't get any closer to their crazy little camp. There's a trail up to the left we can take to skirt around the rest of 'em. It'll take us to the place where we're gonna bed down for the night. With any luck, we won't wake up with a couple of loony scumsuckers cutting our throats . . ."

"Oh hell," Roland whispered. "I think it's Crannigan."

They were lying flat on the lip of a high sand dune, overlooking a shallow valley of sand and scrub. The moonlight was bright, picking out the shapes of Crannigan and his men clustered below. "What'll he do if he sees you?" Cal asked.

"Probably kill me if he can. But . . . might be able to negotiate something. Better if he doesn't see us."

"So . . . shouldn't we get to the outrunner and get outta here?"

"Like I said, you got good instincts. Let's go."

They slid down the face of the dune, and ran toward the outrunner, about ten meters away.

A green-white explosion of energy, expanding in the shape of a sphere, knocked Cal flat on his back.

He found himself dizzily staring up at the oversized moon of Pandora. His ears buzzed, his head seemed to vibrate. What was on that moon? Was anyone there? Were they staring down at him now, with their heads buzzing and vibrating?

"Hey kid . . ." It was Roland, dragging him to his feet. "Get up. We got to try to get the hell out of . . ."

"You're not going anywhere alive, unless I say so, Roland," said someone stepping into view from the shadow under the dune. He had an Eridian rifle in his hands.

"Great," Roland muttered.

Crannigan leered at them. "Well he's able to survive the Primals and he's able to identify me—but he's not able to stay out of my way." He pointed the alien weapon. "Tell me why I shouldn't blow you to hell."

"Because then I'd be in hell waiting for you, Crannigan," said Roland, grinning. "The other reason is—this kid here is worth a million big ones in ransom. And I'm the only one who speaks his language—unless you speak Caucasio Bunkonian?"

Crannigan blinked. "*What* language?"

Cal took the cue. "Carbenosian rafka bukasa?" he asked, stringing random syllables together.

"Carbenosian nofka, ibo," said Roland to Cal, in the same sort of gibberish.

"You claim he's worth a mil in ransom?" Crannigan said, looking doubtfully at Cal. "Who'd pay a million for him?"

Cal almost retorted in his own language. But instead he looked at Roland and said, in a puzzled manner, "Snebozo mucka?" Cal tapped his own forehead.

Roland sighed and shrugged. "Rikbonna forcbusca!"

"What'd you just say?" Crannigan demanded.

"He asked me if you had an injury to your head," Roland said. "I told him I figured maybe you did."

Crannigan scowled. "My head's fine but yours is gonna be scattered all over the landscape if you're bullshitting me about this. Now step on over to our camp. And one thing you oughta take away from this is you can't sneak up on my people without me knowing, I always got lookouts keeping watch. Come on . . ." He pointed the Eridian rifle. "Move!"

"You want a share of the ransom, fine," Roland said, rolling the dice, "but I don't go with you under the gun. We can partner up. You know you're gonna need me—not only to talk to the boy, but also—you're sure to run into some hell out here. None of these chuckleheads you've got with you now are gonna match what I could bring to a fight. You keep me at your side, I can watch your back, Scrap."

"Or shoot me in the back," Crannigan snorted. "Last time we met, I couldn't have made you too happy . . ."

Roland shrugged. "All in good fun. I didn't mind. I handled them."

"Yeah—how'd you get out of that? Outrun 'em in the outrunner?"

"Dragged 'em to a Nomad with a mean streak."

"Nomads are all mean streak." Crannigan lowered his weapon. "Truth is, I don't trust none of my men—so I'll take the chance you're more useful to me than risky. Come on, let's go to camp."

"Crinbonna?" Cal asked, as if puzzled.

"Cringo-ina," Roland said, pointing toward the camp. He turned to Crannigan. "What about my outrunner? I got a Zodiac Turret too . . ."

"A Zodiac, huh?" Crannigan muttered. "That'll be useful. Okay, let's all three get in the outrunner. I'll be on the rear gun. Behind you. So don't get cute. Move it."

TEN

Since coming to this planet, Zac was always a little surprised to wake up in the morning. He was surprised he hadn't been killed in the night by . . . something. Any number of somethings.

But despite his foreboding, he'd slept the deep sleep of aching exhaustion. He'd spent a night in freedom, not tied up, not having to wonder if Berl was going to go mad and kill him, and this morning, stretching, looking around at his surroundings, he felt a surge of improbable optimism. The plateau he'd slept atop was about two hundred feet over the plain, a tableland rising abruptly over the rolling desert; the view, in the blue light of morning, was spectacular. It'd been worthwhile, climbing the steep trail up here with only the moonlight to guide him. It put him out of the reach of most predators—and the vista, from the cliff's edge, was all subtle silver mist broken by islands of blue stone. To one side the moon was setting; to the other the sun was ascending over the horizon. The air was fresh and cool.

Maybe there was hope. Maybe his wife and son were alive. Maybe he would find them, and the crashed alien ship. He would even make it all good with Berl—send him his share. He had no problem with that.

Might be hard to do, though, if Berl killed him before he could find the treasure. Always a possibility. He peered down at the desert, in the direction of Berl's hideout, at least twenty kilometers back. He shaded his eyes, looking for Bizzy. Wherever Bizzy was, Berl wasn't far away. And Bizzy ought to be easy to spot. Just look for a shape like a daddy longlegs as high as a house.

He saw nothing but a movement in the sand, almost directly below the cliff. Big creatures that seemed to swim in the sand, down there: emerging, dipping out of sight, emerging again. Giant purple crustaceans.

And there, a half kilometer off—the rising sun was throwing long, rippling shadows from a group of trotting skags. Farther, rakks wheeled over the horizon. A few clouds scudded. Nothing else moved.

Maybe the old man wasn't coming after him.

But Zac knew better. Berl was obstinate and obsessive. When the old hermit realized what had been taken from the cave, he wouldn't stop till he got back "what was his" or died trying. In time, Zac would have to face him.

He returned to the old surveyor's camp, a hut and a circle of stones, where he'd spent the night. He knew it was an old surveyor's camp because the old surveyor was there: a skeleton, hand still clutching surveillance instruments.

Most of the instruments were rusted, broken. But one, protected by a scrap of canvas bag, looked intact—a small telescope. Did it still work?

He picked up the telescope, brushed off the lens, and looked into the distance. *Yes.* The little telescope zoomed in quite sharply. And it was solar powered, so the power unit was still functional. This instrument could save his life—he could use it to see enemies before they spotted him. Give him time to take cover. It also just might help him find the starship crash site . . .

Feeling like maybe, for once, he was on point with destiny, Zac ate a small amount of the food he'd cadged from Berl, drank a couple of swallows of water from the canteen, and then reached into his satchel, took out the strange helical neon tube–like artifact he'd stolen from Berl's stash. He remembered seeing a spirochete in a microviewer once—this thing was shaped something like that, but large as a man's hand. It squirmed at his touch, turning, shifting, rolling in his palm—to point west.

He put on his floppy hat against the increasing glare of the rising sun, carried the telescope and the artifact to the other side of the plateau, less than a quarter klick away to the west.

Zac approached the edge carefully and hunkered down, not wanting to be seen against the sky.

A warm breeze rushed from the west, fluttering his hair, and bringing the smell of carrion and unknown spices. He raised the spiral artifact, held it loosely on his palm so it could move freely. It quivered, and turned compasslike to point southwest. He set the artifact on the rock of the butte, and lifted the telescope to his eye.

Southwest, a promontory jutted against the sky, rising like a worn tooth above a series of canyon rims. A conical shape, broken on one side—could be an old volcanic cone. Hadn't Rans said something about that?

. . . Now it just happens the crash site is under a kind of overhang in an old volcanic cone . . .

That could be it, right there. Meaning he was in the same area of the planet, in a rough sort of way, as the coordinates he'd been given.

But how far away was the dead volcano? At least fifty kilometers, maybe a hundred. How was he going to get there alive? He didn't have enough food or water . . .

Berl had said a man could eat almost any animal on the planet. He had the shotgun. He could kill game. If it didn't kill him first.

He'd sent the location of the crash site to Marla. It could be that she and Zac had gone there already. They could be there waiting for him. Maybe they'd gotten help—

Or maybe they'd gotten killed. Or . . . remembering the bandits who'd nearly done him in by the DropCraft he felt sure that there were worse things than being dead on this planet. If Marla was in the hands of people like that . . .

No. He had to put that out of his mind.

Zac returned thoughtfully to his campsite. "Well, old boy," he told the skull of the dead surveyor, "sorry to leave you without company. Maybe Berl'll be along soon. No doubt he'll have something to say to you . . ."

Zac gathered up his supplies, stashed them in the satchel, picked up the shotgun and the canteen, and left for the steep, twisty trail that led down to the desert.

An hour later, he was trudging through the shadows of a gulley, headed southwest. He stopped from time to time, to listen, and look. Twice he scrambled under cover of stone overhangs to hide from rakks soaring overhead.

But he kept moving—one step at a time to the southwest. Wondering if he was getting closer to his wife, and son, with each step. Or farther away.

Marla woke in the sheet metal shack to find Vance gone.

The first feeling she had wasn't fear of being left unprotected on this dangerous planet. It was one of emotional abandonment. A deep resonant pang went through her. An ache.

"Oh no," she muttered, looking sleepily around the malodorous little shack. "Don't tell me . . ."

Surely she didn't have feelings for the big lout, did she?

Ridiculous. Despite more than an hour, last night, of . . . bonding. Of a sort.

Sex, sure. But love? Not possible. First of all, she loved her husband, flawed though Zac was. Second, Vance was a felon wanted on numerous planets. Third, he was a big, sweaty thug who'd killed a number of unsuspecting men in front of her—in fact, he'd killed *scores* of them, blowing them to hell on Grunj's Island. True, they were all sea thugs, awful men from what she'd seen, but still . . . the ruthlessness of it was frightening.

And fourth, she had to think of what was best for Cal and . . .

Wait. Why was she having to make this long list? Why wasn't "she loved her husband" enough?

The why was . . . last night. Vance had picked her up in

his arms, carried her easily to the bed of old rags, and he'd taken her, acting as if it were a matter of course—and she hadn't resisted. Just as she'd acquiesced that first time on Grunj's Island. Both times she'd told herself it was because she needed to develop a relationship with him, so she could use him for her own ends—to protect her till she could get back to her family. She needed him to survive, and besides, if she resisted him he might hurt her.

But she'd opened herself eagerly to him; she'd sought out his rough lips, she'd let her hands trace his powerful shoulders as he took her, she'd enjoyed his considerable endowment—in fact she'd reveled in it.

All right, she was a grown woman, the circumstances were unusual, she could be forgiven for enjoying herself, squeezing a little pleasure out of life in this terrifying world. Who knew how long she'd be alive? No reason to be a martyr. She could enjoy the little . . . if *little* was the word, given the ravaged soreness she felt between her legs today . . . that life offered her, on Pandora.

But surely there was no real emotional involvement. Nor should there be. It wasn't *love*making, it was just sex. That was all.

But she ached, seeing he'd left her here alone without a word. There was something primeval here. Her ancient ancestors, hundreds of thousands of years earlier, had been hunter-gatherers, she supposed, traveling the land looking for shelter, for game; the man protecting the woman, the woman doing her part maintaining whatever dwelling they managed, offering him affection, a kind of shelter in her open arms.

The circumstances seemed to call those ancient instincts

up within her. To make her want to follow him, forever, making a fire, arranging a bed for them, watching out for enemies as he slept . . . bearing his children . . .

She shuddered. This was insane. But the feeling was strong.

Then Vance came back into the shack, carrying a bloody carcass slung over his shoulder.

She stood up—and he dropped the dead animal at her feet. Then he took a long, serrated combat knife from a belt sheath, and threw it so it stuck in the carcass. "Marla, you got to clean that, and prepare it, 'cause we're short on food. I had to trade some food for information. I found out where the truck is I want. The one they brought you in on. Same bunch. If you don't like those fuckers, we can kill 'em. Might have to anyway. Meanwhile, we got to have food. Skag meat's not bad if you hang it a couple hours, and salt it. See there, in the corner of the shack? That's a drain. There's a hook over it. Bag of salt on the shelf. You drag it to the drain, gut that skag, and I'll hang it, then we'll let it bleed out, and we'll cut meat and salt it. May as well keep busy. We're gonna be here till after dark . . ." He yawned, and wiped skag blood off his arms with a scrap of cloth. "I'm gonna get some more rest . . . you just about wore me out last night . . ."

He walked past Marla, leaving her in a welter of emotion. Vance was back. That was good. Only . . . *only* . . . because he would protect her till she could get back to her family. It wasn't the bonding thing.

But he wanted her to gut this hideous, large, smelly animal. It looked about the size of a large wild boar, with three oddly splayed jaws, spines along its back, reptilian skin. A horrible reek rose from it, like the repellent smell that garter snakes put out to drive away predators.

Contemplating the dead skag, and the idea of gutting it, her stomach tried to retreat into her bowels.

Still, Vance had gone out and killed the thing, at a risk to his own life. He was going to be protecting her—though she'd have to do some fighting herself—and she had to show him that she was useful. Suppose he decided that sex didn't make her useful enough?

Marla sighed, and plucked out the knife. Grimacing and gagging, she began to carve at the creature's belly.

The hard part was getting the knife into the skin. Once it was in, halfway down the blade—especially in the softer part near its groin— she found she could saw her way up to the ribs. Its general anatomy was not so different from a boar; the skeleton seemed roughly similar. Her hands ached by the time she got the belly split open. She made a cross cut, to open the belly up more . . .

Mottled purple and green, the skag's guts slopped out, with a smell that doubled the repulsive reek of the creature's exterior. Marla's gagging redoubled too, especially when she had to reach into its still-warm, gooily wet interior to cut the guts loose, but she kept from vomiting until, in cutting the thing's stomach off, something popped out . . .

A human hand, bitten off at the wrist.

She rushed to the drain in the corner of the shack, and vomited.

Still bent over, hands on her knees, she turned her head to see if Vance was sneering at her—but he was snoring instead, lying on his back on the raggedy bed, asleep, mouth open. In his right hand was a gun, held across his chest. His finger was on the trigger as he slept. Was the gun a message that he couldn't trust her, clasped there to warn her off—or was it there to protect them?

Marla straightened up, shook her head, and laughed softly to herself, not sure what she was laughing at, and returned to the skag carcass. Looking at the bitten-off hand, the thought passed through her mind that it could be Zac's hand, or even Cal's. But as she looked at it, despite the fact that the skin was half-digested away, she could see it was far bigger than their hands. Some bandit, wandered too far from his buddies, knocked over on his back, had tried to hold the slavering skag's jaws back—and lost his hand for his trouble. To start with. She didn't look into the stomach to see what else was there.

She found an old sack to put the guts and the hand in, using the knife blade to shove them into it. She carried the sack to the door, opened it slowly, and looked through. A sunny morning. A blessedly clean wind in her face. In the distance, down a series of stony slopes, she could see the ocean. Something flew through the sky over the sea—a rakk?

She saw no other movement but the slow nudging of clouds.

She dragged the sack of offal out in the open, tossed it behind a boulder. She hoped the smell wouldn't attract scavengers, but there was no way she was going to share a shack with a pile of rotting skag guts. After a moment's thought, she used her hands to cover it with sand.

She lingered outside, standing by the doorway, taking deep breaths of air. Then she went back inside, closing the door behind her.

"Vance?" she called. "Wake up! You going to help me hang up this skag carcass, or what?"

• • •

"Roland . . . ," Cal whispered.

"Yeah kid?" Roland was barely audible, both of them trying not to be heard by the others. Roland was cleaning sand from the engine of his outrunner, Cal bending over it beside him, pretending to help. He glanced over at the mercs.

The mercs, twenty meters away, were mostly still gathered around the smoky campfire, grousing as they drank their morning coffee, some of them casting disapproving glances at Roland. Crannigan was up on the dune's crest, talking to the sentry he was posting. Another was trudging sleepily down to get some rest.

Cal lowered his voice a notch more. "You think Crannigan buys the thing we told him about, uh, you're gonna get money for me and only you can speak the language and . . . all that crap?"

"I think he half-believes it," Roland whispered back. "But pretending he believes it—that's just cover. More likely he's decided he needs me—he's expecting trouble these thugs can't handle. I guess he knows me well enough to figure, if I say I'll stand by him in a fight . . . I will."

"You will? A guy like that?"

"Sure—long as I need him too. He's on his way to where we're going. Could be he's doing the same thing we are—checking out the place your dad came down. Ol' Scrap's being mighty close-mouthed about it all. We'll see. And once I don't need him—I'll tell him so. And I'll tell him to his face. Then all bets are off. Him and me, we'll go toe to toe. I'll give him a little something special from my old pal McNee."

"Crannigan and his men are going the same way we are?"

"That's the way I heard it."

"They work for Atlas?"

"They're subcontractors, you might say. Atlas has its own men—Crimson Lances. But when they're trying to keep something real quiet, they'll use mercenaries. Guys who soldier for pay. Usually means they got some real dirty work to do . . ."

"Hey . . ." Cal lifted his head, listening. An anomalous keening, humming sound vibrated from above.

He peered up at the sky, half-expecting a swooping predator. But instead he saw a square of silver, growing bigger, bigger, as he came down toward them. "Something's flying down to us! A transport!"

Roland stepped back and they both craned their heads to look. Within a minute, a silvery vehicle, about the size of a four-bedroom two-story house, was slowing to hover over them. About forty meters up, it was shaped like a step pyramid of silvery metal and glass, point upward, with oval pulsers at its four lower corners. Cal guessed it was an orbital landing craft, probably from a starship. He'd seen this model in pictures, but never in person.

It slowed, hovered, then eased over to the nearest hilltop, opposite the big dune, and settled down, extending struts to straighten it, hissing steam, its shimmering repulsion fields raising a cloud of blue dust. Along the lower tier of the metal step pyramid was the corporate logo, red against silver:

THE ATLAS CORPORATION: OTG VESSEL 452

A port opened, and a ramp extended. Down the ramp came four men. Two of them were bodyguards in heavy armor—one silver, the other blue—their faces unseen behind opaque plasteel helmets, sleek Atlas rifles in their hands, heavy boots clanking on the ramp. They kept watch over a scruffy red-faced older man with lank hair, who limped as he walked, and a polished-looking young man in a clingsuit stenciled with a coat and tie; an executive, Cal supposed. The exec wore light blue sunglasses, a friendly, soft smile on his affable face.

"Well I'll be damned," Roland muttered. "That limping old duffer there is Rans Veritas. I know him from New Haven, and Fyrestone. Sneaky old hustler mostly. The guy with him—don't know him. Got to be an Atlas exec. Come on, let's see if they'll let us listen in . . ."

They walked casually toward the shuttle. "Who're the guys in the armor?" Cal asked, in an undertone.

"Canned soldiers, we call 'em. Probably Atlas elite. Usually more cold-blooded than a viper."

Scrap Crannigan hurried up the slope to meet the men standing at the bottom of the ramp. Roland, Cal, and the mercs stood in a quiet group near the vessel, listening.

"Scrap, how are you?" called the slick guy in the blue sunglasses. "Rans here says he can take you to the site. You'll go with him, cross-country from here."

"That right, Gorman?" Crannigan seemed to be holding himself back as he spoke to the exec. He looked at Gorman with a dull, sullen hatred. "Why don't you just take us up in that thing and set us down near it?"

"We haven't got the exact coordinates. We had it down to a few hundred square klicks . . ."

"I know. And we've looked nearly every square centimeter . . ."

"And," Gorman went on patiently, "Rans here says if we get too close to the ET site from the air, it'll shoot us down. Uses some kind of beam we can't shield against. We tried a drone, and we lost it. Never found out what happened to it. But it seems if you approach it from the ground . . ." He shrugged. "It's possible."

"Yeah? How long you had this information?"

"Not long. Rans here—he was trying to do an end run around us. Gave the info to an old associate of his. The guy crash landed between here and the site. Might be alive."

Cal thought excitedly: *He's talking like Dad is alive . . .*

"When we took Rans into . . . protective custody," Gorman went on, "he offered to show us in person. This is as close as we can get from the air. We need you to get in there, run interference. Take down that thing's defenses."

"I saw a starship break up in orbit . . ."

Gorman nodded. "The *Homeworld Bound*. Signal from down here took over their security. We think it was the alien ship protecting itself."

Roland snorted. "Liar," he muttered.

"You still have those outriders we gave you?" Gorman asked.

Crannigan shrugged. "Still got two of 'em. Lost the others when we got nailed by some Primals. They were after"—he glanced over at Roland—"somebody else. They lost some pals, came after us instead. Kinda caught us by surprise."

Roland smiled.

"We can give you a couple of sandtrackers," Gorman said. "I'll have my men offload them. It's all we brought but it should get you to the vicinity. Check out that

DropCraft—we don't want anybody else messing with the site, if you get my meaning."

Crannigan nodded. "I got that message already. We're heading there today. Let me tell you something, Gorman—there better be a payday at the end of this. You bastards have been holding stuff back."

"Mr. Crannigan, I'm afraid I just don't like your attitude. Remember that you work for us. You're on salary—and you get the bonus we talked about if you succeed. Have no fear—it'll make you a very rich man indeed."

"Uh-huh. I could use some more men. How about these metal monsters of yours?"

"The bodyguards remain with me." His affable expression became coldly ironic. "But you can have Rans Veritas. Maybe he's good in a fight. Anyway—he's your guide. It's not just a question of location, as it turns out. It appears you've got to know just the right way to get into the alien ship. That's where Mr. Veritas here comes in."

He turned to go.

"What about those sandtrackers?" Crannigan demanded.

The exec replied as he walked up the ramp, not even turning around. "I'll see they're sent out."

The bodyguards clanked up after him, one following close behind him, the other walking backward, keeping a wary eye on Crannigan.

The ramp withdrew into the ship, the port closed. The onlookers stood back as the shuttle took off.

Rans Veritas stayed behind. And he was staring, with a sort of dull hostility, right at Cal.

ELEVEN

Zac was pretty sure something was stalking him. Trouble was, it was underground.

Spiderants, maybe. Or some of the other creatures Berl had told him about. Larva crab worms.

He was heading southwest down a mostly dried-out riverbed, stopping only once to refill his canteen from one of the few patches of water left. And every so often the ground trembled under his feet.

Now he felt the vibration underfoot again and looking behind him he saw the sand hump up in spots, as if something large was coming close to the surface. Something that was tracking him.

He stood stock-still, suspecting that whatever it was, was tracking his footsteps across the ground.

The trembling in the ground subsided. He had a feeling, an intuition, of something waiting for him to move . . .

Could he stand here, frozen, unmoving, till they went away?

He assessed the area. The dried river seemed to fork just ahead. One fork went southwest, the other bore due south. If he could get these things to assume he took the south fork when he took the southwest . . .

To his immediate right the bank of the dry riverbed beetled with an outcropping of loose rock. Several smaller boulders lined up, in the riverbed, in a sort of natural flagstone pathway to the outcropping. There was a shadowy place behind the outcropping he might hide—or he might be trapped and killed, if the things caught him there.

A rumbling came from the ground to his left. The sandy soil shook, and humped up. Suddenly two purplish jointed probes thrust above the sand like periscopes.

Zac shouldered his satchel, arranged the canteen, got a good grip on his shotgun, and turned to leap to the nearest low boulder, in the row leading to the outcropping. He jumped to the next "flagstone," and the next, hoping his impacts were absorbed, muffled by the stone. On the third rock he nearly tipped over, almost dropping the shotgun . . . swaying like a drunk on the uneven stone till he got his balance.

At last he got to a big rock jutting from the riverbank, climbed onto it, slipped down behind, then peered over it just as the creature emerged bodily from the sand . . .

Larva crab worms, boy, Berl had said. *Mean, purple sons of bitches, bigger'n a big man. Like giant crustaceans they are but with one big glowin' purple eye! Spit acid at you, they will, burn you down, cut up your remains, drag you down to their burrows below the sand. They burn off your limbs, snip and snap through spine, and then eat you! Eat you nice 'n' slow, they do!*

That's what he was seeing: A single large, dark purple,

glowing eye in the thing's head—and forearm pincer-claws, each pincer big enough to cut through a man's neck, and all bristly. The thing wormed and humped eagerly along, hissing to itself, clacking, clearly hunting for food. Those antenna-like probes extended from its mouth, to poke about the sand where he'd been a moment before, examining the rocks he'd jumped onto.

Zac ducked down, trying to think. Maybe the crab worm was intelligent enough to figure where he'd gone. Then it'd trap him here in this stone niche and snip him into pieces or burn him to an easily digestible ooze with a thick squirt of its corrosive phlegm. Or both. He might be able to kill it with his shotgun before it killed him—or he might not.

He noticed a small pile of stone rubble at his feet. If it was true that the things followed surface vibrations . . .

He picked up a rock the size of a softball, and hefted it, slowly straightening up to peer over the top of the outcropping. There were two larva crab worms in the riverbed now, each one about the size of a large crocodile, clicking and hissing and screeching along as they searched for him. They seemed to staring down the passage to the south-west—as if thinking he might've gone that way. And that was the way he was planning to go.

The chitinous purple creatures humped toward the southwest fork in the dry riverbed . . .

They weren't looking his way. If he climbed out of his hiding place, right now, they might spot him, and drag him down.

He got a firm grip on the rock, and threw it overhand with all his strength, as far as he could, down the south fork of the riverbed.

It struck the ground about fourteen meters away with an audible thump. The larva crab worms turned that way, chittering excitedly, humping quickly down the south fork to investigate. He waited till they'd moved well down the fork, then he crept slowly out of his hiding place, and went in the other direction, stepping on rocks where he could, till he was well down the other fork. He looked back, and saw no pursuit.

He continued another kilometer until the riverbed no longer headed southwest—it veered off sharply to the southeast.

Zac sighed. He climbed up the crumbling bank, out of the riverbed, and started across open desert. He was far more exposed now.

But he had to keep on to the southwest—where the half-shattered volcanic cone loomed dark blue against the horizon: tantalizing, inviting, and sinister.

Gnawing salted skag jerky, Marla waited in the cab of a rusted old tractor, a construction vehicle abandoned by the Dahl company and long since stripped of useful parts. She looked out through the cracked window of the cab, squinting at the dark trail that Vance had taken between the piles of trash and mine tailings. Was he even coming back for her? Did the big lug really care what happened to her?

Stop it. It didn't matter if he cared about her. All that mattered was using him to stay alive till she found her family.

But that ache was there, inside her . . .

She'd read about a psychological syndrome that might

apply. A prisoner learned to identify with their captors, in order to survive. Vance wasn't exactly her captor—but then again, he was. She had no doubt he'd knock her flat if she tried to run away.

So maybe . . . Maybe she'd gone a little crazy, lost in these endless borderlands. Maybe the whole nightmare had traumatized her more than she'd realized. Maybe her feeling for Vance was just a twisted strategy to survive.

If what she'd seen on this planet had traumatized her— what was it doing to Cal?

She felt her eyes burning with unshed tears. *Cal.* She couldn't do a thing to help him. Not sitting here.

She ought to simply slip away on her own, and try to find her son. If she kept to the shadows and stayed alert, she just might survive. She drew her pistol from her coat and looked at it. One clip was not much protection on this planet. Should she try it?

But that's when Vance came trotting back down the trail. He waved, teeth flashing as he grinned in the moonlight. He climbed up on the wheel axle, leaned near, whispered, "They're there—and they're drunk! Someone made a run into Jaynistown and got some booze. Ought to take the edge off their sentries. Come on, let's steal that truck. Then we head for the alien treasure horde!"

"If this bunch used to work for you, Vance . . . maybe they'd still take your orders."

"Naw, they worked for Grunj. They took orders from me, sure. But not no more." He took a communicator from his pocket and waved it at her. "I've been listening in to the sentry chatter. The bastards know I blew up the island. There were survivors. Not many, but enough. Turns out

Dimmle's still alive . . . and he's looking for me. Told 'em to shoot me on sight."

"But—you've got that money you stole from Grunj. Couldn't we just go to a settlement and *buy* a vehicle? I mean—why borrow trouble with this bunch?"

"Long way to a settlement—where I just might be shot dead for being an outlaw, anyhow. There's a price on my head. If your old man knew about the alien ship—then so do the corporations. I'm gonna get there before they do. This'll get us transportation fast. Now come on—let's do this!"

Marla groaned to herself. It seemed her mind was made up for her. She climbed out of the old tractor and they moved quietly as they could toward the bandit camp, picking their way through rock and trash and old metal debris.

The night was eerie in the vivid moonlight; the debris seemed transformed by the moonlight into abstract metal sculptures. She caught a glimpse of an attenuated fountain of sparks rising against the dark sky: the campfire of the bandits.

It wasn't a campfire so much as a big bonfire she saw as they approached a ragged ring of rusted metal around the camp. They squatted in the darkness, watching the bandits. There seemed about twenty of them gathered around the bonfire, passing bottles, laughing. They had taken off their masks and goggles so they could drink and their deformed faces seemed strangely naked without the masks. One of them nudged the bandit to his right and hand signaled, *Watch this!* Then he took a handful of bullets from his pocket and tossed them onto the other side of the fire. A splash of sparks—and the bullets, swallowed in flame, detonated almost immediately. A man screamed, others shouted profanities and ran from the fire.

Vance swore as a bullet zipped overhead and flattened down; Marla flattened, too, but watched the bandits through a rust hole.

Bullets ricocheted from stone and steel. Another man shrieked. The man who'd thrown the bullets laughed in drunken hysteria, slapping the ground. He turned to the man beside him, the one he'd signaled to watch . . . the man lay dead, a bullet through his brain. The bandit who'd thrown the bullets gaped—and then erupted into even louder mirth. The others returned to the fire, laughing and cursing both, shaking their heads at their crony's sense of humor. What a card.

Vance signaled to Marla, and they crawled through the shadowed debris, about five meters from the fire. They'd gotten most of the way around the bonfire when Marla saw the truck, just a few long paces away. It was a simple flatbed truck, solar powered, and there were two sentries leaning on it, talking and passing a bottle.

Vance whispered a suggestion to Marla. She rolled her eyes, but shrugged and crept up, alone, to the front of the truck. She was on the side opposite the sentries, blocked from the view of the men at the bonfire. She stood up, walked around to the sentries, pulling up her shirt as she went. "Fellas—do these round plump pink things on my chest mean I'm a girl? I've wondered for years."

They gaped. They stared at her exposed breasts. They both took a step toward her.

Vance stepped up behind them and hit them on the back of their heads—*hard*, judging by the crunch sound—with the butts of two pistols, one in each hand. They went down, eyes crossing, gazes still fixed on her breasts.

Vance holstered his pistols. "Good job," he whispered. "Put those things away before someone else gets hurt."

"Just one of the many degradations offered to women visiting the planet Pandora," she muttered, covering herself.

Vance looked over the top of the truck at the bandits whooping and laughing at the bonfire. "Seems like a good time. Let's get out of here . . ."

"How you going to start the damn thing?"

"I know the code. This was my bunch, don't forget."

"What about the others? If you drive off they'll see it go. I noticed some big weapons back there. They couldn't miss that truck."

"You think strategically," he said, grinning. "I like that. But I've got it covered—I hope. They gimme the idea themselves. Go on, into the truck."

She got into the passenger side and watched as he hunkered down and went to the other side. He opened the driver's side door, then took a large clip of bullets from his trouser pocket. He turned toward the bonfire, took careful aim, and threw the clip underhand, through the air, a good long throw. It came down from above—anyone who saw it wouldn't know where exactly it had been thrown from.

The clip bounced into the midst of the fire, and the men jumped up, cursing, accusing one another—and then diving to the ground as the bullets in the clip went cracking off, firing randomly from the flames, trailing fire into the dark sky.

Vance jumped into the truck, tapped a keycoder, starting the engine. Marla gripped the dashboard as he floored the accelerator and drove the truck off into the desert, while the bandits at the bonfire behind them shouted, swore, and started shooting—at one another.

Marla looked through the back window to see if there was any pursuit, anyone firing at them. She saw nothing but the receding firelight. Soon the fire's flickering light was swallowed up by the night.

It wasn't yet noon but the sun was hot on Cal's head and his backside hurt from the long ride in the jolting, open-air sandtracker. He shared the ride across the rolling plain with the driver and two other mercenaries. The sandtracker's oversized six wheels were ridged, flexibly axled to get traction on sandy terrain and crumbling rock. Another sandtracker, carrying three mercs and Rans Veritas, rumbled along five meters to their left. The outriders, much faster, were flanking the big sandtrackers, sometimes moving ahead or dropping behind to check their perimeters. Roland was up ahead driving the outrunner with Crannigan on the turret gun. Cal wished he could be up there riding with Roland. This was one tedious ride. He couldn't even talk to the mercs in the sandtracker without giving himself away. If they said anything to him he said, "No mezucka Englitchy!"

So far they seemed amused by him. What would they do when they found out he was a fraud?

Wiping dust from his eyes, Cal glanced at the other sandtracker—and caught Rans Veritas staring at him again. Rans lifted his binoculars and looked through them, right at Cal. From that close, looking at him in binoculars—the guy had to be trying to identify him.

Cal smiled, waved, and gave Rans the finger. Then he turned and looked toward the outrunner. What was Rans thinking?

He'd heard him talking to Crannigan, earlier, mentioning his father. *"Finn set out for the same site. Don't seem like he got there. It's waiting for us and Atlas now . . ."*

If Rans had known his father, maybe his dad had shown him pictures of his family. That's something his dad liked to do. Dad bored lots of people with family holos. So if the guy knew he was Zac Finn's son, he'd know that the stuff about the colony he'd come from—and the language only Roland understood—was all crapola. Had Rans told Crannigan what he knew?

A machine gun rattled up ahead—that was the outrunner's gun. Cal thought: *What if Crannigan, riding behind Roland, decided to get rid of him?*

Maybe that's what that gunfire was. People were so treacherous on this planet . . .

But the helmeted, rawboned merc riding beside him looked up ahead with his own binoculars. "Looks like they shot some scythids. No big deal."

Cal almost responded in the language of the homeworld, wanting to talk to someone. Anyone. But he bit his lip and kept quiet.

Instead, when he saw a group of creatures flying over a nearby cluster of rocky hills, he pointed at them and asked, "Mezka rakks?"

"You asking if they're called rakks, them birds? Nope." The man removed his goggles, so that his sunburnt, lined face showed pale goggle marks where the dust was missing around his eyes. He spat on the goggles and wiped them off with his sleeve. "Nope, those is what they call 'trash feeders.' Almost like big, leathery birds. Some can train 'em as attack birds. Mean little bastards when they're mad but they won't bother us unless we shoot at 'em. Least how, that's what I heard." He looked at Cal shrewdly, probably trying to figure out if Cal understood what he'd said.

Cal remembered to shrug and say, "No mezucka Englitchy!"

The merc looked at him suspiciously but only shrugged and put his goggles back on.

Another hour in the rumbling, jolting sandtracker, grinding past the torn, strange bodies of a half-dozen dead scythids; past the cold camp of a Nomad who had retreated to watch them from high on a purple bluff; through a maze of small canyons, and then a small forest of the saguaro-like plants . . . and then up a barren, steep trail, till they pulled up beside Roland's outrunner waiting on the edge of a ridge.

Cal was glad to climb out of the hot, dusty sandtracker. He stretched, and watched as Roland walked with Crannigan over to a group of mercenaries to talk. Rans joined the men. Cal wanted to go over and listen but since he supposedly couldn't understand them that would look pretty suspect.

He crossed to the edge of a nearly sheer slope, overlooking the plain below the ridge. It was a remarkably flat plain, starting about fifty meters below the ridgetop. It looked as if a nuclear bomb had gone off down there, in some phase of prehistory, and turned the plain's sand to coarse, cracked glass. It was hard to tell from up here for sure, with the glare of sunlight on the glossy surface, but it looked as if the cracks were converging, like windshield cracks around a hole. Maybe that was the epicenter of the ancient blast, ground zero.

And rising over it all, far away across the cracked flatland, was the dark purple broken cone of a mountain, probably an old volcano.

Specks moved across the plain, far away. Skags? Scythids?

Flying creatures wheeled over the plain, just silhouettes against the sky. Looking at them he decided they were bird-shaped, and not rakks—probably trash feeders.

"Hey kid—how'd you like riding in that sandtracker?" Roland asked.

"My ass is killing me—uh-oh." He had answered without thinking—and Crannigan was there, standing beside Roland, with Rans Veritas and two mercs. Crannigan was smirking—and Roland was grinning.

"Don't worry about it, kid," Roland said, clapping him on the shoulder. "Crannigan figured it out. But he just hired us both on."

Cal blinked. "Me too?"

"Sure," Crannigan said. "We might need you for a hostage. Or we could trade you to the Psychos for a bottle of booze."

The mercs laughed and wandered off, Crannigan with them.

Rans remained, staring. "I know this kid. I remember now. Zac Finn sent me a picture, when we were talking on warp mail. He sent a holo of his wife and kid. And this is the kid, right here!"

"Yeah?" Roland said, turning a warning glare at Rans. "So what?"

"So—he's a liability! Might be anybody out there looking for him! Bringing trouble down on us! They'll find out about the crash site!"

"We all work for Atlas now," Roland pointed out. "The company'll watch our back."

"I say we get rid of this kid, dammit!" Rans insisted. "If his old man is alive the kid might do anything! He might sneak off and help his old man get what's ours!"

"You the one talked my dad into coming down here?" Cal demanded, staring.

"I made him a deal and it didn't work out!" Rans snarled. "Don't be mouthy, boy! I did what I had to! I got myself shot half to pieces for this thing . . . and I'm not losing my share! Not for anyone! Your old man is out of the picture now!"

"Maybe," Cal said, looking him in the eyes. "And maybe not."

Roland chuckled. "Don't get on the wrong side of this kid, Rans. He's a pistol. And learning to use one too."

Rans snorted and stalked over to the men making a temporary camp at the ridgetop.

Roland glanced over at the other men standing with Crannigan. He pushed his goggles back on his head. "Looks like we'll stop for something to eat, get our breath, then move on, when we figure out how to get the vehicles down off this ridge . . ."

"What'd he mean about a hostage?" Cal asked.

"Just talk. Nothing. Unless he's thinking ahead to the possibility that your old man is alive—and trying to get hold of the same thing he's after. He could trade you for the rights to the find, see."

Cal grimaced. The thought made him uncomfortable. "Crannigan figured it out—about the language thing?"

"Yeah. Pretty early on. Now they all know—but nobody cares. Give 'em something to laugh about around the camp at night. I heard a couple of 'em trying out your 'No mezucka Englitchy' and having a good laugh."

Cal shrugged. "So—it just gave you time to show Crannigan he can trust you?"

Roland nodded. "You're a pretty smart kid. That's about it. But"—he lowered his voice—"there's something else." He glanced over at Scrap Crannigan, then stepped closer to Cal, and spoke almost inaudibly. "Crannigan figures he's gonna rip Atlas off. And Rans. Everyone. He figures he can't do it alone—and, since I ain't given to false modesty, I will admit I'm about the best man with a gun this side of Pandora. So Crannigan offered me a split. I join with him . . . we catch the mercs by surprise, kill 'em off." He started counting the plan's points off on his fingers. "Call the Atlas shuttle down. Kill everybody on board the shuttle. Take the goods from the alien ship, load 'em on the shuttle, head up to orbit. We surprise the crew up there, take *that* ship over. Atlas ship's mostly automated so—not many crew . . . Then we take the goods and offer it to Dahl, or one of the other corporations—and me and Crannigan split the full price, not the little cut Atlas is offering. After that, he figures he'll retire to the homeworld . . ."

Cal studied Roland's expressionless face. Was he really thinking of taking the deal? He'd said, *Kill 'em off . . . Kill everybody on board the shuttle . . .*

Like it was nothing.

Cal had to ask, "Would you—really *do* that?"

Roland's smile was twistedly ironic. "Naw. But Crannigan doesn't know that. And we don't want him to know that until the last moment. So keep your trap shut. All he knows is, I said okay. And I told him I wouldn't tell you about it. But I figure you got to know what's up. When the time comes, Crannigan'll get what's his. And it won't be an ET treasure."

"Suppose you'd said no right to his face, right then? What would he have done?"

"He'd have shot me dead. Or waited for the first time I turned my back. Just to keep me from telling the others. Then he'd claim I was up to some shit so he had to kill me."

"What about my dad? Anyone hear anything, see anything . . . ? Of him—or my mom?"

"No word yet. But maybe he's on his way to the site. That's the, what you call it—the hypothesis, right? We see either one—we'll do our best to protect 'em. Put you back together with your folks."

"You don't want any of that stuff from the crashed ship?"

"Kid—I don't know if that alien ship is really out there. It might be all skagshit. If it's there—I'm not gonna murder a buncha guys in their sleep, or whatever Scrap's got in mind. But I'll *get* my share from it—and I'll see that Crannigan pays his debt to McNee. Don't you worry. The problem is going to be living long enough to sell the stuff off, once we get it. But if we live, you'll get your cut, kid. You'll clean up."

"Yeah?" Cal wasn't particularly excited by making

money on this trip. Not right now. He'd trade any amount of riches for a sight of his family.

"Yeah. Alien artifacts from anywhere are worth a pretty penny. Especially if there's tech involved. Trouble is, all these bastards are thinking the same thing. I figure half these damn mercs are thinking like Crannigan. They're thinking maybe they can take the thing for themselves. The word has gotten round that there's riches out there, in that volcano. But lots of times I see people go after riches, they end up as meat for scavengers."

Cal closed his eyes, controlled his impulse to start crying. But it must have shown on his face. He felt Roland's big, rough hand laid reassuringly on his arm. "Take it easy. I didn't mean your dad ended up that way . . ."

No? But his dad had gone after riches . . .

And he might already be bleached bones somewhere in the desert.

TWELVE

Zac was out of water, nearly out of food, and running short of hope.

It was early evening. He was in the shadow of an overhang under a ridge, on the edge of a glassy plain, still a long way from the volcano cone. And there was no hope of getting across the glass plain without being spotted by some predator. No cover at all. No water likely out there in that flat emptiness. As for food—he was more likely to *become* food.

Zac took out his telescope and turned it on the horizon, made out some skags, off in the distance between him and the volcano. Flying creatures circled over the skags.

He swept the horizon but saw nothing else. Then a sound prompted him to look up at the ridge. Dust was sifting down from the edge of the ridge, about an eighth of a kilometer away, and light glinted on metal. He turned the telescope that way and after some fiddling with it, made out an outrunner poised on the top of the ridge, and a couple of men standing near it—judging by their outfits, they were mercenaries. Maybe ex–Crimson Lance.

Great, he thought as he lowered the telescope. *Now what do I do?*

If he set out across the plain, they'd probably see him and head out after him. The presence of mercenaries suggested one of the big corporations—they had their own little armies but they used mercenaries when they were trying to keep something quiet. They were probably after the same thing he was. Maybe they worked for whoever had sent the security bot to sabotage his DropCraft.

They were looking toward the old volcanic cone, just like he was . . .

And maybe they were looking for him too, so they could finish what they'd started on the Study Station.

Even if they didn't go after him, he'd run into those skags and rakks out there, and who knew what else. There was no cover on that plain.

There was one chance—a slim one. He could wait here, till it got dark. Then head out in the dark and hope to elude both the human predators and the animal ones.

Of course, the mercenaries would go on ahead. But this was Pandora. Who knew what they'd run into?

A squadron of mercs in big outrunners, they'd call attention to themselves. They could draw off whatever he might have to face—they just might accidentally keep him safe . . .

He'd come too far to give up now. He had to try it. He would go after dark—the moon had been setting earlier at night, so it'd be mighty dark. If the moon set and he got lost in the dark, he'd use the alien artifact that pointed the way to guide him. The night would be his cover.

But that meant he would have to wait here, right here, crouching under this outcropping, until nightfall . . .

Zac sighed. He had a little food. He had no water. But now, anyway—he had a little hope. Just a little.

The flatbed truck emerged from a canyon and Vance brought it to a skidding stop on the edge of a cracked, glassy plain. The sunlight, in this spot, threw glare back from the enormous shards, so that Marla had to shield her eyes with her hand.

"What *is* that?" she asked. "Ice?"

"Nah," Vance said, handing her a pair of tinted goggles. "It's melted what-you-call-it—silicon. I've been out on it, about a quarter klick, once before. It's just a coating over the rock and sand. Solid enough."

"Where'd it come from?"

He stuck out his lower lip and cocked his head. "Ain't nobody knows for sure. But a year or so ago, Grunj took a scientist guy prisoner. One of those archaeologists. There's a lotta bones of archaeologists scattered around on this planet. Anyway, the guy had been working out here on this thing, came out to the Trash Coast looking for something else. I talked to him some. He said this here was from some old nuclear blast—happened thousands of years ago. Ain't radioactive anymore. There's a crater out in the middle of it. Not sure if some alien visitor did it—or some old civilization used to live here. He said he figured those big ugly bastards—the Primals—were degenerates, left over from that bunch. Mutated, kinda . . . mentally messed up . . . Their ancestors weren't so beastly-like."

"What, um . . ." Marla suspected she was going to regret

asking this. "What happened to the archaeologist Grunj took prisoner?"

"Oh, him? He was kinda young. Eventually Grunj decided not to sell him, or ransom him out. See, if Grunj takes an interest in a young guy—he don't last long. I think he was already dead, though, when he fed him to that big ol' skag of his . . ."

He opened a canteen—she automatically put out her hand for it, but he drank from it first, before handing it to her.

Lot of differences between this guy and my husband, she thought, as he finally passed her the canteen.

"I don't see anything out there," she said. "Is it safe?"

"Safe?" Vance said, as if puzzled by the idea of a place that was really safe. "No place is safe." He fell into a brooding silence. Then after a long pause, he growled to himself and said, "When I was a kid, I lived in a place that was supposed to be safe. Luxury space colony called Highbuckle, on the moon of Thora. We had security guards with big guns. We had an automated defense fortress in orbit right over us. We had cops and a militia. We had a protection pact with Thora. We had a force field projected from the fortress. We had walls and big doors and locks and computer surveillance—lady, we had it all. But the Wastemakers didn't care about that stuff. They found a way into the autodef fortress, took it over, dropped our shields, turned the fortress's guns on us. Killed most of the colony. Then they came down and killed the rest. Except for one or two . . ."

"The Wastemakers. I've heard about them. I thought they were a myth . . ."

He shook his head. "Crazy cult bastards. Think they got to cut and burn and ream their way across the outer colonies, because their priestess told 'em that they're the promised people waiting for the Blonde Goddess to return from the Silver Screen of Heaven. And she's gonna take them up to this Silver Screen, whatever the hell that is—and until then they're the only real human beings around, see. They can kill anybody they want and take what they need till the Goddess returns. 'Cause they're the only . . . goddamn . . . human beings."

"Sounds like you heard about their religion from them personally."

"Yeah. They take kids prisoners, for the fresh genetics, see, sometimes. They have this ritual that makes you 'human' all of a sudden so they can use your . . . your seed. I was with 'em a year, when I was eleven, while they waited for me to get to puberty. But I managed to kill the bastard that kept me prisoner, and I got in a robot shuttle, told it to take me someplace else, went into suspension. When I woke up it was a year later and I was in the hands of Sky Pirates. They coulda killed me, or sold me, but Captain Flench needed a cabin boy—a servant, like. When I was sixteen, I joined their fightin' crew. Became a raider."

She looked at Vance with a new understanding. "So—you saw the Wastemakers kill your parents?"

"Yeah. And my brother. In that safe little haven of spoiled rich people. Safe and protected Highbuckle. No place is safe, lady. No place." He noticed her staring at him, and he scowled and looked away. "Let's get a move on—we're gonna go around the edge of this plain. It's the long ways but . . . we'll be too easy to spot out in the middle of that big flat nothin'. We lose a day . . . but we'll get there. Might be better if we got there second so's we can make sure we got the jump on 'em . . ."

He accelerated the truck, turned it sharply, cutting back toward the grittier edge of the plain, skirting its glassy surface. They skidded and fishtailed at first on the slick surface, and then he had the truck close enough to the curving wall of rock enclosing the plain—here, sand and dust had blown into soft moraines that gave the vehicle better purchase. They bumped along over the snaking sand, at the edge of the glass plain, following a curving, indirect path but still generally toward the coordinates Zac had sent her.

Thinking about Zac, she asked, "Vance—what'd you mean, if we get there second we can get the jump on them?"

He chuckled. "You're thinking of your old man. You got the crazy idea he might be alive, right? Chances of that are about as good as rolling a six on dice that only got snake eyes. Better forget him, girl. He's long dead."

Marla felt a chill quiver through her. "You know that? You heard it—on that communicator of yours?"

"No," Vance admitted. "But that's just how it is on this hellhole. Probably died in the crash and if he didn't—he's skag droppings by now, girl. Sorry but . . . that's how it is. Ain't nothing and no one safe. Unless maybe the guy with the biggest gun and the eyes in the back of his head. And not even then."

"That communi—" She broke off, grabbing for the dashboard as the truck hit a sand dune and jolted. "—communicator of yours. Can you call orbit with it? I mean—if you can't, how are you gonna get off the planet, once you've got what you want, if you're afraid to go to the settlements."

His grin faded and he turned her a cold look. "I'm not afraid of *anything*. I'm just not gonna be stupid." He frowned at the windshield, steered around a pothole, and added, "Don't you worry, I'll get off this rock. Maybe I'll take you with me—if you don't ask stupid questions, and if you don't try and steal that communicator. That thing won't call orbit anyhow—it's just for local transmissions, and only bandit frequencies. You can get that idea out of your head."

They drove for another half hour, along the curving edge of the plain, in the shadow of the natural stone wall around it, bumping over short sand dunes, and all the time she wondered, *Is he lying about that communicator?*

"What the hell is that?" Vance burst out, stopping the truck.

They'd come to a barrier of boulders, about ten meters high, with spikes sticking out of it, thin shards of glass each about a meter long. It extended from the cliffside out about forty meters into the plain, and then stopped out there like an unfinished wall. It almost looked like it could've happened accidentally. But then again, looking closer . . .

"Somebody put that damn thing up," Vance said. "Looks like they brought down part of the cliff . . . stuck those glass spears in there."

"What would be the point? We could just drive around it, onto the plain."

"Yeah. Seems like. But what's on the other side of it? Maybe some kinda ambush." He backed the truck up a few car lengths and put the truck in idle. "Listen," he whispered, getting out of the truck, "stand just outside the truck, Marla—and talk to me as if I'm right in front of you and we can't decide what to do. Do it kind of loud. Like we're about to turn back or something."

"What?"

"Just do it." He walked softly toward the wall.

She shrugged, got out of the truck, took a deep breath, and, almost yelling, said, "Well dammit man what are we gonna do, are we gonna stay here or what? Are we going around it? Are we going back? I mean, what the hell? I mean shit, why don't we make up our goddamn minds? What? What? What kind of way is that to talk to me?"

As she bellowed this, Vance was climbing the wall, easing up between the glass shards, picking out his footing with great care. He looked over his shoulder and silently mouthed, *"Keep it up! More!"*

She went on, "I mean, Jeezis, can we get off the dime and get movin' here, man? You know, this is just like you. I do and do and do for you and you sit there behind the wheel yawning and scratching your nuts . . ."

Then he was at the top of the barrier, peering carefully through a space between two rocks down at the other side. He shook his head, then climbed quickly down.

"And another thing . . . !"

"Forget it!" he told her, hurrying over. "Nobody over there."

"So who was I yelling for?"

"Somebody who might've been there. To cover for me as I took a look."

"I know, but—who put this barrier up? What's it for?"

"My guess is, somebody was setting up something here and they got killed before they could finish it."

"You sure? Maybe we should go back a ways, then head out on the plain, take a long circle around it, Vance. It's just too . . ."

He looked at her with narrowed eyes, seeming irritated. He'd made his decision and she was second-guessing him. "That'd take too much time, and it'd expose us too much. We're going around the barrier right here and we're moving on the way we were going. We're already taking the long goddamn way to the crash site . . ."

If there is an alien crash site, she thought. The whole thing could be a boondoggle.

They got in the truck and he started around the barrier, heading out onto the glass plain. The wheels skidded a little on the slick surface, but driving carefully he was able to make good progress, passing the barrier. They had gone a truck's length past it, turned toward the edge of the glass plain again—when cracks appeared in the glassy surface, all around them, making *crick-crick* noises as they opened. The cracks spread out from the truck in every direction, like thin ice breaking under a weight.

"Oh shit!" Vance burst out, flooring the accelerator. The wheels spun in place—and then the truck fell, straight down, through the shattering thin glass surface.

A second later the truck's wheels struck the surface below with a jarring thud that cracked Marla's teeth together, whiplashed her neck; a flailing grab at the dashboard saved her from cracking her forehead on it.

Engine dead, the truck sat on all four wheels in a thin cloud of dust. Light angled sharply down from above;

to either side were rough columns of stone. As the dust cleared Marla could see the chisel marks—the stone had been hollowed out here.

"Get your gun ready!" Vance barked, turning to get the combat rifle from the back window shelf. "It was a tunnel rat trap! I fell for it like a green dumbshit!"

"What?" Still dazed, she fumbled for her pistol. "What are tunnel rats? You mean actual rats or . . ."

"People!" He opened the truck door. "They went degenerate in the tunnels! They eat human flesh!"

Vance was already climbing onto the truck cab roof and immediately firing at the dark tunnel mouths revealed by the settling dust. Hooded faces drew back into the shadow at his burst of gunfire.

Faces? Not exactly. More like goggling glass eye sockets, rubbery snouts in place of noses . . .

Instinctively, she pushed the passenger side door open, stepped out behind it, fired her pistol through the open window, blasting blindly into the darkness.

Muzzle flashes lit up the figures in the tunnel as they returned fire with pistols and shotguns. She saw they were indeed human in shape, though gas masks made their faces look snouted and rodentlike.

Bullets cracked against the armored door of the truck—there were flashes overhead as rounds impacted on Vance's shield. She had no shield herself.

That's another thing Zac would've done, she figured—first thing he would've given her his shield. The one they'd scrounged for her from the dead bandits had run out of power.

She fired again, emptying her clip, then looked up to see

Vance firing his rifle at the wall of dirt and rock to his left. Why was he doing that? Trying to cause a cave-in?

In a way, that's just what he was doing, she realized—the soft, already undermined rock crumbled under the impact of his bullets, and a rough ramp of stone and dirt tumbled on his side of the truck.

"Come on, girl!" he yelled, leaping up onto the tumble of rocks.

"Help me up!" she yelled, as the tunnel rats came at her. She tried climbing up onto the truck cab, got onto her knees on it as Vance kept climbing, ahead of her, up toward the daylight just about two and a half meters above. Bullets splashed into his shield, making it flicker. Two tunnel rats clambered up onto the heap of rocks and grabbed at his legs. He smashed one in the goggles with the butt of his gun, cracking the glass and driving in the shards so the tunnel rat screamed, blinded; Vance shoved a pistol into the other one's mouth, pulled the trigger, blowing through the back of the tunnel rat's head.

Marla got to her feet, started to follow Vance—and then clutching hands grabbed her ankles and jerked her off her feet.

The wind knocked out of her, gasping for air, she clawed at the rooftop, tried to call out to Vance. The clutching hands were pulling her back, off the truck. Claws dug into her legs and dragged her painfully, inexorably, back down . . . to the floor of the tunnel. One of them clawed her gun from her hand . . .

She looked up past the truck to see Vance, silhouetted against the sky, standing on the rim of the break in the glassy surface of the plain—he fired a burst down at a tunnel rat near her, shot the top of its head off. She tried to stand—but saw that four other tunnel rats were holding her down, their visages completely enigmatic in the gas masks.

"You will be with us, we will share you, in many ways," hissed one of them.

"Vance!" she screamed, as terror licked up in her like flame in dry kindling.

She caught a glimpse of him looking cautiously down into the pit. He fired at a tunnel rat, then jumped back from return fire. Bullets strafed past him.

Who sells these horrid creatures guns? But she knew. People like Grunj would sell guns to tunnel rats—people like Grunj and Dimmle, and probably Vance . . .

Another burst of gunfire from Vance. He was shouting at her. She couldn't make it out. She caught only one word—*sorry*.

The tunnel rats dragged her, struggling, away from the truck, into shadow and then deeper darkness. In the last scrap of light, up above, she could make out Vance, crouching to peer down at her from up on surface of the plain. He cupped his mouth and shouted, and this time she heard, *"Sorry, girl! Too many of 'em! You were a good—"*

That's all Marla heard—a wiry arm crooked around her head, muffling the rest as she was dragged backward.

Tunnel rats hissed and muttered as they clutched at her. A necrotic stench closed around Marla, making her gag— the stench choking her exactly as the darkness of the tunnels closed around her and clawed fingers began tugging at her clothing.

THIRTEEN

Crannigan, Roland, Cal, Rans Veritas, and the mercenaries were camped in the thickening dusk; in the crater at the center of the glassy, cracked plain. The floor of the crater, about sixty meters across, was coated with dust. It was just the height of a man from the floor of the crater up to the glassy surface. They stood around a small campfire between their tents, the men talking over security. They were using a chemical fire here, poured from a can, no other fuel to burn.

"What are Guardians?" Cal asked, when the conversation lulled. He'd heard the mercs in the sandtracker talking.

Rans Veritas turned to glare at him, and didn't answer at first. His face twitched. He looked around fearfully, then looked squint-eyed back at Cal. "You got all the information you need to have, boy. Ought to keep your flapper zipped."

"The Guardians, Cal," Roland said musingly, leaning back against a sandtracker, "are alien entities. Eridian based. Maybe artificial, maybe not. They guarded the area around the Vault—another alien site. Guardians are dangerous as hell. There's more'n one kind of 'em too."

Rans's face was twitching. "They don't apply here! That's a whole different set of aliens. There won't be any Guardians. What we're going to see has *nothing to do with the Vault*! I'm telling you, I had a couple artifacts, had 'em tested and they're not Eridian." He pointed at Crannigan's Eridian rifle. "See the shape of that alien gun there, the material it's made of? Everything, even the power source, is Eridian. Eridian guns are made for something that has hands not so different from us. But this ship, out there— it's nothing like that. Maybe these critters were enemies of the Eridians. I dunno. But they're *different*—and that means, no Guardians at the crash site!"

"No *Guardians*," Roland pointed out, "doesn't mean no *guards*. That ship could be protected by something else. That suit from Atlas claimed it wasn't safe to approach the crash area from the air. Which means it's got some kind of protection."

"How dangerous *is* it to go at from the ground, Rans?" Cal asked. "You were there, so—"

Roland winked at Cal. "Good question, kid."

"I've briefed Crannigan about that," Rans snarled, glaring at Cal. "I don't need to answer questions for this pain-in-the-ass boy."

"Then answer it for *me*," Roland said icily, looking steadily at Rans.

Rans looked at Roland, licked his lips nervously.

"You may as well, Rans," Crannigan said, stroking the Eridian rifle thoughtfully.

Rans shrugged, then said, "You can get pretty close to

the ship, approaching on the ground. There's a debris field where you can pick up a few things. That's as close as I got. You can see the main fuselage of the ET ship from there, see, down under the volcano shell. But . . . if you try to move in real close, things get ugly. There's a thing that flies around and grabs things . . . changes 'em sometimes, makes 'em its servants. Now, a force of men like we got here—I figure they can shoot their way in, get some good stuff, more proof of what's there . . ."

"In short," Roland said, "you chickened out and ran, and you don't really have a goddamn clue what's down there. You didn't get that close."

"So what?" Rans said sulkily. "I can take you there, that's the main thing."

"Atlas already knows where it is."

"I can show you how to get close pretty safely, I can tell you about a *lot* of stuff—but I'm not telling you anything else in advance." His hooded eyes flicked at them suspiciously. "I know what could happen if you bunch figured you don't need me no more . . ."

With that he turned and limped toward a tent.

Looking up at the crater rim, Cal could see the upper edge of the moon rising. "Going to be dark soon. You figure it's safe down in this crater, Roland?"

"Safer'n some places, anyhow," Roland said. "This impact crater's pretty close to the volcano. We'll head out there fresh tomorrow . . ."

Cal's heart lifted at the prospect. His dad could be there—alive.

The moon was rising. The stars appeared over the plain of cracked glass. Shotgun in his hand, Zac kept scanning the horizon, hoping to see skags before they saw him. No real cover here. If he did see predators, best to flatten down, hope they overlook him. He could kill one or two skags with the shotgun, but if they came in a pack, he was done for.

Zac stopped, catching sight of a faint, dancing light off to the east. A campfire, he figured, a half kilometer away. He lifted the small telescope to his eyes—in the scope he could just make out an outrunner parked on the edge of a crater. Sweeping left, he saw the silhouettes of squat, big-wheeled vehicles, probably sandtrackers. Chances were, that was the mercenary camp. They had vehicles, protection—they could stop for the night. That was a luxury he didn't have.

They had other luxuries too. They'd have water. Food. But . . .

There was no chance of any kind of friendly reception there. They'd probably interrogate him, and then kill him. And even if they weren't completely hostile, they wouldn't know where his wife and son were.

Better to steer way clear of them.

Zac angled away from the distant firelight, heading a bit out of his way to give a wide berth to the merc encampment.

He trudged on, glancing at the sky for rakks, scanning the horizon for skags, or the birdcage shape of a drifter; he licked his cracked lips, trying not to think about water.

Then, looming up ahead, purple in the evening, he saw the bluffs of stone encircling the plain. Why not follow the edges of the plain around to his goal? It would be farther— but safer. He might well be able to retreat into those rocks for cover. There could be overhangs, boulders, caves near them. There might also be water there.

He pictured a spring of water, crystal clear, enticing, trickling from a crevice in the bluffs. He imagined the stream falling glitteringly into a clear pool. He'd find it, he'd throw himself facedown and bathe his dust-stung eyes, and drink deep . . .

Zac moved toward the bluffs with redoubled energy. Feet hurting, he marched onward, stumbling sometimes in the cracks on the glassy surface. The edge of the plain seemed to get no closer. The night, however, got darker. The moon was no longer full and it was dipping close to the horizon, threatening to set; clouds had come to shutter the stars.

His legs began to ache and he coughed with dust. He felt as if he were growing heavier, as if gravity were increasing around him. He was wearing out. He wanted to lie down and rest. But he was afraid he'd go to sleep here—good chance he'd wake up with a skag or some other creature slavering over him. *Keep going.*

He looked down at the glassy surface of the plain, and watched his own feet trudging, on and on. It was hypnotic . . .

After a timeless time he stopped, staring . . . past his feet. He had come to a place where the ground under the glassy surface seemed to change color. No—the ground down there was absent, he realized. He was standing over a covered pit of some kind. The surface was scratched and dusty and discolored but it admitted a little wan moonlight. And down below, through the translucent glaze, he could just make out what looked like a chamber, carved in rock, with tunnels at either end. Was it an illusion? Maybe just some mineral pooled in the glaze of stone?

But then he saw something moving down there. Though distorted by the uneven surface like an image seen through a primitive window, the shape seemed human. Then it looked up. Were those two big, round, dark eyes, like the eyes of a giant rat? Was that a rat's snout on a man's head?

Zac stepped hastily back, hoping the thing hadn't been able to see him.

He felt dizzy, deciding that fatigue and dehydration were getting to him. He must be seeing things.

Still, he circled around the dark place under the glassy surface, walking only where the glaze seemed supported by stone.

He saw no more of those dark places. And at long last, he thought he was making real progress. It looked like only another half klick to the edge of the plain.

But something else was up ahead. Was that a wall, jutting from the bluffs? Difficult to tell in the darkness. But it looked like a wall, or barrier of big stones. Something glittered, spears of glass, in the barrier of rocks.

Maybe there was shelter there. Perhaps a spring . . .

Zac picked up his pace, gasping the last half kilometer, his throat rasping—and he almost tumbled headlong into a large hole broken in the plain, near the end of the jutting barrier. He swayed, and then got his balance, and stepped back from the hole. The break in the surface was clearly delineated in the moonlight. There was a pit down there, this time—and it was open. And something else down there caught the light. It was dark, difficult to make out exactly what it was. But . . . it looked like a *truck*, down in a pit. A flatbed truck.

Had someone been driving through a tunnel down there? Then he saw the tire tracks in the thin layer of dust spread intermittently over the glassy plain. They led up to the edge of the pit. They'd driven here—and crashed through, it looked like, maybe forced onto this spot by driving around the barrier. They'd been caught in a trap.

He remembered the ratlike face on a man's body, and shuddered. Whoever'd been in that truck—one of those things had them. Hadn't Berl once said something about "tunnel rats"? Seemed like he had, and with a tone of real disgust.

"Hello?" Zac called, not too loudly, in case there was someone lying low in the truck.

No reply. He shouldn't be calling out, attracting attention to himself. He should get away from this spot, and quickly.

But what if there was water down there, in that truck?

No. No, it would be a trap for him too. He mustn't venture any farther.

He backed away from the pit, and looked for its edges, made his way carefully around them, feeling the surface, with his feet, for springiness, testing for too much give where it might break under him.

He moved past the pit and found more solid footing. He reached the end of the barrier of rock, followed it back toward the bluffs. He hoped to see a silvery trickling in the moonlight. Nothing.

What had he expected? No reason there should be water in this spot, particularly.

But he couldn't go on any farther. He was exhausted. *Got to. If you don't, you'll die right here. Keep going.*

Zac groaned, but forced himself to move onward, along the edge of the plain, just under the bluff, watching for tunnel entrances, pits, hoping to see water. Seeing nothing but dust, sand, rock, and, to his left, the glassy edge of the plain.

He seemed to get heavier and heavier. He thought of dropping the shotgun, his pack, the artifacts, everything. Just to feel lighter.

No. Find a place to rest . . .

He rounded a gentle outthrust in the bluff . . . and felt himself pitch into despair.

Four skags, bigger than any he'd seen, were just thirty paces away. And they were sniffing, turning their ungainly heads toward him.

He'd come all this way for nothing. Pandora had been tormenting him, playing cat and mouse with him. Now it was done playing . . .

"All right you hellhole, swallow me up!" someone shouted.

Zac realized he'd shouted it himself. He raised the shotgun, cocked it . . .

He could take a couple of the repulsive creatures out before he went down. Then if his body was found, maybe his son would know that he'd fought to the end.

His son. His wife. The deal with Rans Veritas. The Drop-Craft. Failure. Shame. Futility . . . Death.

The skags suddenly charged him, coming in a phalanx. He fired the shotgun and the nearest one squealed, one of its three jaws shot away, but it kept coming. Zac squeezed the trigger again—

Nothing. The shotgun was jammed.

Zac shouted, "Damn you!" And he raised the shotgun by the butt, to use it for a club. He waited for the oncoming skag, just a few bounds away from him . . .

Then he heard a hiss, and the skag stumbled, its whole body twisting, contorting in pain as it sizzled in a purple puddle. A combat rifle stuttered a series of bangs, and the other skags squealed with pain, turned to run. Another hiss, another splash of purple, and the nearest retreating skag was splashed with acid, rolling in agony on the ground . . .

Zac stared, blinking, wondering if he was dreaming all this. Then he said, "Oh."

"*That's* right," said Berl, behind him. "'Oh.'"

Swaying, Zac dropped the shotgun and turned slowly around, wiping dust from his eyes. In the dimness he could see the glowing eyes of the drifter, above Berl, not far away. Bizzy had fried the skags with his toxic exudate. And Berl had fired the combat rifle—which he was now pointing right at Zac. Berl was standing underneath Bizzy, between the stiltlike legs, like a bird in a warped cage. His combat rifle gleamed in the moonlight.

"Well, I'll say this, young fella, you've got guts," Berl declared. "You were ready to go down fightin'. You might get the chance to die proud pretty quick here. Only reason I ain't shot you is, you're carrying my goods. And I don't want them busted up by stray bullets. You push me though, I'll just see if I can put one in your head . . ."

"Berl . . . I'm sorry." Zac spat dust, spoke in a raspy burr. "But you know, you had me tied up. I was your prisoner. I couldn't stay there like that. And I could've taken more than what I did, when I left."

"I wouldn'ta cared none about the shotgun, nor the water. I've got weapons and ammo and water. But you took something that matters to me, more'n anything, Zac Finn! The artifacts! Includin' the one that points toward the crash site. Now, *that* was one big fat mistake, boy. Also it was a big fat mistake not to cover your trail better. Because here I am! And now it's high time I figure out exactly how I'm gonna deal with you."

FOURTEEN

You can be food or you can be a child bearer," chuckled the tunnel rat. The wizened, wiry man pointed a clawed, dirt-crusted finger at Marla and added thoughtfully in his whispery voice, "*Or*—you can be *first* a child bearer . . . and *then* food. That is the most likely outcome. Yes, yessss . . ."

Trying to cover herself better, though her clothes were badly torn from tunnel rats' claws, Marla cringed back against the wall of the stone cell, telling herself: *At least they're not going to eat you right away. There's hope.*

Maybe Vance would come, after all, fight his way to her, and save her from them.

But she knew he wouldn't. Vance was just the wrong kind of guy for that. He was tough, and brave, but he was not going to take that big a risk for her—or for anybody else.

The tunnel rat had removed his gas mask when he'd

first squatted down to inspect her. His face was rather rodentlike itself, but human. His eyes were large; his nose pronounced, his chin weak. He was bald, except for an occasional random bristle of hair. His skin was pallid, and speckled with crusty sores. A smell came off him like week-old roadkill. He wore a leather jerkin over a long-sleeve shirt of some synthetic, its glossiness dulled with dirt. His trousers and boots were worn, coming apart. As he inspected her he toyed with a machine pistol of some kind, itself so dirty she marveled that it could work. The tunnel rat had a shield on at his waist, its energy field glowing faintly.

Behind him, holding up a dim lantern, was another tunnel rat wearing his gas mask and carrying a very large shotgun. He seemed dressed in a hodgepodge of clothing, probably taken from various victims. Hanging from his belt loop was a string of five sausage-like objects. After a moment she realized they were human fingers. They were brown and dried, like the jerky she had made of skag meat. Finger jerky—for a snack, she supposed. Whose fingers were they? Had they ever imagined their fingers would end up as dried meat on a tunnel rat's belt?

A third tunnel rat was a shadowy shape in the opening behind the one with the shotgun. No hope of slipping past these three for now. The only way she could hope to do it was through cunning, biding her time. For that, she needed time to bide. Which meant she'd have to start stalling.

Especially as the one hunkered in front of her was creeping closer . . .

"Maybe . . . I will test your possibilities for mating," said the tunnel rat, scooching closer. "I have the status to mate with you! I'm the chief tunneler here!" He showed his yellow, filed teeth in a rattish smirk. "It was I who engineered the trap that captured you!"

"Oh really!" Marla said, mimicking excitement. She raised her hands to hold him back—but trying to make the gesture look as if it were saying, *Wait, I'm very interested in hearing about this.* "That was brilliant! However did you do it? I mean, isn't it solid rock around here?"

"Here? No, much about here is soft sandstone, not so solid, with pockets of dirt. I can tunnel through it with my bare hands. But I don't use my hands much—I have tools, I have a good tunneling equipment! We took it from the miners who were here—after we killed them. But before we ate them." Sequence seemed important to him.

"So—what did you do first with the pit?" she asked, feigning interest as best she could. Keeping the quaver of fear out of her voice wasn't easy. "I mean—to set the trap you used to catch our truck."

The tunnel rat scratched the bristly place where his chin should be. "Well of course, we have tunnels everywhere in this area—because the long-ago explosion here, long before men came to this world, created many cracks and possibilities of tunnels hereabout. So, this is where we come for our annual feast! All of us, those who are not the enemies of the tribal boss, come from around the continent, and converge here! My tribe comes early, to prepare! Next full moon—we feast! It was when we came to prepare for such a gathering that we noted traffic in the area! Our vibration forks rang to tell us: Men coming! Trucks, outrunners, outriders, sandtrackers! So we built the barrier—under my supervision of course! Just a few explosives, carefully placed, and a little leverage applied, and there you have it! The ideal method for pushing your truck onto the glass plain! There, we have traps, and tunnels hidden! And we made sure you were likely to drive onto ours! I ordered the pit dug out just hours before you arrived! So fast, so cleverly do we work! And *crack*, down you come!"

"That's amazing!" she said, clapping her hands. "Very impressive!"

"Tunnel droppings!" sneered the tunnel rat with the shotgun. "She's playing with you, Broncus! Toying with your affections! She means not a word of it!"

"Droppings back to you, Flemmel!" hissed Broncus, glancing back at the masked tunnel rat. "More likely she sees a fine opportunity for mating with one who can provide good burrowing, food meat, and warmth!"

"True," Marla said, trying not to gag.

Broncus leered at her. "So—I am desirable, eh? Perhaps you may live longer than we had planned!"

He moved toward her again, and she asked hastily, "But . . . tell me this—you wear gas masks, yet the air seems breathable here. More or less. So why . . . ?"

"The masks? They are badges of honor! Like the helmets of ancient heroes! Once we needed them, in the old days, when my grandparents, and the others, they were attacked by the Psycho Midgets—terrible things happened to them. So they hid underground, in the mines they'd come here to work in, where there were many poison gases. And they chose not to go up again where the vicious little brutes dwell! How we hate them! How we love to sneak out at night and capture them as they sleep and bring them back for our cooking spits!"

"You only go out at night? Except for the traps?"

"Only at night! The sun is cruel!"

Interesting, Marla thought. *They dislike being in direct sunlight.*

Flemmel growled. "Listen to her—she wants information! She is interrogating you, Broncus! You cannot trust her!"

"Of course I don't trust her! I trust no one!" Broncus snapped. "But I know when a woman desires me!"

"You have never had a woman," Flemmel sneered.

"I had one! She was dead when I found her, but I had her!" Broncus protested. "I know how to . . . to do it. What is done with a female!"

"Ha! To a dead body, yes!"

Marla thought it imperative to change the subject, and fast. "I'm sorry my companion Vance killed some of your people back at the truck. He was just trying to protect me. What will happen to the truck? Will you be able to get it out of the tunnel so you can drive it—at night?"

"Oh, perhaps we could, but more likely we will strip it for parts, use them in the many devices we make down here! We have many skills! The body of the truck will make a good tunnel brace, for shaky places!"

"Female, if you are so eager to please Broncus," Flemmel said, "perhaps you might tell us where your friend has gone! This Vance of yours. If we knew where he goes to—we could capture him more easily!"

"Oh, he was looking for something out here," Marla said, shrugging. "An alien ship. He gave up trying to get to it. He said he was going to find the nearest way out of the glass plain and head back to . . . to the Trash Coast." It seemed absurd to be protecting Vance. He had abandoned her. But she couldn't help herself.

Broncus was scowling—a revolting sight as it made his teeth project crookedly over his lower lip. "Did you say . . . an *alien* ship? That one? If he had found it—he would not be alive now! Even we do not dare to go near it! That vessel does strange things to those who approach it!"

"You give her information with every babbling word!" Flemmel complained. "You are a good tunneler, but you never could control your tongue! Babble babble babble!"

"Silence, Flemmel!" Broncus spat. "I am in charge here! You are next down in status, one lower than me, and do not forget it!"

The evident rivalry between Flemmel and Broncus might be of use, she mused. If she could talk to Flemmel alone . . .

"Now, I will rut with you," said Broncus. "Lie on your back to facilitate the process."

"Ah, yes, well," Marla said, "let me just, uh. . . ." She was stalling as she pretended to remove some of her clothing.

She wondered if she could grab his gun and kill him and the other two. Probably not. If she got one, at least one of the other two would shoot her dead. And she would prefer that to letting this thing violate her.

"You there, Broncus!" shouted someone from the door-way to the cell.

Broncus turned. "Who? Ah!" He stood up, and made a peculiar rat-clutching kind of genuflection to the new visitor with his claws. "Engineer Gluck!"

A tunnel rat pushed past Flemmel to stand over Marla, looking balefully down at her.

He wore a rubber gas mask on his head, complete with snout filter and goggling eyes. But it was more elaborate than the others, studded with gold, and crested with a silver spike. His leather and metal outfit seemed a bit cleaner too, and his shoulders were decked out in braids. He reached up with a gloved hand and pushed the mask back on his head to get a better look at her.

He was a little cleaner, a bit less obviously inbred. His lean face with its pointed chin and small eyes seemed not as rattish as Broncus. But as he spoke, she saw Gluck's teeth were filed to points. "What goes on here? This is clearly a *premium prisoner*! All such are to be brought to me, for assessment!"

Broncus wrung his hands, and ducked his head repeatedly, cowed by this superior being. "Yes, yes, Great Engineer, it is so! I was just checking her to make certain she had no weapons hidden on her person!"

"Did I not hear you making your plans for rutting with her, Broncus? You do not have a tunnel status that gives you the possibility of rutting with a premium prisoner unless I sign off on it, in triplicate!"

"I . . . I only spoke of rutting in the most *maybe, possibly, could-be, might-be* sense, Great Engineer!"

"You are a subengineer—a mere tunnel digger! You have pretensions to be more!" sneered Gluck. "Don't think I don't know it! If you were not occasionally useful . . ."

"I'm sorry, Great Engineer, but please be assured . . ."

"Great Engineer—may I speak?" Marla said timidly. "I have information that may be of use to you."

The engineer—clearly the leader of this tribe—looked at her in surprise. "Oh, and what's that, prisoner?"

"Your man there, Flemmel—he *tried* to tell Broncus that he did not have sufficient status for such a thing! But Broncus would not listen! Flemmel, though—he was truly fiercely loyal to you."

"Indeed!" The engineer tittered skeptically. "And what do *you* know of tunnel status, sun-basker?"

"I . . . have longed for the safety of the tunnels," Marla said, as sincerely as she could manage. "I ask here, and there, of those who might know . . ."

"No one knows but the Tribe!" insisted Gluck. "And as for your hopes—don't get them too high!"

"Of *course*, Great Engineer!" Marla said, genuflecting in the way she'd seen Broncus do. "But I cannot help thinking . . . that I am destined for the honor . . . the supreme tunnel status . . . of bearing your children!"

"Pretentious creature!" Broncus said, slapping at Marla.

"Silence, Broncus!" Gluck snarled. "*I* will decide this matter! Bring more troops, Flemmel, and take this prisoner to a locked cell. Have her securely guarded there! Indeed, guard her yourself! The tribes will soon converge! We have preparations to make for the feast. And we shall see what her part is to be in that feast . . ."

The attack came at dawn, coming over the rim of the crater with the first sunlight, moments after Cal woke, rolling from his bedroll under a sandtracker.

The chatter of the Zodiac Turret was what announced the attack: Roland's tripod automatic weapon, set up to watch for enemies on the crater rim, hammered at the charging enemy. Wounding one; taking one down. Not stopping all of them.

They came from the blaze of the rising sun—Psycho Midgets riding Primal Beasts. Six of them got past the Zodiac Turret, bounding over the rim, one of them heaving a barrel of explosives as it came. The explosives hit an outrider and covered it in flame. A man just waking up beside the outrider woke to find himself on fire—and ran screaming past Cal, flailing at himself.

Cal gaped at the oncoming Primals—the bizarre sight of the midgets riding on the backs of pumped-up four-armed bipeds. A thrown axe whizzed past Cal's head—then Roland grabbed him, pulled him out of the way of a Primal that stampeded past, the maniacal midget on its back cackling madly.

At almost the same moment Roland fired a combat rifle from his hip, shooting a Psycho Midget off the back of a Primal. The little lunatic went down, but didn't die immediately, and began crawling in circles as the Primal ran off in confusion.

But Cal turned to see the other Primals rending their way through the mercenaries, smashing, crushing, slashing as they went. Primal picked up a mercenary and threw him at two others just as one of them was preparing a hand grenade—the grenade blew up, shattering all three men.

Debris flew, smoke drifted, men screamed, guns boomed. Crannigan fired his Eridian rifle sloppily and missed—he was still disoriented from sleep and surprise—and then threw himself aside to avoid being trampled.

Cal saw a merc grabbed by a Primal thundering by, the

Psycho leaning down, whacking at the man's neck with a short axe, severing it as the Beast dragged him along. The Primal tossed the severed head in the air, its neck streaming blood, spinning so the blood made red spirals; the Psycho, on cue, used the axe to strike the head like a baseball striking a bat, knocking it out of the crater.

The Primals raged back and forth, around and around, crushing, slashing; their riders threw axes and shrieked in glee—and mercs fell. Shields flickered here and there, but most of the men had turned theirs off for the night to save power. The sentry had been killed almost instantly, at the beginning of the charge.

Cal found he had his pistol and fired it at a Psycho Midget, then saw a red flower blossom in the center of its forehead. He threw himself flat, firing at the Primal as it thumped past. It bounded, screaming, out of the crater.

Cal looked up from the ground to see Roland vaulting onto the back of a passing Primal, right behind the Psycho Midget riding it. Roland jerked the Psycho from its saddle and threw it in front of the Primal Beast so the Psycho's own mount trampled it to death. The Primal reached back and slashed at Roland—who blew its brains out even as he rode it, and jumped off as it went tumbling down, the Primal plowing headfirst into the dust, skidding on its belly . . . dead. "Mess with the bull and you get the horns!" Roland shouted. "Come on, boys, spray 'em and slay 'em!" He pulled a sidearm and opened fire at another Primal.

Then only two Primals were left, along with their shrieking Psycho Midget jockeys. They circled inside the crater, clockwise and counterclockwise, smashing equipment and heads. One of them unstrapped an explosive barrel from its lower back and tossed it at Crannigan, who ducked under it, so it exploded behind him.

Crannigan came at the roaring Primal and the cackling Psycho with his Eridian rifle—Crannigan was firing into them, almost point-blank with the Eridian rifle, while another merc was firing at them with the rocket launcher. Two kinds of explosions merged, and the Primals went down.

The Psychos were dead; the men converged around the Primals and crushed their skulls with the butts of their guns. It was a memorable sound, the crushing of skulls with gun butts. Cal was very much afraid he'd never quite forget it.

At last it was done. It was quiet, then. Rans Veritas crawled out from his hiding place under an outrunner.

Cal gagged and rolled over, to look at the sun rising above the rim of the crater. The purifying sun. The sun glared back at him. He closed his eyes and pretended he was back on the homeworld, lying on a beach . . .

"Hey kid," Roland said. "You okay?"

Cal sighed, opened his eyes, and sat up, looked dully around at the blood and spattered brains and shattered bodies. "Yeah. I'm okay."

"You're not hit or nothin'?"

"No, I'd have been trampled, at least, but you pulled me out of the way. Thanks."

A gunshot—they both looked over to see Crannigan, pistol smoking, standing over one of his own men. He'd shot the man through the head. He glared at them. "What?"

"Is that necessary?" Roland demanded.

Crannigan shrugged. "Yeah. He was too badly hurt. We don't have regeneration supplies we can spare. Couldn't take him with me. It's triage. What was I supposed to do?"

"I'd have given him my supplies."

"I'll tell you something else—he was our sentry. He dozed off right before they attacked."

Roland turned away in disgust. "Whatever. Let's bury our dead."

It took them a couple of hours. The enemy dead they left for the skags and the trash birds.

The only ones left alive in Crannigan's camp were Rans, Roland, Crannigan himself, Cal, and one merc, an older guy named Rosco.

"Hey!" Rosco said. He was a stocky, scarred merc with a flattop haircut and fatigues. "What's that comin' outta this Psycho's head?"

He pointed at one of the fallen Psychos. They all gathered to stare at the dead Psycho Midget's body.

"There," Rosco said. "You see? In the back. The other Midgets have it too! They all do!"

Something twisted out of the Psycho Midget's body, just at the back of the skull—tech of some kind. Something no human being had ever created.

Something alien.

FIFTEEN

’m only giving you water, you understand," Berl was saying, "because I need you to not die on me before I figure out how best to kill you dead."

"Sure, Berl," Zac said, taking another drink as he looked at the rising sun. He was just glad Berl had let him out of the ropes; had given him a canteen to drink from. A chance to rest. "I know that."

They were sitting up in the rocks, overlooking the plain, Berl a little behind Zac where he could keep an eye on him. They'd spent an uncomfortable night on this shelf of stone under the watchful eyes of Bizzy, who was squatting atop a large boulder nearby, legs sprawling over it to the ground.

Berl asked, "You figure—that family of yours . . . they're alive?"

Zac turned around and glared at him. "They're alive. Don't question that. You can shoot me right here, goddamn you, I don't care. But don't say my family's . . ."

Berl gave him a snaggle-toothed grin. "Sure, young feller. Whatever you say. I hope they is. But *you*, now—"

"I know, Berl. You told me already. You're gonna kill me. When you get ready to do it, just do me a favor and shoot me. I really don't think anybody deserves being melted by Bizzy. If you don't want to waste the bullet, then bash my head in with a rock. Make it a big one so it's over fast."

"Now don't start feelin' sorry for yourself, boy. Tell you the truth, I'm starting to think that maybe it was lucky you did what you did. I was thinking for a few years there, I'd like to go get me some more artifacts. Only, it was too moth-erbuggerin' dangerous. Now maybe I got me a way . . ."

"What do you *do* with the artifacts, Berl? They your re-tirement plan? Save 'em up and sell 'em sometime?"

"Why, I'm long ago retired. I tried for a long time to find the Vault. Got clues but . . . couldn't get close enough. This—this is *my* Vault. It's not made by the same alien critters—and that suits me. And them artifacts . . . I just . . . I just *like* those things. You wouldn't understand. They call to me!"

"Wait . . ." Zac looked sharply at Berl. "What do you mean, 'Now maybe I got me a way.' Looking at me like that."

"You wanted to go there and get some more o' them alien artifacts, right?"

"Maybe. I was going to verify the crash site and, if I could do it safely, get one or two. I needed to get a sense of what was there before I could . . . Dammit, Berl, what have you got in mind?"

"Fishin'! You ever go fishin', young fella?" Berl's

chuckle had a particularly evil sound, just then. "I intend to go fishin' right here on this planet! Using Mr. Smartass Zac Finn for bait!"

"You're going to cut me up and put me on hooks?"

"No, no, *I* don't need to kill you. Why, the Ship'll probably kill you for me! But if I can use you to lure the monitor over to one spot, why, *I* can slip in the back way and grab me a few things. Then, maybe, if you're still alive . . . and you might be . . . and if it hasn't screwed with your brain . . . why, I might let you go. You could go right to hell for all I care, after that—or go off and find your little boy and that sweet squeeze of yours."

"Fishing. With me as bait . . ." Zac turned away so that Berl wouldn't see his growing fury. Leave it to the cunning old hermit to come up with the most misanthropic way to degrade a man. He had to play along till he got a chance to disarm the old guy. Bizzy had to go off without Berl and hunt now and then. The chance would come . . .

But there was another possibility too. Maybe all this was a break, after all.

Then he looked out across the unforgiving landscape of the borderlands, and he snorted to himself.

Sure. Tell yourself whatever you want—but this blighted planet is never going to cut you a break . . .

"Here you go, boy," Berl said, tossing him a small bag. "Have some skag meat. And I'll even give you a nice Primal ball to chew on. Testicles make a man strong, ha ha! We *need* you strong! You're gonna need *all* your strength, Mr. Smartass. You wait and see. Because if you're not strong and fast—it'll finish with you, one way or another, real quick and real ugly. Yessir. Real ugly."

• • •

Marla paced the confines of her cell.

It was seven paces by five. A shelf was cut from the wall; it could be a bench or for sleeping. On it was a pile of old rags, probably clothing from former prisoners. *I guess when you're taken out of your cell to be eaten, you don't need clothing.*

The cell was on the corner of intersecting carved-out corridors. The wall behind the bench was about a third of a meter thick, with the corridor on the other side. The other wall seemed carved out of a big piece of stone. The three walls were stone, scored by scratched-in graffiti: *Kiss your ass good-bye; I'm going to poison the one who eats me; A Loving God would not have left me here; All Hail the Great Engineer.*

The floor was uneven stone, covered with a thin layer of dirt; a little light came through the steel bars that made up the cell door, from a lantern on a stone shelf in the narrow carved-stone corridor.

Marla went to the door and tried it, hoping it was loose in its socket, or its lock rusty, but it held firm. She looked down the corridor and saw no other cells.

Just inside the cell door was a tin bucket, crusted with old waste matter. This was presumably her toilet. Nearby was an identical bucket about half full of water.

She cupped some water in both hands, smelled it, and made herself drink some. She used another handful to try to clean her face, and press her hair into place. She needed to seem attractive—it was helping her stay alive.

But again she vowed to herself that she'd die before she'd ever let the tunnel rats use her. After she was dead, the execrable Broncus could do as he liked with her. And probably would.

"Move back from that door, prisoner!" growled Flemmel, stepping into view around a curve in the stone corridor. He was carrying a submachine gun. He was wearing his gas mask, and she only knew it was him by his voice.

She took a step back. "Why? You afraid of me?"

He pushed his gas mask back; it sat there like a hat, so she could see his scowl. He was as pale and chinless as Broncus; his nose was even larger, even more suggestive of an animal snout. One of his eyes was blue and the other brown. His upper incisor teeth were so long they'd cut into his jutting lower lip. "Afraid of *you*? It is merely a matter of procedure."

"You tunnel . . . *people*. . . . are a study in contrasts, Flemmel. Your talk sounds more educated than a lot of people on this planet and you seem to have a pretty good understanding of mechanics. But you're . . ."

"We're what?"

She'd been about to *say you're more barbaric than the other people I've seen, except maybe the Psychos.* Instead, she went on: "You're isolated down here. How do you maintain your, uh, high standards?"

"We are descended from those who designed the mines. We are mining engineers. We pass on that knowledge, that speech. We know many things, many things. And you need to know nothing more—except that we know how to flense flesh from bone! So don't try to tinker with my wingding as you did with Broncus! You cannot get around me!"

She nodded resignedly. "I know a man of character

when I see one, Flemmel. I find some reassurance in the fact that you're my sentry—you're guarding me as well as keeping me in here, after all."

He blinked. "Reassurance?"

She turned away, smiling to herself at his bafflement, and went to sit on the bench, keeping her back to him.

Suddenly, the suppressed emotion of the past day swept over her. She found herself silently sobbing—the weeping too powerful to express itself aloud—and she saw clear mental pictures of Cal, and Zac, on the gray beach of the Homeworld's polluted ocean, Cal very small, Zac swinging him about by his wrists, the boy laughing. The mental image was more vivid than any holovideo. She could feel the sand under her bare toes . . .

"*Cal,*" she sobbed, trying to speak to the images of her husband and son on the beach. "*Zac* . . . Look at me. I'm here . . ." But Cal tumbled to the sand, laughing, and ran off, Zac smilingly running after him . . .

Were they dead now?

All she knew was, she was in a stone cell, underground, in a place that smelled like a sewage treatment plant, shut away from the sun as well as her family. With only cannibals for company.

Probably Zac and Cal *were* dead. So why should she live on without them? Even if the tunnel rats were to spare her—why would she want to live on, here, to bear their hideous, doomed children and slowly go mad?

Why wait to die? She would never get out of here. Even if she somehow got past Flemmel, the tunnels were surely thronged with these vermin. She couldn't get past all of them. Why shouldn't she kill herself right away?

She could lure Flemmel close and grab his gun—he'd probably shoot her if he did that. That would get it done.

Idly, trying to decide how best to get herself killed in short order, Marla poked a finger through the rags, vaguely thinking to see if they contained lice. She saw nothing of that sort. They stank, though. Her hand struck a small, hard rectangle under the rags. She exposed it with a flick of her hand—and saw that it was a little notebook in a metal binder. She glanced over her shoulder at Flemmel, who was standing slumped against the wall, across from her cell door, staring at the stone floor, muttering inaudibly to himself. He wasn't looking at her.

She looked back at the little book and flipped it open. Instantly, she saw that it was a diary. Most of the pages were ripped away. She'd opened it to the remaining few pages.

There was a date, from several years earlier, with a question mark after it. And then it read:

Hymus is coming for another of my fingers today. They seem to have some superstition about my fingers because I'm a technician. They're very primitive, except for a few little peculiarities. They have odd superstitions. They apparently believe if they eat my fingers, it'll increase their technical prowess. They let me work on one of their trashy, wired-together mining machines.

But if they keep lopping off my fingers I won't have anything to work with—or to write with. I found this empty diary book and this pen in the pocket of an old coat left by a previous prisoner. It's someone to talk to besides the tunnel rats—I guess I'm talking to myself, and whoever might find this later. Good thing the rats can't read much.

I might also use the pen to gouge out Hymus's eyes at some point, if I'm swift. But I only have two fingers left on my left hand and four on my right, to do it with. Fortunately he gives me a spray of deadener to stanch the pain before he cuts it off. It doesn't hurt so much. What hurts is despair. It's strange how physical the feeling of despair is.

I wonder who Hymus is selling my fingers to? I know he's eaten at least one himself. I look at him and think of him chewing on my severed finger. He hopes to be the Great Engineer here soon, I understand.

I hope he chokes on one of my fingers, and dies from it. I'd take such delight in that, were I to see it happen.

Perhaps I might convince him my finger's more potent if he bites it off when it's still attached. Then I can shove it down his throat and choke him . . .

But before I do anything that desperate, I must think about the soft stone about the ancient columns. There might be a way to dig at the cell's corner, and get out to one of the corridors. They do sleep during daylight hours, though it's always night down here. There are sentries at all times, but I could slip past one or two.

Probably that's a dream. But if I give up hope, I die all the sooner. I won't give them the satisfaction. Keep looking for a way out! Keep looking! It must be there!

It was signed. *Two Finger Frank Finackus.*

Marla stared at the page. Were they going to start lopping off her body parts?

But something else arrested her attention. *There might be a way to dig at the cell's corner, and get out to one of the corridors. They do sleep during daylight hours.*

Frank Finackus. Had he died here? Or had he escaped from this cell? And—was there a way out?

Cal was relieved, *very* relieved, to get out of that crater, away from the stench of death, the memory of skull-crushing crunches . . .

"You guys figure out what that thing was?" Cal asked, getting in the outrunner beside Roland. "I mean—that stuff sticking out of the Psycho's head."

"That stuff" had been like jointed worms made of a strange, iridescent metal, short tendrils whipping out from the back of the skull . . .

Roland shrugged, starting up the outrunner. "I'm not sure, kid. We got nothing but theories." He drove up the ramp of sand that led to the edge of the crater, and over into the sunny morning, the light glancing painfully from the glassy surface of the plain. Behind them came Crannigan, Rosco, and Rans Veritas in the only other surviving vehicle, the sandtracker. It was slow, so Roland held the outrunner in check.

"What kind of theories?" Cal asked, holding on as they bumped over a wide crack in the crude glass surface.

"Well—Rans has seen skags with implants. Anyway, he says it *seems* to be implants of some kind. You know, wiring stuck in your head. Like that colony world Singularity where everyone's sixty percent gear. Cyborg types—I never could stand those snooty bastards. And I never needed any extra anything stuck in my brain. Anyhow, he says it's the same technology as the crashed ship. It's the same aliens. But . . . he says don't touch it. Not that stuff. It can crawl right up your arm. So they're not taking it as a sample. Some of the alien artifacts are safe to handle—and some aren't."

"But—did the Psycho Midgets put that stuff in there themselves . . . or did something put it in there for them?"

Roland glanced at him, eyebrows raised. "Can't get anything past you, kid. You're a quick study. Yeah. Seems like those things were *put* in there . . . Rans claims it's the alien ship itself that does it. Maybe some kind of computer on the crashed starship, see. And it manufactures these gizmos, uses 'em to take control of people and animals, sends 'em out, sometimes, to protect itself."

"So it was watching us somehow? It knew we were getting close?"

"Must've been watching us—or listening to transmissions. I don't know for sure. Rans talks like he knows. But I don't think he does."

"I don't trust him."

"That's another good call, kid."

Ahead of them the volcano loomed, its lower slopes perhaps twenty kilometers away. Roland had told him the volcano was their destination. It looked like it had been a complete, hollow cone, later broken open on the eastern side, its interior dark and misty. Anything could be waiting in there . . .

Cal turned around, looked back at Crannigan and the others, riding in the sandtracker. "We're getting pretty far ahead."

"Yeah. I'm keeping about this distance between us. I

don't trust any of those three. Rosco might be all right. But the other two . . . I hate to have them at my back."

"They need you, after that mess back at the crater. All those men killed. They're shorthanded now."

Roland grunted assent. "True enough, kid. They need me for a while. And I need them for a while. But that's one treaty that just isn't gonna last—whoa, better slow down, what the hell is that?"

Roland slowed the outrunner, brought it to an idling stop on the edge of a dark spot in the plain. He got out and walked up to the edge of the big blot on the glassy ground.

Roland stared down at the slick ground, shook his head, and growled, "What the hell! Kid, stay in the vehicle."

Cal was annoyed at that—but he'd learned not to argue with Roland when he used that tone.

Roland turned and waved at the sandtracker, signaling them to come, but slowly. In a couple of minutes the sandtracker caught up. Crannigan switched the engine off. "What's going on? We need to get moving!"

"Not through here," Roland said. "Looks like something's hollowed out the plain in this spot. Kinda looks like it might've been done deliberately."

"He's right," Rans allowed, getting carefully out of the sandtracker. He studied the glassy surface, then walked gingerly over to Roland and looked down at the dark blot. "They've expanded their tunnels. They didn't used to be this far out. Might be true what I heard—they have some kinda tribal gathering out this way . . ."

"Who's *they?*" Crannigan asked, getting out and walking over with Rosco.

"Tunnel rats," said Rans, spitting.

"I was afraid of that," Roland said, lifting his goggles to wipe dust from his eyes. "Goddamn tunnel rats."

"Which is what?" Crannigan asked.

"Screwballs who live down in tunnels, most of which they dig themselves," Roland said. "Went kinda wacky, hiding out from the Psychos. Never came back up. Inbred and mean and filthy motherbuggers. And if that wasn't enough—cannibals."

"They stay down there, out of our way?"

Rans Veritas shook his head. "Can't be sure they'll stay down there. They come out at night and nab people. And they lay traps . . . which might be what this is. One thing for sure, if Roland hadn't spotted it, it would've collapsed under him. He'd be down there with the kid right now . . ." Rans turned to look at Cal in a speculative way that made Cal shiver. There was something sinister in that conjectural look.

Crannigan was giving Rans a sour look of his own. "You didn't know about this? We didn't get any warning about it from you. And you're no good in a fight—you hide under the vehicles! So what good are you?"

"You'll see," Rans grumbled. "You'll all see when we get there. Right now we got to find a way around this."

"Let's get back in the outrunner, and drive around it," Roland said, shrugging.

"Looks like these dark spaces go on a ways," Rosco said. "Branching out all over. Hey—is that someone down there?"

Cal stood up in the outrunner to try to see what was down in the sheathed pit.

He couldn't see much in the glare of reflected light on the slick ground, just a sense of depth he hadn't noticed before on that glassy plain.

"Yeah—looked like a tunnel rat to me," Roland muttered. "Let's get out of here."

Tunnel rats, Cal thought.

His father might have come this way. For all he knew his father, or mother, was already down there.

Vance got in the outrunner; the others got in the sandtracker. Roland backed up a little more and drove around the edge of the dark spots in the glassy surface.

They hadn't gone more than thirty meters before the silicon sheath underneath them began to crack. Roland stopped the outrunner, backed up a little, and watched the glassy surface. The cracks stopped spreading.

"Can't go on that way . . . Hard to see with all the sunlight shinin' off the glass. We're gonna have to head over to the edge of the plain and go the long way. Makes me nervous, though, taking the extra time. Too many people seem to know about the alien crash . . ."

"Roland," Cal said, "I've got an idea. Suppose you give me some tinted goggles. There's a pair in the sandtracker. Then I walk real slow up ahead of the vehicles. I don't weigh much—I probably wouldn't break through. I can point you to a safe route."

"Kid, you don't know for sure you don't weigh enough to break through. Those little bastards might've undermined it so almost anything'd fall through."

"Looks solid enough for someone my size. Come on, Roland. I want to be good for something out here."

Roland looked at him with a grim seriousness. Then

he sighed. "Can't argue with that. That's what any man should want. Okay. Get out and wait by the vehicle."

Roland went back on foot to the sandtracker, found the tinted goggles, and brought them back to Cal. He tossed them over, and Cal put them on. The world shifted into a cool blue. Details he hadn't been able to make out before came through. Rocks that had looked blue now looked gray, or flat black, or reddish.

"Okay, kid. You're on. Head away from those cracks— off that way, toward the edge of the plain."

Cal swallowed hard, but walked out in front of the outrunner, in the direction Roland indicated, testing the ground as he went. Treading lightly, he moved slowly to the west, away from the cracked areas. Even more slowly, the vehicles followed him, inching along.

There were a good many dark areas, indicating under-mining tunnels. But with the goggles, and being close to the plain's surface, he could see a way past them, on the glassy ground where there was solid support. They kept going roughly the way they had been, but wending carefully between the dark tunnels, visible in outline beneath the translucent surface.

At last they reached the end of the maze on the glassy surface. Up ahead, between here and the volcano, it looked mostly clear.

But to his left, in the single dark shaft still visible under the scratched, translucent glass, something moved. He peered down through the glass—and caught a face goggling up at him.

Tunnel rat. Manlike, but with a rubbery face and glass

eyes, the creature clasped its hands together, wringing them . . .

Suddenly it pointed up at him and gestured with its clawed finger. *Come here.*

Something about the tunnel rat's gesture hinted that coming down there was Cal's destiny.

SIXTEEN

W e may be going the long way around," Berl
was saying, as sunset began to turn the glassy
plain a streaked, rusty orange. "But we're more
likely to get there in one piece than any of them others.
Sure, I seen 'em too, boy. Mercs. And way far off I spied
some folks in a truck. I asked Bizzy was it you. He said no.
And those mercs ain't gonna make it, no sir. The tunnel
rats, and the ShipGrowth—that'll get 'em. But the way
we're going . . . we're good. Up to a point, anyhow. Ha! Up
to a point . . ."

They were tramping along the curving edge of the
plain, Zac carrying most of their baggage, getting closer to
the lower slopes of the old volcanic shell. Bizzy was well
ahead, ranging back and forth, looking for trouble. Zac
wondered if he could knock Berl down, take the gun—use
it to control the old man. Berl would keep Bizzy off . . .

But how would he know what Berl said to his pet? One

222 | JOHN SHIRLEY

spit of that corrosive venom and Zac would be a mass of dying, bubbling flesh.

It occurred to Zac, then, that he was going to where he'd planned to go anyway. When he got close enough, he could turn the tables on the old hermit.

An undertow of excitement began to tug at Zac. He was going right to the alien crash site. Maybe he would die there. Or maybe it would make his fortune. With enough money, he could find his family.

Because they *were* alive. Definitely. They had to be.

"Now—you see that wall of rock up ahead?" Berl asked him suddenly, pointing to the cliffs under the foot of the volcano shell. "Tell me, boy—how you think we're gonna get over that?"

"I dunno unless Bizzy can carry us. You got a jetpack on you?"

"See that fold in the rock there, not much more'n a crack from here? Don't look like much, do it?" Berl chortled. "Just you wait. Let's pick up the pace—it'll be dark soon. Want to get in the pass before dark."

They trekked onward, and at last, as the half-moon began to rise, they came to the cliffs abutting the glass plain. The cliffs beetled over them, leaning out above the plain as if about to rush it. Bizzy had already climbed the cliff, was poised at the top, looking down at them, his yellow eyes glowing against the deepening night.

The seam in the rock Berl had pointed out appeared to be just that. They came closer, and Berl skipped ahead, and seemed to disappear.

"Berl?" Zac looked up to see Bizzy staring down at him. There was no running off now, even without Berl to watch

BORDERLANDS: THE FALLEN | 223

him. Because his giant pet was watching. And Bizzy always knew what Berl wanted.

Berl's head seemed to appear in the wall of stone, jutting out sideways. "Get on in here, boy!" He vanished again.

Zac reached out, touched the stone, and felt his way along it—and suddenly no longer felt the rock under his hands, though he could still see it there in front of him. He stepped through what had seemed like impenetrable rock—but it was just an image. Something shimmered, and then he found he was standing in a shadowy crevice just wide enough for two men, a little light shafting down from overhead.

Berl was there, combat rifle in hand, grinning at him. Zac turned and looked back at the plain—and saw an open entrance, a meter wide, as high as the cliff, the "seam" he'd seen earlier. "Some kind of optical illusion?"

"It's more'n that, boy. Someone way long ago hid that entrance there. I think it was the ship done it. And I think it did it so it could bring its took-overs up here without anyone seeing where they went."

"What are took-overs?"

"The Vault had its Guardians—these aliens do it different. Come on, there's a way up, nice 'n' smooth. When we get to the top, there's a cave we can spend the night. We'll want to go about our 'fishin' early in the mornin'. Let's just hope we don't run into any took-overs on the way."

Berl gestured with the rifle and Zac went on ahead. They climbed a ramp, at the widening back of the crevice, that zigzagged upward in short switchbacks, up and up . . . to the foot of the hollow volcanic cone, and the outer region of the alien debris field.

• • •

"We can't drive up any higher than this?" Cal asked as they stood at the edge of the plain in the moonlight-damaged darkness.

"Nope, not in either vehicle," Roland said. "The passage is too narrow. Way too steep. Anyway it'll be stealthier this way. And we've definitely got to be stealthy. And I think we oughta go and have a look right now. See what we can see. We'll be too visible come daylight. May as well use the night to our advantage."

Rans snorted and complained, "We could fall into a damn crevice or something, in the dark!"

"There's just enough light," Roland said patiently. "I think we'll be all right . . ."

They were at the foot of a short cliff, maybe forty meters high, below the rugged foothills under the shell of the volcano. A break in the wall opened up in front of them; a tumble of broken rock offered a route up to the top of the cliff. It looked like loose rock, and a dangerous way to go. But it was the most expedient.

"Let's go!" Cal said. He was excited on several levels. First the possibility existed that he might find his father up on the volcano. Second, the sheer excitement of being at the end of a journey. And then there was the mystery, the alien mystique, nestled in the ancient volcanic cone . . .

Rans glared at him. Cal could only see his eyes in the uneven light. "We stay here and rest! I've got a bum leg— I'm not going to climb that now! We can go up just before dawn. It'll still be dark."

Crannigan shook his head. "You've lard-assed your way through this whole trip, Veritas! Now you want to lie around some more! We need to move! We're burning moonlight!"

"I ain't going, I tell ya! I haven't been able to pay for a rebuild of my leg! It hurts like the devil!"

"Oh hell, let's rest, I could use some too," Rosco said.

Roland nodded. "We'll have to move the vehicles out of sight, around that point there," Roland said. "They'll attract too much attention if we leave 'em here. Me and Rosco can do that. It'll take us a half hour or so to walk back. Cal, you help the others set up camp—see there, up the crevice, there's a shelf of rock. We'll camp there. But a cold camp—no fires. That was our mistake last time . . ."

Cal opened his mouth to object—he didn't want to be left here with Rans, even for a few minutes, without Roland. Some instinct warned him against it.

But he saw Roland looking at him and decided he didn't want to seem weak.

"Sure, okay," he said. "I'll start moving the tents."

He and Rosco took the camp supplies out of the vehicles, and then Roland and Rosco drove off toward the point where the cliffs thrust out into the plain.

Cal, Crannigan, and Rans—who was carrying as little as possible—toted their gear up the crevice, over the shale and loose rock, toiling in the darkness, sometimes falling and barking their shins.

At last they reached the shelf where they'd take their rest. They set up camp, and then Crannigan said, "I'm gonna climb up, see if I can see anything. I wanna know if any of those weird brain-controlled bastards are hanging around up there. Keep an eye on the kid, Rans, will ya? Roland'll be back soon."

Cal snorted. "It's not like I need anyone to keep an eye on me."

Crannigan ignored him and started climbing the rocks, vanishing into the darkness above them.

Cal was looking for something to eat in the packs when a big, grimy hand closed around his mouth, clamping down hard. "Hold still, kid," Rans said, "or I'll break your neck right now."

Cal stopped struggling—and bit Rans hard in the hand. "Ow!"

Then came a thumping crunch, and a big splash of darkness, as Rans hit him hard in the back of the head—and Cal lost consciousness.

He was on his back, moving backward on the slick ground . . .

Someone was dragging Cal along by the collar. He was no longer at the camp. He was out on the glassy plain. He could see it stretching out to his left, and the half-moon rising over it. The moon was reflected, dull and smeared, in the surface of the plain.

That's when the pain hit him. The throbbing in the back of his head crackled with a piercing hurt.

Cal reached back, tried to pull his collar loose from Rans's grip. He wasn't strong enough.

"Forget it, kid," Rans said. "The thing is, I don't like loose ends. And you're one. Your old man's gotta be dead. And that means you and your family'll blame me. If you come out of this alive—you'll come after me. You or some other Finn putz. And another thing is, I don't like the way you talk to me. No respect."

Cal struggled again, trying to wrench loose. It hurt to do it but he had to try. "You're just guilty, that's all—you know what you did to my dad! You don't like me around to remind you!"

Rans twisted Cal's collar angrily—the kid had hit a nerve. "Shut up, boy."

"They'll know—Roland'll know what happened. He'll figure it out. And he'll kick your ass up over your head!"

"Naw. I'll tell them about the skags that jumped us and dragged you off. Happens all the time on this planet. And they're sure not going to find you where you're going. Bye, bye, kid."

Marla guessed it was near dawn because of the way that Flemmel was sagging. The tunnel rats were accustomed to sleep during the day. No one came to relieve Flemmel, and eventually he squatted down, leaned back against the wall. Soon he was snoring, clutching his submachine gun to himself much the way a sleeping child hugs a stuffed toy.

She'd slept fitfully, her stomach burning with the bitter mash of seed pods and roots they'd brought her to eat. There had been meat too, but she'd picked that out and put it in the waste bucket. She didn't know what—or who—it might be.

The lantern was still glowing, but weakly now. She had just enough light to see what she was doing, as she got up, stretched, wincing at her aching muscles, then went to the far, darkest corner of the cell, half-hidden by the stone bench. Here she was partially concealed from anyone who might watch from the corridor. She might be able to dig a certain amount . . . but with what?

She scraped at the wall near the floor with her fingers, and found it was indeed fairly soft stone here—not quite soapstone soft, but almost. But she could make no real progress with her hands. She soon had bloodied nails.

Then she remembered the diary. Checking Flemmel again, and finding him still asleep, she pulled the diary from under the rags, removed its metal cover—noting a corner of it seemed bent, and dirty—and used it as a crude shovel. Now she made real progress, using the small metal rectangle to dig out the soft stone.

She might try to slip out, find a way past the tunnel rats, without even dealing with Flemmel. But . . .

No. She would need his mask. His clothing. That was the way to do it. Disguise herself as a tunnel rat. She'd have to kill Flemmel to get his mask and clothing.

No problem. She'd grab the gun from him, and smash his head in with its butt before he had time to think. It wouldn't do to fire it and make a ruckus, draw other sentries here.

It could work. It *had* to work.

She glanced at him, and saw he was still squatted down, and snoring softly.

She went back to scraping at the soft spot in the wall. It was even softer than she'd supposed, sometimes falling apart without her having to push hard. Which suggested that it had been dug out before, and filled back in.

This was the darkest part of the cell—much of her digging had to be done by touch. But by degrees her eyes adjusted a little, just enough to see a piece of paper, barely visible, buried in the soft material of the wall.

Marla stared. Then she dug the paper carefully out

and brushed it off. It appeared to be one of the pages from Frank's diary. She checked Flemmel—he was still asleep—and held the paper up to read the writing on it in the dim light from the lantern:

You've gotten this far. I'm going to put this page in the wall, and then close up the wall after me—if I have time—so they won't see someone's gotten out. I'll try to pile up the rags so they think I'm sleeping. They don't watch very well during the day. I estimate that it's late morning. When I was taken out to work on their machines, I memorized the route to the nearest escape. You go out this hole, head right, take a left turn, then a right and go all the way to the old elevator shaft. The elevator may or may not work.

The problem is, the escape takes you close to the volcano, and there are other dangers there. But I'm going out that way if I can, because it's the shortest way. I have one of their gas masks, I've swiped it, and I can use it to conceal my identity. I'm sorry I ever came to this accursed planet. I yearn to be back in the good old chemical works on Toxic Tomb 7. Sure, the atmosphere of that planet is deadly poisonous, and except for our dome there's no life on that world—but there were no murderous cannibals there, and no skags, no rakks, and no crab worms. I hate crab worms. If I escape this world, I'll try to go back to work on Toxic Tomb, perhaps stop off on the homeworld to get some new fingers regrown.

Until then, I am sincerely yours (whoever you may be),
Two Finger Frank

She smiled, feeling a flush of hope, and then folded the paper up, tucked it in her blouse, and murmured, "Bless you, Two Finger Frank."

She scraped away at the lower corner of the wall for another hour. It was dark here, it would be hard for him to see what she was doing, with the bench in the way, but she was hoping to get all the way through before her tunnel rat sentry woke.

But then he moaned in his sleep, and looked sleepily about, smacking his lips and yawning. She hid her simple tool and went to lie on her bench.

"What are you doing there?" Flemmel asked sharply, squinting through the bars at her in the dim light. "You were doing something in the corner."

"I had to pee, if that's okay with you."

"What? There's a bucket right here!"

"I don't wish to do my business in front of all the world. I found a shallow hole in the corner to pee in. And to do a bit more than that. Would you like to *examine* it?"

"No, no, not I, what a revolting thought. You suppose we have no niceties here? You think we defecate just anywhere like . . . like rats? In our own quarters we have vacuum toilets and privacy." He yawned. "All right. It is daylight, so you'd best lie down. You must acclimate yourself to our hours if you are to bear children for us. Personally I think you may grace the feast table instead—we have little enough to sustain the feast. But it's the Great Engineer's decision to make . . ." He yawned again, muttering to himself. "Great Engineer . . . Broncus . . . the scum . . . Imagines he can . . ."

She stretched out, every muscle tense, waiting. Listening and praying for Flemmel to go to sleep . . .

We have little enough to sustain the feast.

She had to get out of here and soon. Or die trying.

A few minutes passed—and then came the scrape of booted feet. She looked over and saw Flemmel was standing at the cell doors, glowering at her through the bars, his eyes large and moist. "I could not get back to sleep. Not with the injustice of Broncus's pretentions—and the feelings you bring out in me. Why should Broncus think he could mate with you? Why not I? Because he is slightly higher in tunnel status? Bah! If they're likely to feast on you anyway—why should I not know the touch of a woman first?"

She sat up, trying to block his view of the corner where she'd done her digging. "Daylight's nearly done, Flemmel! It's nearly time for someone to check on us. They'd catch you at it if you . . . had your way with me. You'd be doing it without the Grand Engineer's permission! I wouldn't want you to get in trouble."

"They won't be along for a while." He turned a key in the lock—his gaze fixed on her. "If you are discreet about it, I'll see that if they do plan to cook you, your death comes quickly and with little pain . . ."

Now is my chance. When he thinks he's about to take me, grab the gun. Crack him over the head . . .

She nodded resignedly. "I guess . . . I *would* like to have one more . . . one more experience of carnal, ah, delight, Flemmel, before I'm . . . I'm to be provided for the feast. Tell me—can you really protect me from a painful death? How do they normally do it?"

"Ah! It's a serious matter. It depends . . ." He opened the cell door and stepped in, closed it behind him, glancing over his shoulder. The gun was loose in his left hand. He was quite confident of himself. "There is a traditional tunneler belief that boiling a prisoner alive makes it possible to drain all their juices of creativity and personal power into the broth." He put the key in a jerkin pocket. His large eyes glittered as he stared at her. "But some prefer a simple roasting, on a spit. With the Psycho Midgets—they're small, perfect for turning over an open flame. We simply cut their throats first. You might be small enough—I will try to arrange the spit for you. That way, not a long, painful death. Now then . . ." Flemmel licked his lips and started toward her.

She raised a hand to keep him back—but as coquettishly as she could. It was hard to pretend to be cute and sexy in filthy clothes, in a jail cell, with your hair matted and in disarray. "Wait—let's . . . let's lie down and be comfortable. I'm sure you'll have a better time."

"Then—before we lie down—take off your clothes. I've never seen a woman without her clothes. Not a live one."

"Won't you—help me get undressed? There's a zipper in the back of my top. I'll turn my back and you can find it and unzip me . . ."

Her plan was risky but it might work. He would fumble about, looking for the nonexistent zipper. Then she would spin quickly to her right, grab the gun from his left hand, raise it up, and hit him sharply several times in the forehead with the gun butt. She couldn't risk the sound of a gunshot. She would have to use all her strength when she crushed his skull, to shut him up fast. One yell from Flemmel would bring the other sentries.

She turned her back. He approached her. She tensed . . .

"Flemmel! What are you doing there?" Broncus shouted, from the corridor.

She turned—and saw Broncus, on the other side of the bars, pushing a bound prisoner ahead of him. The prisoner was small, his head a little bloodied, and bowed. A moment later he lifted his face to look around . . .

Marla gasped. *"Cal!"*

"Mom!"

SEVENTEEN

The morning sun brought out green glints in the flinty rock of the ancient lava field. Zac and Berl gazed over it from its outer edge; Bizzy loomed up behind them, clicking to himself.

"This here field of lava," Berl said, "it must've flowed right out of that volcano, why, millions of years ago. Hard and sharp as a stone axe it is. But there's a way through, even here, young fella. And just on the other side is the ship's debris field, right outside what I call the auditorium . . ."

"All this sharp rock, it'll take us days to get over it," Zac said as he chewed a dried testicle.

"No, I'm telling you—I've got a way. I'm going on ahead but I'm gonna tell Bizzy to follow close and spit a sizzler on you if you make a move on me."

"You don't have to worry about that. I had every intention of coming back later and giving you your share of anything I found out here."

"Ha! Like I'd trust you! All right now . . ." Berl turned to Bizzy, touched his alien-tech collar, and gave a series of long whistles. Bizzy assented by bobbing on his gigantic stiltlike legs.

Berl led the way around a spiny, man-high stone and across a rugged field of volcanic rubble. The lava field seemed a mix of the gnarled, pitted black rock, the lighter, porous, dull red volcanic rock, and green-black volcanic glass. Only a few sparse patches of plants grew. Mostly the prospect ahead was barren, deathly dry, the lava bed crunching loudly under their boot steps. The volcano—just a particularly large cinder cone shaped like a giant blue-gray broken-open eggshell—rose up on the other side of the lava field, with a few twisted humps of ancient lava flow wrapping its lower slopes.

The shadow of Bizzy fell over them as they went. But Zac was actually glad to have Bizzy along, to protect against rakks and other creatures. He felt dangerously exposed here.

They had to pick their way, stepping carefully over the large chunks of sharp-edged volcano glass. The sun rose, and so did the temperature. There was almost no shade, and the sunlight blazed back at them from countless rock surfaces.

"Here we go," said Berl, after about half an hour. "See this? Kind of a natural ramp, like. Right up here and it gets to be easier going . . ." He pointed to where an ancient lava flow had hardened into a kind of twisty pathway up the flank of the cinder cone.

The going got easier on the pathway, but it was still a long, hot trudge up onto the base of the cinder cone. After working their way up about a quarter kilometer, Zac was relieved when the path stopped rising, flattening out, and the air suddenly got cooler. They'd ascended into an altitude where winds blew in from the sea, which was just visible on the horizon. Even Bizzy, still teetering along after them, seemed to move more springily, as if enjoying the coolness.

At last they followed the old lava flow around a natural buttress of stone—and they stopped, gazing at the scene spread before them.

Down to their left was a deep gorge. But it was what was directly ahead that captivated them. The hollowed-out cinder cone made a kind of enormous natural amphitheater—Berl's "auditorium"—not quite a kilometer in diameter around its boulder-strewn floor of black hardened lava. Parts of it were in inky shadow; other parts were brightly illuminated by the sun coming through the break in the stone shell. Something gleamed inside, near the back wall; something slick and translucent and shifting in color, like mother of pearl one moment, purple iridescent another—something big. It was hard to tell how big it was from here.

In the dark rubble of the broken cinder cone's side, smaller, oddly shaped objects shone brightly, twinkling enticingly. No two of them were formed alike.

The overall shape of the broken volcanic cone made Zac think of shrines he'd seen, back on the homeworld. But the idol in the shrine was something truly celestial. It was like looking at a gigantic temple to the alien.

"You can see what happened," Berl said. "Long time ago, fer one reason or 'nother, the ship came down at a slant, smashed into that old cinder cone there, busted that big gap through the side. Some of the ship broke off, parts of it came out in that rubble. That's what I call the debris field. The main body of the ship is inside, on the floor of the cinder cone. It sits on top of all that column of old, hardened lava. Never have gotten very close to it. Those folks in orbit can't see the ship from up there, it's too far under the shell. This angle here, where we're at, that's how you see it . . ."

Zac nodded, feeling past words.

After a few minutes they continued silently onward, working their way along the lava flow pathway, till at last they drew near the debris field. To their left the deep gorge of coarse volcanic rock fell away steeply. Bizzy came along behind, looming over them, his shadow a cage.

"Watch this now," Berl said. He paused and took out the artifact Zac had stolen, the spiral that was never only a spiral. Immediately it leapt in his hand and pointed quiveringly at the site of the crashed alien ship. "It's damn excited to be home."

He put the artifact away and they moved onward, along the edge of the gorge, getting close to the top of the cliff that was the beginning of the debris field. The pathway wound along the mountain's flank to their right.

They were approaching the clifftop and the debris field . . . when Zac felt something grip his ankle. He looked down—and stared in frozen horror at something serpentlike, about twenty centimeters long; it was headless, made of the same peculiar translucent, iridescent material as the pointing artifact. The serpentlike living artifact was winding around his ankle like a small constrictor, moving upward, twining its way up his leg.

He let out a wordless shout and shook his leg, trying to get the thing off.

"Dammit, boy, hold still!" Berl commanded him. Berl tugged a knife from his own boot and used it to pry the thing off Zac's leg.

Before it could wind around his hand, Berl grabbed it by the lower end and flipped it into the gorge to their left.

"What the hell was *that*?" Zac asked, gasping, trying to calm himself.

"ShipGrowth, is what it was. One of the ways it protects itself." Berl chuckled grimly. "You know what it means?" He nodded toward the crashed alien ship. "It means that thing in there knows we're here."

Marla sat beside Cal in the cell, struggling with her emotions, trying to focus on a plan for escape. She felt an enormous relief that Cal was alive, relief alternating with horror at his ending up a prisoner of tunnel rats too.

Broncus had taken over the sentry duties from Flemmel, who had been sent away in disgrace. At the moment Broncus marched back and forth outside their cell with an affectation of great importance, clutching a submachine gun and wearing his gas mask.

"If you'd got here a moment later," Marla whispered to her son, who was seated beside her on the stone bench in the cell, "you'd have seen me smashing that tunnel rat's skull."

"*Whoa,* Mom," Cal said, staring at her. "Being here has changed you."

"In some ways," she admitted, softly. "But not really. You know—parents can't be terribly honest with their kids about the real world. Not at first, when the child's too young. Otherwise—you'd be scared all the time." She sighed. "But I assume that by now, this planet has shown you everything we wanted to keep from you."

He thought about that. "Yeah. Probably most of it."

"So—you haven't seen your dad?"

He shook his head sadly. "How'd you end up here, Mom?"

She told him about the collapsing surface of the plain, the pit that had swallowed the truck. She didn't tell him everything about Vance. "How'd they get you, Cal? Just fall in like I did?"

"Not exactly. I was pushed. The guy who got Dad to come down here to Pandora—Rans Veritas—he's working with some mercs from Atlas. Anyway, me and Roland fell in with 'em . . ."

"Wait, who's Roland?"

"He's the . . . the free agent, sort of, that I met out in the world. I was trying to steal some supplies from him. He caught me. I thought he was going to kill me for sure but—he's treated me all right. Saved my life. He's been helping me—and I've been helping him."

She smiled. "Good. Almost enough to make me believe in God."

"What? Why?"

"Never mind. So this Rans . . ."

"Rans Veritas. He . . . didn't like me. He thought I was going to turn him in or hatch some kind of . . . what do they call it . . . revenge scheme against him. And when Roland was out of the camp, Rans cracked me over the head and dragged me off." He grimaced. "Head still hurts . . ."

"Oh! How do you feel?"

Cal shrugged. "Kind of nauseous. A little dizzy. Not too bad. Felt worse when I got to the bottom of the hole he shoved me in. It was like a chute or something, these tunnel rats use to transfer stuff down to their colony. I sat up at the bottom—and tunnel rats were staring at me. I heard they're cannibals and I thought they were going to eat me, like, first thing. But then they brought me here . . . now I don't know. But I'm sure glad to see you."

She put an arm around him and hugged him to her. "But I bet you've got mixed feelings about seeing me here."

"Yeah. I do."

"Yeah. I know just how you feel. Let me see about that bump on your head . . ."

She brought over the bucket of water, and used an almost unsoiled swatch of her clothing top to cleanse the knot on his head. He winced, but made no sound. "He could've killed you. Broke the skin, bruised your head. But we did get the vaccination against all the local organisms when we hit orbit, here, so probably you won't get an infection."

"I'm okay."

"Chances are you've got a mild concussion. But we have to kind of pretend it's not there, for now, if we want to survive." She glanced at Broncus, then pulled Cal closer and whispered directly into his ear. "Listen closely, Cal. I'm going to talk to that inbred scumbag over there. I'll keep him distracted. While I do that, you look at that hole in the corner. It's almost broken through. A little pushing and scraping, it'll open into the corridor around the corner. I couldn't fit through it. But you could squeeze through. If you do it, make it quick."

He nodded, wide-eyed.

Marla kissed her son on the cheek, winked at him, and stood up. She was a dozen times more determined to escape now. It would take ten tunnel rats, maybe twenty, to hold her down. Her son was here.

She strolled over to the door of the cell, took hold of the bars, pressing her breasts casually against them. "*Bron-chus . . . ?*"

He stopped marching and came wearily to look at her. He pushed his gas mask back so it became a hat on top of his head, and stared at her with his large black eyes. "Yes—what is it? Why are you not resting, woman? You need to sleep now, adjust to our cycle! You might not be eaten, you know, now that the boy is here. He will provide enough feast, along with a Midget we caught." He paused to yawn and rub his eyes. It was day, well into tunnel rat sleep time. "Not being eaten brings with it great responsibility."

"I'm sure it does! Listen, Broncus—if I'm *not* eaten . . . I'm not counting on anything . . . I mean, I know it's the Great Engineer's decision . . ."

He started to glance past her, toward her son, and she moved to hold his gaze with hers. ". . . but if I'm not eaten . . . and they decided I was worthy of bearing . . . tunnel children." *Don't retch,* she told herself. *That'll give it away. Do. Not. Retch.* "Well—is there any chance I might end up . . . if I happened to be very lucky . . . with a certain . . . Broncus? With *you?*"

"Ha, well, I . . ." He straightened up and glanced at the ceiling. "I suppose so. I mean—it is Flemmel, really, who is in disgrace. I am, after all, higher in tunnel status than

Flemmel anyway. I am the one who created the very trap that trapped you!"

"Right! It's only fair . . ."

"I was thinking along the same lines. And so my dear . . ." He reached through the bars with his free hand and touched her forearm. The grime and grease on his fingers left a mark on her skin.

Don't retch.

Broncus frowned, aware of a movement to his left. He looked—and she reached through the bars, grabbed the gun. She had a good grip on it by the muzzle.

He squawked, made a hasty grab for the gun—and someone clasped him roughly from behind. It was Cal, using all his strength to try to hold Broncus in place.

She knew he couldn't hold Broncus long. The tunnel rat opened his mouth to shout for help—and she swung the gun, hard, down between the bars, onto Broncus's forehead—with all the strength of a mother desperate to rescue her child.

His eyes crossed, he made a gargling sound . . . and slumped in Cal's arms.

Cal let the tunnel rat drop. "Is he dead?"

"He's still alive. If I had a knife . . . never mind. You're right—this planet has had an effect on me. Just get the key to the cell from his pocket—and get the gas mask from him. We'll find something to tie him up and gag him with. We'll need his clothes too . . ."

They dragged Broncus into the cell, used a belt and a dirty strap from his clothing to tie him, gagging him with some rags from the cell. Marla stripped him, forced his clothes on over hers, and put on the mask.

The whole process only took about ten minutes but it felt like a lot more—Marla was expecting the other tunnel rats at any moment. But it was daytime, and no one came to check on them. When they were locking the cell door, Broncus began to wake, wriggling and moaning through his gag.

I should kill him, really, to make sure he stays quiet, she thought.

But she couldn't do it with Cal there. He'd seen enough. He shouldn't have to see his mother slit a helpless man's throat.

"Come on," she muttered. "Put your hands behind you, Cal."

He obeyed, and she tied his hands loosely behind him, with pieces of cloth. Hopefully no one would look closely at his bonds.

"But which way do we go?" he asked.

"Keep your voice down, son. I know which way to go. Two Finger Frank left me a message . . ."

"Who?"

"We've got a lot to tell each other later. Go on. I'm gonna poke you in the back with this gun to make it look good . . ."

"Okay, Mom."

"If we run into anybody, keep your mouth shut, and for God's sake don't call me Mom."

"Mom, I'm not stupid."

She took the lantern in one hand, the gun in the other, and prodded her son, muttering directions to him. She kept her finger away from the trigger.

They started off down the dark stone corridor and turned right, following Frank's directions.

You go out this hole, head right, take a left turn, then a right and go all the way to the old elevator shaft. The elevator may or may not work.

They got past the first two turns without encountering a tunnel rat. They encountered only roots dangling from the ceiling in one spot, and a heap of human bones. The last corridor led to an elevator, like an old freight elevator, near the end. It was open; a lantern hung inside, throwing light down the corridor.

But there was a tunnel rat, dozing with a shotgun cradled in his arms, leaning against the wall near the elevator, his face mask pushed back. She didn't recognize him.

Marla's finger moved closer to the trigger on the submachine gun. Cal kept walking. She kept walking, past the tunnel rat. The elevator was just a few steps farther.

"That elevator's broken," the tunnel rat said suddenly.

She nodded, stopped her son by grabbing his shoulder. In her best imitation of Broncus's voice, she hissed, "Not that way, prisoner."

"You going to see the Engineer, huh?" the tunnel rat asked, scratching himself.

"Yes . . . ," she said, afraid to say more.

"We going to eat that one? Scrawny. Hope we eat the woman too."

"Yes. This way, prisoner." She pushed Cal to the left.

"Wait—that's not the way to the Engineer!" the tunnel rat said. "And you've got Broncus's markings on your mask but the voice . . ."

She turned on her heel, fingering the trigger, and fired from the hip. She caught him across the middle, stitching him with bullets. The shots sounded insanely loud in the corridor. The tunnel rat seemed to dance in place against the wall, then he slid down, eyes glazing, leaving a smear of blood.

"Wow," Cal muttered.

"Never mind!" She pulled the loose bonds off Cal's wrists. "Get the shotgun!"

He grabbed the gun and they dodged off to the left— unsure where they were going now. Hoping for a stairs . . .

Shouts came from behind them, down the corridor. The voices were high-pitched, near hysteria. "Gunshots! Prisoner escape!"

Then Cal said, "This is the way they brought me—that room with the chute . . . Look, there it is!"

He led the way to the right, into a storeroom cut out of sandstone. A lantern on the ceiling illuminated odds and ends of equipment and one dead skag all piled in a corner. In the opposite corner a metal chute, somewhat dented, slanted up to the ceiling. It reminded Marla of a children's slide. At the top a closed hatch fitted flush with the ceiling.

"Go on, Cal! Up!"

"You first, Mom!"

"Just go, you can help me through after you get up there!"

He climbed partway up the chute, holding on to the side and using the dents, but it was too difficult with the shotgun and he slipped, slid back down on his stomach, using words she'd thought he hadn't known.

She took the shotgun. "Go on!"

He climbed again—and now she heard running feet from the hall outside the room.

"Hurry up, Cal!"

He got to the top, held on with one hand, the other trying the bolt lock on the hatch.

She turned toward the door, in time to loose a burst from the submachine gun at the tunnel rat stepping into view. He shouted and spun, and another stepped up—then dodged back as she fired the shotgun with her other hand, bracing it on her hip. The recoil made her stagger, almost fall, and the shot went wide but the tunnel rats were momentarily cowed, holding back.

"You go, Grinkus! You have the big gun!"

"I? You go, damn you, Skoink!"

"Mom—I got it open! I . . . who's that?"

She turned—and saw someone reach down through a dazzling square of light, grab Cal by the collar, and drag him up. She emptied her clip at the door, then dropped the guns and turned to the chute, clambered up it as best she could. A gunshot sounded behind her and a bullet hummed by her right ear. Then she was at the top of the chute, and someone was pulling her out into the sunshine.

They stood blinking in the bright light, gaping at Vance and their surroundings. They were at the base of a cliff, on the edge of the plain. Above them rose the broken blue cinder cone.

"Get out of the way," Vance growled.

He pushed her aside and fired a combat rifle down through the hatch. Someone down there screamed. Vance kicked the hatch shut and turned to grin at her.

"Thought I'd forgotten all about you, huh?"

She stared. "You're out here, not down there. But I appreciate the help."

"I've been hanging around here, thinking about going down, looking for you. Just about had myself talked out of it—then I saw the hatch open."

"We better get outta here!" Cal said, looking around. He found what he was looking for—a large rock, just small enough for him to lift it. He dropped it atop the hatch. "Might hold 'em awhile."

"Those bastards won't come up no-how," Vance said. "Not in the daylight." He looked Cal over. "This is your kid, huh? Sure is—"

"I'm not scrawny," Cal interrupted. "Thanks for your help, mister. We're gonna find Roland. I think I know where the camp is . . ."

"Naw, kid. You're coming with me. You and the lady here are valuable to me. For different reasons. You might make a good hostage. And your mom—well, she proved herself useful lotsa ways."

Marla felt her face flush but she said only, "All we want is to find a way off this planet. We're not interested in that crashed ship. You can have all that, Vance."

"I do plan to have all that, yeah," he said, grinning. He pointed the combat rifle at her. "I found a way up to that volcano. And we're gonna see what's up there."

"That site's dangerous," she said. "We're already too close to it. Two Finger Frank said that it was . . ." Her voice trailed off. She could see by his expression she was wasting her breath. He was going to do everything his way.

He cocked his head, eyebrows lifted. "You say *Two Finger Frank*? I knew that guy! He worked for my gang for a while—then he swiped some guy's DropCraft and left the planet. You sure get around, Marla girl. Yeah Broomy almost killed him when he ran out on her, one night, and he just kept going. Stole an outrider from Grunj . . . It's a long story. Maybe later. We're going to follow the base of the cliff, that way." He pointed east. "You won't believe what I found . . . tracks that disappear into a wall!"

"I've gotta find Roland!" Cal said. "Come on, Mom. I don't think this guy's going to shoot us."

He took her hand and tried to tug her away—the direction opposite the one Vance wanted to go in.

Vance strode up and backhanded Cal, hard, so the boy fell on his back, nose bloodied.

Marla shouted and ran blindly at Vance, raising her fists—he struck her down too. Then he stood over them and said, "Kid's right about one thing. I won't shoot you—because I don't *have* to shoot you. I can beat you to a pulp and drag you along on a rope. Or you can do what I tell you. Your choice."

EIGHTEEN

Berl and Zac were hunkering behind a boulder, within thirty meters of the edge of the debris field.

"Now, young feller," Berl said, "what we're gonna do is, we're gonna use you to keep the monitor occupied."

"What's the monitor?" Zac asked.

"You'll see it soon enough—and you'll know it when you see it."

Zac shook his head. "Where's that combat rifle of yours?"

Berl frowned, reached under his pack, and pulled up the rifle. "Right here. You're not thinking I'm gonna let you have it, are ya?"

"No. Point it at me and shoot me. Because I'm not doing a thing till you give me more information. The more I know—the better my chances."

Berl's frown became a scowl. He glanced up at Bizzy,

standing close by, leaning close as if listening. He looked back at Zac. Then he said, "The monitor is something the ship uses to keep watch on the area around it. It's shaped like a kind of flyin' manta ray, if you ever saw one of them—I saw one in an aquarium once when I was—"

"Berl? Let's stick to the main ideas, man. Hey, how come you talk about the ship like it's a person?"

"I expect it's the ship's computer doing all this. And it's what they call an artificial intelligence. An AI. It's the computer's job to keep the damn ship going—though chances are whoever rode in that ship is long dead."

"The monitor—does it have weapons on it?"

"Not exactly weapons. Tentacles, like. And—it can order the UnderBodies around. Like one of those things that grabbed your leg. And the ones that get into people's heads—they can control the Psychos, some animals . . ."

"Wait—is that how you control Bizzy?"

Berl smiled sheepishly. "It is. I kind of fibbed about where I found him. It was hereabouts. He wandered over here from his own territory, the ship took control of him. He was about to kill me—was spittin' that venom at me and I got a splash on my arm. I got a scar here, let me tell you, a big one. Well I was in the debris field and he was gonna do me in. But then I put my hand on this . . ." He touched the artifact hung around his neck. "And I said, 'Don't kill me you big ol' daddy longlegs!' And he stopped right there. He heard me! Ever since, I've been developing our . . . what you call it . . . a rabbit, a rap it . . ."

"You mean *rapport*?" Zac said.

"That's it. We got one of those, Bizzy and me. It seems to help to whistle at him. But see—he hears my thinking, kinda, through this alien doohickey here. It's some kind of telepathic telephone thing, I figure."

"How do you come by terms like UnderBodies and ShipGrowth? That's not something that sounds like you."

"Why, it comes from the ship. Sometimes, maybe through Bizzy—I hear it thinking!"

"Yeah? What's it thinking now?"

"Oh I can't hear it all the time. Just sometimes. I don't understand most of it. It's not in our talk. But after a while some of the meaning of the words, it kinda filters down to me—in my mind you know."

"Berl—about that rapport of yours. Originally, the ship had control of Bizzy, right? So what happens if it takes over again?"

"Oh, don't worry about that, young fella, I got it all worked out. You see, you get a half klick from the ship, it don't control Bizzy no more. Now—"

"Wait, hold on—we're closer to the ship than that right now!"

"Well yeah, I s'pose we are, but you know, I got the artifact around my neck here. Long as it's on me, it kinda runs interference for me, and Bizzy turns to me first. I reckon he thinks I *am* the ship, or some kinda part of it. If he seems like he's faltering, well, I just touch the artifact here with my hand and I whistle to him and we do our rat-pour, and we connect again, see. Berl 'n' Bizzy, Bizzy 'n' Berl, right? So don't worry your empty little head, boy."

"That's not very comforting, Berl. Seems to me like you could lose control of him. And he could fry us both with a spit of that bright blue tobacco juice of his."

254 | JOHN SHIRLEY

"It's like I said, me and him, we're tight now. It don't matter he's got alien tech in his head. But if he does waver . . . I'll call him back! He'll come right back to me, you wait and see. Him and me are old pals . . ."

Zac sighed. "You'd better be right. What else you know about the alien ship?"

"The monitor notices you more if you move. And . . . there's one other thing I've been noticin'."

"What's that, Berl?"

"Don't you see it? The ship is lighting up! It's shining out more than it was. I've noticed it since I come here. It had a twinkle or two but really the ship used to look kinda dead except for the monitor, and the UnderBodies. That alien ship is coming alive!"

Late afternoon and Roland, Crannigan, Rosco, and Rans Veritas stood in a tense group at the entrance to a gorge leading up to the foot of the broken volcano.

"We're not wasting any more time looking for that damn kid," Crannigan growled. "We're moving on. Face it, the skags had a nice meal and left us alone. So he was good for something."

Roland almost punched Crannigan at that last remark. He surprised himself, feeling that strongly about it. He must've gotten too attached to the kid. Stupid to get attached to anyone on Pandora. Look what happened with McNee.

Roland kept himself in check. Rosco was on Crannigan's team and Rosco was good in a fight. He was watching Roland closely, eyes narrowed. Crannigan was a deadly fighter himself, and he had that Eridian rifle in his hands.

Roland's shield wouldn't stand up to it for more than one good pulse.

Roland had his own Eridian weapon, taken from the bandit cache—a Thunder Storm electric shotgun—but it was stowed in the outrunner as he didn't like handling Eridian weapons too often. He suspected contact with Eridium of causing the mutation of ordinary miners into Psycho Bandits.

"Rans here tried to find the kid," Rosco said. "You tried. Can't be done. It's too damn late, no matter what."

Roland snorted. "Rans says he followed the skags that took the kid. I found drag marks, and Ran's footprints—for a while, till he got to the glass plain. Didn't find any skag tracks anywhere. And skags don't range that far from their dens. No sign of 'em around here for two or three klicks at least."

"What are you saying?" Rans demanded. "You're saying I'm a liar?"

"Never doubted you were a liar," Roland said calmly. "From the moment I met you. And you didn't like that kid. He worried you, for some reason."

"What you think I did, sell him to the bandits?" Rans said, grinning nastily. "You seen any bandits around here?"

"No. But . . . I've seen tunnel rats." He watched Rans's face as he said it. And there did seem to be a flicker of tension there. A sick feeling went through him. Had the shifty old hustler turned the boy over to tunnel rats?

If he did, the kid was probably dead. Which would give Roland yet another score to settle.

Roland groaned inwardly, annoyed with himself for

getting soft. But he had to know what happened to Cal. That kid had counted on him . . .

On the other hand—the boy's father might be in the area. The kid could have stumbled into him. He might be with him now—which meant he might be at the alien crash site. Looked like it was going to be necessary to cover both possibilities. And he did want to see that crash site. His interest had gotten ever more piqued.

"Tell you what I'm gonna do," Roland said. "You go on ahead and I'll catch up to you—maybe in a few hours. Follow the gorge up toward the volcano. I'll leave the outrunner here—but I'm taking the Zodiac Turret with me. It won't be of much use to you anyhow—it's attuned to protect me and me only."

"That wasn't the deal," Crannigan said coldly.

"I'll be there when it gets rough," Roland said, giving Crannigan a significant look. "We've got a deal."

"Okay, whatever," Crannigan grunted. But he wasn't pleased.

Roland just stood there, waiting, unwilling to turn his back on Crannigan right now.

Crannigan shrugged, and led the other men away, grumbling to himself. "A fucking kid. Should have known that'd fuck things up."

Roland waited till they'd moved off far enough up the trail, then he turned, retrieved the Zodiac Turret, which he'd set up on their backtrail; he folded it into carry mode, slung it on his back, and jogged down the trail and back to the glassy plain. A half hour of sweaty trotting took him to the outrunner. He found a water jug, drank about half of it, then got in the outrunner and started it off, following the sandy fringe of the glass plain—almost immediately running into scythids. Some of them spat venom at him, burning a hole in the seat next to him. He ran over four of them till they got the idea and dove into the sand.

Another few minutes and he reached the opening to the trail leading up through the bluffs where they'd made camp. He parked the outrunner where the others could see it, got the Eridian electric shotgun out, and started off along the glass plain toward the tunnel rat maze.

He cut across the glass plain, some of the way, to get there quicker, putting on his tinted goggles against the sunlight gleaming on the glazed ground. He leaned into it, going as quickly as he could . . . and came to the nearest of the rat tunneler excavations visible from above.

"Still time to talk yourself out of this," he muttered. "This is close to suicidal . . ."

But there was no talking himself out of it. He knew damn well he was going in.

He had three protean grenades. Time to use one up getting in.

He backed up, flattened down, activated the grenade, and tossed it at the dark spot on the glass plain. He covered his face a split second before the explosion. Crude glass splinters zinged over him; debris rained down.

Roland sighed, thinking: *That'll bring the sons of bitches running. No hope for sneaking in . . .*

He got up and checked his weaponry. Zodiac, Eridian Thunder Storm, a pistol on each hip, knife. However this came out, there would be fewer tunnel rats, come the end.

"Well," Roland said, "I'm just burning daylight. So . . ."

He ran to the hole blasted through the surface, over the

excavation. Just big enough. He stepped over and dropped, landing with a grunt on the balls of his feet three meters down. He recovered his footing and looked around. The corridor he'd landed in was flooded with sunlight from above—but the farther doorway was dark. Behind him— just rock. This branch of the colony tunnels ended here.

Good thing he'd gotten a night-seeing mod for his goggles at Fyrestone. Roland switched it on, and the darkness became a sharply defined green and red tunnel—with the reddish shape of a tunnel rat running toward him, gas mask pushed back, oversized buck teeth bared. It had a pistol in its hand, firing. Roland's shield repelled the bullets.

He couldn't see a shield on this rat. No sense in wasting recharge time. When the tunnel rat got close enough, he simply smashed in its head, crushing his skull completely with the butt of his gun. It folded up at his feet, stone dead.

But the three coming at him from down the tunnel were quite alive—and firing larger-caliber weapons.

The rounds hit Roland's shield, making him stagger back, his shield flickering. Roland snarled and shouted, "Mess with the bull and you get the horns!" as he fired the Thunder Storm. The electric pellets flashed out and struck the first tunnel rat straight on, penetrating his shield, so that he was flung backward. The others were struck by the rebounding shots ricocheting around like tiny meteors in the corridor, coming at the tunnel rats from every angle, tearing into them, making them dance with electrical charge. One of them, staggering, had a strong shield and got through, eyes ablaze with electricity, shaking but firing a submachine gun at Roland.

Roland returned fire, blasting at the rat's legs so the shot would not only take him out but would ricochet to take out the taller tunnel rat coming around the corner behind him. Down both tunnel rats went, screaming, crackling, electrocuted and bleeding, their wounds spitting sparks as well as spurting blood.

There were half a dozen bodies in the tunnel now. The tunnel rats would be worrying about adding to that pile—so they'd try rockets or grenades, if they had any. He needed to forestall anyone coming close enough till he had a chance to figure out how to get an edge on these scraping scumbags. He could hear them arguing back there, in the tunnel, their feet scuffling on the floor.

"We must charge him again! He cannot kill ten!"

"He is big, he will make a fine meal!"

"You wish to be in the forefront of the ten, Broncus? I thought not!"

Roland unshipped the Zodiac Turret and set it up, fast as he could. It did some of the work itself and soon the tripod was humming, the gun conning back and forth, looking for enemies.

He retreated into the room at the end of the tunnel, a few steps behind the turret—just as a phalanx of tunnel rats tried a charge. The gun chattered and spat bursts of bullets, a powerful caliber that penetrated most shields—the tunnel rats went down, or scurried back, yelping with pain and fear.

Roland chuckled. "I love that damn thing. It's like having another soldier in the field." He stepped closer to the archway and shouted, "Tunnel rats! You listening down there!"

"We are not rats! We are men!" someone shouted back. "We are tunnelers! We are members of the Sacred Guild of Mining Engineers!"

"Right, right," Roland said. "But there's like ten of you at least that are dead mining engineers about now! You want there to be more dead mining engineers? Or you going to give me what I need?"

There was considerable muttered discussion. Then he heard, "Do you really think you can kill all of us? If we must we'll drown your tunnel in fire! We'll use every bomb we have stored away!"

"I got the best shield there is!" Roland yelled, lying through his teeth. "I can take down a hundred of you creepy little bastards before I fold up! And if you bitches creep away, I'll just hunt you through the tunnels! Or you can cooperate—'cause what I want from you ain't so much!"

More muttering. Then, "What is it you require?"

"I'm gonna tell you what I want to know and if I don't get honest answers I'm going to start using my *big* weapons! Now listen—you had a kid in there, right? A boy! You caught him recently! Right? I wanna know, is he alive—or dead!"

A long period of muttering, argument, hissing. "We cannot agree . . . we send the one responsible to talk to you . . ."

The one responsible? What did they mean by that? Roland wondered. "Send him unarmed then!"

"You must neutralize your turret!"

"I'll do it—but if any more than one comes it fires again!"

Roland looked around the stone corner, down the

corridor. He couldn't see the tunnel rats but he could make out their shadows, from around another corner. He reached out, reset the turret. "It's set to let one through! Just one!"

Another lie. It didn't have that refinement. It was completely neutralized. But there were so many weapons modifications, the tunnel rats couldn't know for sure.

Roland drew back, and waited.

In a moment, a tunnel rat, in a gas mask, came up the tunnel, his grimy, clawed hands raised.

"And who the hell would you be?" Roland asked, stepping partly into view and pointing the Eridian shotgun.

"My name is Broncus." He rubbed his hands together nervously, wringing them. "We had the boy. And his mother. But . . ."

His mother? "Yeah, what happened to them? You digesting them right now?"

"No, unfortunately. They escaped."

"I told you I'd know if you were lying!"

"I'm not! The woman used a disguise, a gas mask, and . . . I don't want to discuss it. But she took the boy with her. It was tragic! Right before the feast!"

"Yeah? Well . . ." He noticed the tunnel rat looking speculatively at his muscles as if wondering how juicy the meat would be. "You can forget eating me. I'll burn myself into a cinder before I end up in your intestines. Now listen—I've decided you're telling the truth. Just tell me this, how long ago was this?"

"I don't know. Some hours. It was daylight, not quite sun-overhead. They went out the farthest-most southeast entrance, near the cliffs!"

"I gotcha. Okay, you cooperated, so back you go, down the tunnel. Hey!" He called to the others. "Your pal Broncus here just saved you about thirty lives, at least, so you better thank him and make him your head negotiator or some shit! Now all of you back off and . . . wait. Hold on . . ."

It occurred to him that he didn't want to go through the tunnels to find a way out. That'd leave him too vulnerable to sneak attack.

"One last thing!" Roland called out. "I know you 'engineers' gotta know about ladders, right? Get me one and I'm gone! Nobody else dies! And just think . . . these other losers here I killed . . . they'll make a nice feast!"

"Very true!" said Broncus, brightening. "Everyone should be of service . . . or be a serving . . . to the colony. I will see about your ladder. It's such a shame you can't stay for dinner . . ."

NINETEEN

An empty satchel strapped over one shoulder, Zac was creeping through the debris field, on his hands and knees, wincing as the rock ground into his kneecaps.

He crept up to a boulder shaped like a giant's anvil, to find himself in the shade of the inner shell of the volcano. The shade was a relief—the late afternoon sun fairly blazed into the "auditorium" of the volcano shell.

He heard a beeping, a humming, and glanced up to see the monitor flying slowly over, making those sounds as if they helped it search. The monitor did look roughly like an airborne manta ray, one big as a small car, but semi-transparent, lights twinkling inside it, and with four long transparent rubbery tendrils whipping about from its front end. It was eyeless, but Zac suspected it was *all* eye, in a way. It was the roaming eye of the crashed alien ship.

Was it in fact just the surviving main computer of the

ship that was maintaining the monitor, as Berl supposed—
or were there aliens alive in there, somehow?

Was the monitor itself an alien? A creature? As Zac
looked at it, he thought it seemed, really, more like a so-
phisticated, prehensile floating machine than like an organism.

It drifted slowly over, and Zac held perfectly still, even
holding his breath, remembering what Berl had said about
the monitor being sensitive to motion. At last the monitor
veered off to the right, like a kite changing direction, and
he lost sight of it.

Zac let out a long, relieved breath, and raised himself
up just enough to look around for artifacts. Something
rippled with light, in those rocks over there. But could he
get to it?

What Berl had in mind was his keeping the monitor
busy—when it was far enough off, Zac was supposed to
throw rocks, then hide, do whatever he could to keep it
snooping curiously over here—while Berl slipped in from
another side and grabbed some more artifacts. Zac had his
own satchel and hoped to find a few himself. They could
be worth a lot of money to Atlas, or Dahl, or Hyperion.

Of course, Zac was taking a far bigger chance than
Berl was. But Berl's rifle and his trained drifter were
persuasive—Zac was in no position to argue.

Zac picked his way through the rocks, hunched over,
constantly glancing at the monitor, still turned away from
him. He stepped onto a pile of rocks, a shelf of rock near
the closest artifact—and the rockpile slid apart under him,
with a noisy clatter. He glanced at the monitor, saw it turning his way to investigate the noise.

He flattened, rolled partway under the shelf of rock, and lay still, holding his breath again. He wasn't completely hidden but if he lay still, he might go unnoticed.

Zac heard the monitor whispering wordlessly, hummingly to itself as it moved slowly by overhead; he felt a tingle as it passed over, as if it were probing, and a formless pressure on his eyes. He smelled something odd, too, like rancid pickles. His head ached briefly . . . and then the effect vanished. It had gone.

He breathed again, aware that his pulse was thumping in his ears, and slowly eased out from under the stone.

He rolled onto his stomach and got his feet quietly under him, stood partway up, little by little—

There. The monitor was about seventy meters off, poking at a different end of the debris field.

Licking his dry lips, excited to be here and scared and angry at Berl all at once, Zac turned and climbed the shelf of rock as quietly as he could. On the other side was an object as big as a man's head, not quite spherical, shaped like a flawed pearl. It was translucent, iridescent, and small lights flicked on and off in it. He reached for it—and as his hand got close, the warped sphere extruded small spikes, made of the same material as its body, like a sea anemone. He drew his hand back—the spikes disappeared back into it. Was it safe to pick this thing up?

Zac took off the empty satchel, turned it inside out, then used it as a kind of loose glove to pick up the artifact. It didn't spike out when he picked it up that way and he found it only as heavy as a baseball. He closed the satchel over it and glanced around for the monitor.

The strange delta shape, glimmering within itself as if

thinking visibly, had come to a dead stop hovering over the debris field; it was turned away from Zac, about sixty meters off.

He suspected that the artifact had called to it in some way. The monitor seemed to be thinking it over . . .

Zac hurriedly slid off the rock, taking the satchel with him; he crawled back under the stone shelf and waited. Again that rising hum, the wordless whispering, the pressure on his eyes, the strange smell . . . It lingered a little longer this time. Then it was gone.

He waited as long as he could bear it, then crawled out from under the rock and looked around. He couldn't see the monitor.

He had no idea what the artifact he'd found was good for. But it was going to have to do Berl for now. His heart was stuttering in his chest.

Still one thing to do—and the timing should be right. He lifted up so he could see the monitor, drifting over the debris field now about forty meters to his left. Berl wanted him to throw a rock to distract the thing—but that would be stupid: this thing would probably track the source of the rock.

No. He was going to be more obvious than that and hope he could move fast enough to get where he needed to go.

He crept through the rocks, keeping low, looking around for the monitor, and when he was near the edge of the debris, he saw Berl, waiting near a cluster of artifacts, about halfway across the field. Berl had one hand on the artifact hanging around his neck. Bizzy was nearby, within spitting distance, literally, of Zac: about thirty meters away.

Zac waved at Berl, meaning, *Okay—now!*

Then he jumped up and howled.

He waited till the monitor turned, then he spun about and ran, leaping from rock to rock, jumping behind boulders. He heard the humming, the whispering. Felt the probe . . .

Faster.

Gasping, Zac redoubled his speed, plunging into the sunlight, reaching the pathway of ancient lava flow around the debris field. He leapt up onto it and darted between two rocks, and then behind two more. And shading his eyes against the sun, turned to see if something Berl had said was true: *The monitor won't leave the debris field.*

It did seem to have stopped on the edge of the debris field. Behind it, he could see Berl scrounging among the artifacts . . .

Then he saw the monitor approaching Bizzy.

Berl, dammit, pay attention.

But the old hermit was greedily harvesting artifacts, his attention fixated on his treasures . . .

The monitor got within a few meters of Bizzy and then began to gleam, to flicker inwardly . . . and Bizzy straightened up on its legs, shook itself, and turned toward Zac.

Bizzy stalked over toward Zac and began spitting glowing blue corrosive venom at him in meteoric globs. The stuff burned through the air, hit the stone next to him, dissolving its way through it . . .

"Oh fuck," Zac said, turning to scramble away. Bizzy came after him, quickly gaining ground.

Zac ran down the pathway of melted stone on the edge of the gulch, thinking: *Maybe it's simply time for me to get the hell out of here.*

He hesitated, looked back to see Bizzy—and saw he'd turned away, was stalking toward Berl—and spitting venom.

Good luck, Berl.

Zac turned to run down the pathway. Then he heard a long, pealing shriek, from Berl, in the distance. *"Zaaaaaaaaac! For God's sake, boy! Help me!"*

Zac slowed . . . and stopped. "Oh come on, dammit . . ."

"Zac! Help me! He's not listenin' to me! He's got me cornered! Zaaaaaaaaac! You gotta come back here!"

Groaning, Zac turned around . . . and stopped. "No, goddammit, that old man was ready to shoot me down . . . he cracked me in the head . . . He tied me up . . ."

A particularly piteous cry. *"Zaa-aa-aa-aaaac!"*

He shook his head. There was no living with this if he didn't try to help.

Zac started back toward Bizzy, not sure what he could do to help the old hermit. Another long hot jog up the path of ancient lava flow—and there was Bizzy and the monitor, both of them focused on an igloo-shaped rock. He couldn't see Berl at first—then caught a movement in the shadow of the rock. The boulder was tilted up, at the bottom, resting on another rock, leaving a space in which Berl sheltered. There were smoking, steaming spots on the rock, and in puddles around it, where Bizzy had spat his caustic venom.

Berl tossed a rock out, trying to distract them away. It didn't work.

Bizzy spat a glowing blue wad that struck Berl's shelter. The corrosive bubbled and steamed, and the rock began to pit and burn away under it.

"Zaaaaaaaaac! He doesn't obey me no more! You gotta do something!"

Bizzy was bending down now, trying to aim his toxin into Berl's hiding place, like an exterminator trying to get at a rat hiding in a wall crack.

There was nothing for it. "Bizzy!" Zac shouted. "Goddammit he's your friend! Leave him alone!" On sudden inspiration he took off the satchel, reached in, and took the risk of touching the artifact. He felt it spine up but nothing that hurt him. "Bizzy! Back off him!"

The artifact pulsed . . . and Bizzy turned toward him. The drifter seemed to hesitate, clearly torn, confused.

But the monitor, spinning toward him, didn't hesitate. It rushed toward Zac—and just as he thought: *It won't pass out of the debris field . . .*

. . . It did. It was capable of improvising.

Zac turned to run, then heard the humming, the whispering, felt the probe. And something whickered down and snapped around his shoulders, his upper arms, his chest. He felt a paralyzing pain go through him . . . and then his feet left the ground.

He was lifted upward, upward . . . He looked up to see he was close under the monitor, and it was turning. It was carrying him. It carried him past Bizzy and Berl.

The monitor carried Zac right to the crashed alien spacecraft. And deposited him within it.

It was hot, in the glaring sunlight, as Marla trudged with Cal up close to a featureless cliff of bluish sandstone. Vance was close behind, his gun not pointing at them—but ready, just in case.

This whole journey felt so pointless to Marla. The more she thought about it, the more she doubted that Zac was anywhere around here. She doubted he was alive at all. They should be trying to get to a settlement. And suppose Zac was up there? What would happen to him? Vance didn't like rivals. Chances were, he'd—

"Watch this, Marla," Vance said.

Vance grabbed her son by the collar and the back of his pants, lifted him off his feet, and threw him at a wall of stone.

She jumped to her feet—she'd been resting on a hump of sand—and then, instead of hitting the rock head-on, Cal vanished into it.

She swayed, staring. *"Cal?"*

After a few seconds he thrust his head into view—it appeared that his head was sticking out of a natural sandstone cliff. No body was visible, just the head.

"I'm okay, Mom . . . There's some kind of hidden place in here . . ." His head vanished into the wall.

Vance grinned. Marla didn't return the smile. She walked over to the wall of stone, put her hand out—and her hand disappeared into it.

"Some kinda generated illusion thing," Vance said. "I think it's used to protect that alien ship. I found it following some tracks here. Was about to go up there—then I thought I'd go and have another look to see if I could get into that tunnel rat colony and look in on you. Only . . . I had to think it over. Then—there you were, popping up outta the dirt!"

She glared at him. "You threw my kid at a big rock."

"Hey, ease up, pretty lady," Vance said, flashing his big

smile. "I was just funning with you and the kid. I knew it wouldn't hurt him. It wasn't a real rock."

"Funning? Yeah? Like when you threatened to beat us into pulp and drag us with a rope, was that just funning?"

"No," he admitted. "It wasn't." He shrugged. "Whatever. Go ahead on in, I'll be right behind you so don't try to run off."

She shook her head, thinking that Vance wanted complete control, and he wanted to be liked too, even loved, and maybe that wasn't so unusual—but it was a toxic combination.

It was not surprising, given his history and what had happened to his family. But she couldn't trust him again.

Marla turned to the wall, closed her eyes—and walked through it. She opened her eyes and found herself in a narrow pass through the stone; a sort of crooked natural corridor leading to a pathway climbing steeply toward the cinder cone. It was cooler in here, in the shade.

Cal was just walking back toward her, down a twisting ramp of stone.

"Looks like it goes up toward the volcano, Mom. Could be Dad's up there . . ."

"Wouldn't count on it, kiddo," Vance said, coming through the wall. "Maybe he is up there—what's left of him. Or maybe he never got there."

Cal nodded. "I know. The chances aren't good. But . . . it's what we have."

Marla looked at her son and smiled. Cal sounded like a man now.

She hoped he'd understand what she was going to do next. "We're not going up there," she said. Both Cal and

Vance looked at her with surprise. She shook her head. "Cal and I aren't going. You shouldn't go either, Vance. There's death up there."

"Mom—Dad could be—"

"Cal—he's just as likely to be on his way here. Or somewhere around his crash site. Maybe even back on the Study Station by now. He could be in Fyrestone or New Haven or some other settlement looking for us."

"I don't know what you think you're pulling," Vance growled. "But it's not going to work. We're all going. The two of you are . . . useful to me. I'm not leaving you here. You need me to protect you, anyhow."

"My son has a concussion and you threw him like a stuffed *toy*—"

"Get over it, Marla! He's all right now, come on, I patched him up, I fed him, I gave you both food. And I'll tell you something else. That money I took from Grunj— you notice I'm not carrying much with me now? You think it was in the truck? Naw. I hid it somewhere else, before then. I'll share it with you—when the time comes."

"I'm not interested in money. I just want to find out what happened to my husband and get off this planet."

"Naw. Not yet you aren't. You're coming with me. Make up your mind—you gonna make me use force?"

Marla hesitated, licking her dry lips. She knew she was taking a big gamble with him. She couldn't tell Cal about her real fear—that Vance really had connected emotionally with her. That his way of wanting her would be to kill anything that got in the way. That he would, eventually, kill her husband, when they found him. She felt sure of it—if they went up to that crash site and found Zac, one way or another . . .

Vance would kill him.

"I can't do it," she said, more gently. "Just let us go, Vance. Just . . ."

"There's something on that path going up the ravine there," Cal said suddenly. "Something . . ."

Vance glanced irritably over at the zigzag path going up to the cinder cone. "I don't see a damn thing. You trying to keep me distracted, kid? What are you two cooking up?"

Marla couldn't see anything up the path either. "What is it, Cal? Where?"

"See? Sparks . . . it was there and gone. I thought I saw something crawling down on its stomach."

Vance snorted. "I can *see* what's up there and—" He broke off, frowning. "Wait. Did you say sparks? Like electricity?"

"Yeah . . . around a shape. It's gone now but . . . you hear that? Something scraping on the rock?"

"You two stay exactly where you are," Vance muttered. He raised his rifle to firing position and stalked slowly toward the twisting pathway of stone and dust . . .

Marla peered past him, puzzled, but then she glimpsed an electrical flicker too, just a kind of bluish, sparking glow around a shape crawling close to the ground. It appeared—and vanished, in a split second. It was near the bottom of the path—and it was coming their way.

Vance moved toward the pathway, and Marla wondered if she should use this chance to grab Cal, drag him out through the entrance, back onto the plain.

Then Vance fired—his assault rifle clattered, and bullets sprayed up the lowest ramp of the rising pathway. Something squealed angrily—and she saw it clearly then. It was about half the size of a grown man, and its front limbs were shaped like a bat's wings—but there was only the smallest trace of leathery wings remaining. Making *err err err* sounds, it dragged itself along the ground with its thin hooked forelimbs the way a bat did, when walking. But its head reminded her of a grasshopper's, only as large as a child's; its plated body was more like a scorpion's, and its long prehensile tail ended in electrically crackling spikes . . . Then it vanished again.

"It's a stalker!" Vance declared. "Only saw one once before. They've got some kind of biofield around 'em—they cloak up invisible when they're going after prey . . ."

Prey? She stepped decisively over to Cal, took him by a wrist, and drew him back toward the entrance. The two of them backed slowly up, afraid to turn around.

Vance fired again—this time up higher, and another stalker appeared out of nowhere, the bullets momentarily knocking out its invisibility cloak. It gave that angry squeal, and a dark fluid leaked from its midsection. Its tail lashed out angrily . . . and spikes flew from it, to clatter off the stone wall over Vance's head. It could whip spikes out of its tail, throw them arrowlike at its target.

"Down, Cal!" Marla said instinctively.

She and Cal flattened facedown on the stone floor. She was afraid that if they ran for the entrance they'd be stabbed in the back by spikes. The things were just too close . . .

"Shit and hellfire, I didn't want to use this," Vance burst out. He was pulling the pin from a protean grenade, tossing it at the spot where he'd last seen the nearer stalker. He dropped down as the grenade exploded—and they saw, then, the outlines of three stalkers revealed by the blast force. An angry squealing, as debris pattered down—and one of the creatures seemed to writhe in the air, its whole body snapping like a whip. The others flickered out of sight—but the nearest stalker was now entirely visible, broken in two, oozing dark fluid from the halves, its severed scorpion-style tail twitching, the head twisting in its death throes.

Vance got up to a flattened sniper position, positioned his rifle against his shoulder, firing—and the bullets exposed the other two. They were closer, climbing over the ruins of their companion to get at their prey. They weren't going to back off. One of them whipped its tail toward Vance and this time the spikes flew dartlike through the air, just whistling over Vance's head, missing by centimeters.

Marla tugged at Cal's arm to get his attention, and signed with her hand, *This way.* She turned and crawled toward the entrance; Cal crawled beside her, the two of them going as fast as they could in this awkward position. She felt like she'd been degraded to a desert creature herself, crawling through dust and rubble.

Vance fired at the stalkers again, swearing to himself. "Shit goddammit, gotta change clips . . ."

As he focused on reloading the gun, Marla got to her knees, signaled to Cal. *Let's go for it.* They were only two steps from the entrance. Cal rushed toward it, vanished into the rock; Marla followed, closing her eyes till she got through.

She was panting, her pulse loud in her ears, as they stumbled out onto the edge of the plain, into the glaring sunlight.

Maybe now was their chance. She tugged Cal onward,

not sure where she was going. They went twenty paces out into the glass plain . . .

"Where you think you're going?" Vance asked, behind them.

Marla hesitated, then turned to see him stepping out of the cliff entrance, his rifle strapped over a shoulder. He called out, "You stay right there, lady, or you're getting these instead . . . My last ones. I'd sure hate to waste 'em on you two . . ."

Vance had two more protean grenades ready, one in each hand. He activated the grenades, turned, stepped back a few steps, and threw the explosives through the entrance—just as a repulsive grasshopper-like head thrust out from the entrance near the bottom, squealing, crackling with energy.

Vance, Marla, and Cal backed hastily up—and the grenades blew. The stalker's head severed from its body, rolled along the ground. Something thrashing kicked up dust at the entrance—and then a dying stalker crawled through. It made a fitful fling with its tail, and spikes darted at them, to fall short, sticking in the ground at their feet, crackling with electricity. Then it spasmed one last time—and lay still.

Vance turned and trotted over to them, taking his rifle into his hands.

"You think . . . that's all of them?" Cal asked.

Vance nodded. "I think so, kid. Nasty motherbuggers . . ."

"I need some water, Vance," Marla said.

Vance turned her a long, cold look. But he took a small canteen off his belt and handed it to her. She drank, thinking that water was as good as wine when you'd met death, and come out alive.

She handed the canteen to Cal. "I meant what I said before. We can't go with—what is it now?"

Vance was staring past her. She heard it, then: the sound of an engine rumbling. She turned and saw the outriders coming, just forty meters off. Two of them. Marla knew there could be two men in each outrider. And that kind of vehicle, with the skulls wired to the front, wasn't likely to be driven by anyone friendly . . .

"Run!" Vance yelled. "The entrance!"

Vance, Marla, and Cal turned and ran—and after just ten steps came to a stop, as an outrider pulled up in front of the cliff, blocking their way, raising a plume of dust as it skidded to a stop.

They turned—and another outrider pulled up to block the route out to the plain. They were boxed in.

The turrets on the vehicles fired—bullets strafed across the ground on either side of them. They froze, waiting—knowing those had been warning shots, since the outriders could have cut them down with the car-mounted machine guns anytime they wanted.

Marla impulsively put her arms around Cal.

The nearer outrider, on the glass plain, suddenly popped its hatch. Two men climbed out, long guns in hand. Marla knew one of them instantly. Mash, the slaver with the misshapen head, was getting out of that one—with a man she didn't know who wore a black patch over one eye, grubby skag-skin leathers, and triple fins of hair on his head. She thought of him as Patch.

Marla looked at the other vehicle. She knew both men

getting out of it. Dimmle and Grunj—Grunj's wild beard was matted with dust.

"Holy *goddess* on a *crutch*," Vance muttered.

"We've tracked you for a long while, Vance," Dimmle said, smiling unpleasantly, patting the breech of his assault rifle as he walked toward them. "That truck leaves a track. Followed it, found our truck in a hole. Had to torture a tunnel rat to work that out. Found your tracks. And here we are."

TWENTY

Zac woke to a flurry of half-remembered impressions.

The monitor had carried him to the alien crash site—to the wreckage itself. He'd been lowered into a sort of hatch—almost like a blowhole, really, or a mouth . . . and he'd screamed. The grappling tendrils released him, he fell, and felt himself grasped, tugged down into a tight tunnel of something that looked like transparent plastic to him. It was as if he were being swallowed by a giant see-through esophagus. He'd been tugged deeper; the smells were unknown to his experience. Sparkles came and went in the alien craft; iridescent, translucent bulkheads pulsed softly with energy all around him, making him think of images he'd seen of electricity passing through neurons. Shapes formed in the translucence, shifted, contracted, expanded—but were never clearly defined.

The humming, the whispering, the probing, the pain in his head going from throbbing to thundering . . .

Then he'd lost consciousness. Peace and darkness—no more horror. *Thank God for death,* he'd thought. His last thought . . . before waking up. Here.

Where was here? He seemed to be suspended in a kind of pocket built into the wall of a large, oval, luminescent chamber. The pocket, seamless with the wall, clasped him tightly from the shoulders down.

Slowly, his eyes adjusted to the glow, the restless, changeable lighting of the room. There were no corners, no sharp edges; the ceiling was curved. There were spiky points, however, on the roughly spherical object projecting up from the middle of the room. It reminded him of the sea urchin shape he'd seen earlier, but writ large, five meters in diameter. The object was not translucent, but pearly, with light flaring restlessly from the tip of one spine to the next, as if thoughts were passing through.

Was the object a computer of some kind, perhaps the automated mind of the ship? Was he in the control room, the brain of the starship?

It occurred to him that the ship might have always been an unmanned drone. If true—that was bad. Hard to negotiate with an AI drone.

Zac tried to speak—and couldn't. His throat was gummed up. He cleared it, over and over, and finally spat out some kind of plug. How had he been able to breathe, with that thing in there?

"Hello?" he said. "Anybody here I can talk to? I mean—you've been observing this world for a while, I guess. Maybe had other prisoners. Do you have a sense of our language? Is there a translation program I could use to talk to you?"

There was no reply. And he felt foolish—you needed a translator to ask for a translator.

He wasn't able to move much—just enough so he could press forward, and see he was hung on the wall about two meters off the translucent floor. The floor gave out a light of its own. Craning his head, he saw another of those blowhole shapes in the wall, big as a door in a house, some distance to his left. It was hard to judge distances in here. The edges of the room's features were so ill-defined . . .

"Hello?" Zac called out, again.

Still no reply. So now what? Would he hang here, stuck in this pocket in the wall, till he starved to death? Would the thing get around to dissecting him—perhaps vivisecting him? Would it take him over in some way—as Bizzy had been taken over?

He pushed down with his feet, trying to get purchase, hoping to wriggle out.

The response was instantaneous. The pocket holding him in place tightened painfully around him.

Zac cried out with fear and anguish, afraid his blood might be squeezed out his mouth, his eyes . . .

Then the squeezing relented. A moment later it came in another, incorporeal form. Zac heard the whispering he'd heard before, a whispering without words; he heard and felt the humming. He felt the unseen pressure on his eyes; the rising thrum in his brain.

And then there came a high-pitched sound that went on for an infinity . . .

Zac knew, then, that something had pushed its way into his brain. It was right here with him, all around him. He could smell it and touch it and feel it and taste it.

He was in the alien ship —and it was in his mind.

●   ●   ●

"I'd really *hate* to just kill 'em quick," Mash was saying, thoughtfully, hefting his Cobra combat rifle. "The girl— I'll sell her to the meanest buyer I can find. Vance—he'll die long and he'll die slow. Big strong fucker'll cry like a little girl before I'm done. And the boy . . ."

"The boy is mine," Grunj said, his eyes alight with sick flames.

"Why sure, Grunj," Mash said affably. "But you got to buy me out on him."

"You don't own him, damn you!"

"We *co-own* this bunch of losers! You'd be buying out my share of the brat!"

Marla was looking desperately at Vance, silently pleading with him to find a way out of this. Vance ignored her, but his hands tightened on his rifle as he looked back and forth between his chief enemies, evidently trying to decide whom to shoot at first, Grunj or Mash.

If Vance opened fire—and she knew he would—it meant an all-out firefight. The chances of Cal coming out of it alive weren't good.

"I'll give you that outrider you came in, for the boy," Grunj said. "That's one of my outriders you're using, you know."

"Done deal!" Mash declared, his misshapen face creasing in his version of a grin. "Now—"

"You guys move an inch," Vance growled, teeth clenched, "and I'll take out one of you—you Grunj, or you Mash. And you don't know which one."

Grunj chuckled. "You can't get through my shield that quick. Yours is weak, it's flickerin' out." He brandished his Stomper combat rifle. "This'll cut right through that shield of yours. We'll shoot your legs out from under you, shoot your arms . . . and then we'll really start in on your . . ."

"He's gonna let me put out your eyes!" Patch said. "That's because that blast you set off on Grunj's Island cost me my eye."

But Patch didn't move. He was looking at Vance's gun, probably to see if it was powerful enough to break through his shield . . .

Marla frantically searched her mind. What could she offer these thugs they didn't have already, to prevent them from murder and rape and atrocity? Nothing. Because no deal they made would mean a thing. They'd do just as they pleased.

"He's got your money, Grunj, remember?" she blurted. "What if he led you to where he's hidden it? I happen to know he hasn't got it on him."

"Marla shut up!" Vance hissed.

Grunj grunted. "Oh he will lead me to it, missy ho, don't you worry! He'll tell me right where it is so he can make the pain stop!" Grunj said. "I don't need to make any deals with him for that!"

She could see the men bracing—Patch was aiming his shotgun at Vance . . .

"What's that?" Cal asked, pointing at the cliff.

"Ha-*haaaaa*!" Patch chortled. "The kid thinks that old dodge is gonna work!"

"No, really!" Cal insisted. "There's something cloaked over there—I saw the sparks . . . coming around the outrider! I think it's a stalker!"

Vance let out a grim laugh. "It seems I didn't kill them all . . ."

"Grunj!" Patch bellowed, "I say enough of this bullshit! Let me take this bastard—*Uck*."

"Take him *uck*?" Grunj said, turning to him, puzzled and annoyed. "What the hell are you—?"

"Uck . . . uck . . ." Then Patch spat blood—and fell face forward, dead, with large, sparking stalker spikes still quivering deep in his back. The electrified spikes could go right through a shield.

The men turned toward the stalker—visible now for a moment—Grunj swinging his rifle instinctively toward the stalker, Mash trying to see it as it flickered in and out of visibility. He fired a burst and a rifle-launched grenade at it—sparks outlined the stalker as the bullets hit it and it gave out that angry squealing . . . and then the grenade struck, blowing its head off. It died with a last, long, furious screech.

But Vance had already seen the stalker, and knew that Grunj was between him and the predator. When the others looked away from him he used the moment to make two moves, in under a second. He planted the butt of his combat rifle on his right hip, swinging it toward Grunj with his right hand—his left shot out and shoved Marla hard, so that she was flung right into Cal—and both of them went sprawling onto the ground.

She was stunned and angry for a moment, but as he opened fire at Grunj she realized Vance had done it to save their lives. Covering Cal with her body as best she could, she watched as Vance slammed his rifle through Grunj's shield, shoving the muzzle into the sea thug's right side, and firing point-blank—a burst of rounds smashing under Grunj's ribs, shattering his insides. Grunj staggered, looking stunned. He coughed. He spat out a bloody bullet. Then he went down like a felled tree.

Vance was already turning toward the others—but by then Mash had fired his Cobra at Vance, roaring with murderous delight as he emptied the whole clip into Vance's shield—and Dimmle did the same with his assault rifle, bellowing with wordless fury: two men blasting Vance with automatic weapons at once, emptying their weapons into him.

Vance was knocked off his feet, rolled over a couple times and lay on his back, gasping, as the guns finally quieted. Vance's shield was gone. His right arm was shot away at the elbow; his neck fountained blood; his big jaw was shattered. His broad chest was pocked with oozing bullet holes. But he was alive, turning his head to look right at Marla.

She got unsteadily up, gestured at Cal to stay down—and walked over to Vance. She sat down beside him, next to his intact arm, in the only spot that wasn't pooling with his blood. She put her hand over his.

"Mom?" Cal said, puzzled.

Marla was dimly aware that Mash and Dimmle were reloading their weapons. But she bent near Vance, to listen as he whispered hoarsely to her, barely audible: "The Trash Coast. Under that shed. The money. When you were out, I . . ."

"Never mind that, Vance," she said softly, squeezing his big, calloused hand. She thought she had hated him. But seeing him die like this—she saw the boy, who'd been dying, in a way, ever since that day he saw his family killed by the Wasters. "Rest," she said. "You . . ."

He coughed blood, and said, "I'm sorry. I don't know any other way to be . . . it's all I . . . it's what I . . ." Then he shuddered, his eyes went blank, and he breathed his last.

"Dammit," Mash said. "Did you hear what he said to her, Dimmle?"

"I did not."

"Well maybe he told her where he hid that money!"

They turned toward Marla—and Mash strapped his rifle over his shoulder. He flexed his fingers. "Don't think I'll need the gun for this. I'll squeeze it out of her."

"Leave her alone!" Cal yelled, throwing himself at Mash's legs, trying to tackle him. The move had hardly any effect—except to make Mash laugh.

He shook Cal off, as if shaking off a poodle humping his leg. "Get away, boy. Or it'll go harder for both of you. Maybe I'll sell you together, if you're good . . . You and mom can be a team!"

Dimmle laughed at that—and then stopped laughing. He looked around, puzzled. "Mash—you hear something? Sound like a gun cocking or . . ."

"You've got good ears," said a deep, amused voice.

Marla turned to see a large muscular black man wearing goggles, standing nearby—how had he crept up without them seeing him? In his hands was a strange-looking weapon, like nothing she'd ever seen. It looked like it had been grown instead of manufactured.

"Roland!" Cal said happily, jumping to his feet.

"So that's Roland," Mash muttered, realizing that Roland had a gun pointed right at him—and his own was over his shoulder. "I've heard. No need to fight, Roland. You can share in the booty—"

"Yeah, in every sense of the word," Dimmle chuckled. "See, booty got two meanings—"

"Shut up, Dimmle, I'm talking. Thing is, Roland, this bitch here is gonna tell us where that backstabbing bastard lying dead over there hid Grunj's money. Seems like she might know. There'll be plenty to go around . . ."

"We'll have a nice chat about it," Roland said pleasantly. "Soon as you drop your weapons on the ground there."

He glanced at Cal in a way that seemed to carry significance . . .

Cal nodded and moved away from Mash, sidling over to his mother.

"I'm not dropping my weapons for no man," said Mash flatly. "Dimmle—nail him and I'll give you a double share of that money."

Dimmle chewed his lower lip nervously.

Roland shook his head warningly.

Dimmle swung his rifle toward Roland—

Who fired the strange, gnarled weapon, blasting both men with a spray of electrified orbs—Dimmle and Mash screamed, their shields shorting out, their bodies jumping spasmodically . . . and then they fell, Dimmle staggering one step so he fell facedown across Mash. Their bodies made an X.

"Only cross you're gonna get from me," Roland muttered, stepping over to kick the bodies—just making sure they were dead. He turned to Marla, smiling, then lowered his rifle.

"Crazy luck," Cal said, "your coming along then!"

"Not really," Roland said. "I've been tracking you since you went missing. Finally tracked you here. There's a break in the glass, a long crack back there, gives a little cover for sneaking if a man slides on his belly." He turned to Marla. "I'm Roland. You'd be Marla—Cal's ma, I'm guessing . . . ?"

She sighed and nodded. "You'd be . . . guessing right." She felt dizzy. Exhausted.

"Mom? You okay?" Cal asked, taking her hand.

"Yeah, I'm just . . . I guess I saw a few too many men die. Especially . . ." She looked at Vance's body—and decided not to say anything more about it. Cal wouldn't understand. She wasn't sure she understood it herself.

"No need to bury those others," she said. "But that one, Vance there—could you help us bury him? There wasn't much good left in the big oaf. But I owe him my life. He saved me—more than once."

"Sure, I'll bury him," Roland said. "We'll find a spot off the glass ground here. Glad to help, you being Cal's mom." He winked at Cal. "That means you're a close associate of my partner. He did a damn good job for me. That kid's got a lotta sand in him, like they said in the old days. Gonna be a hell of a man."

She put her arm around Cal, seeing the boy beaming at Roland. "Yeah. He is."

But she hoped Cal didn't have to grow up without a father.

TWENTY-ONE

Zac couldn't remember having lost consciousness. But he must have. Because he was somewhere else now. In the same room, but moved.

He blinked, trying to clear the haze from his eyes, looking around. He was no longer in that pocket on the wall. He was sitting up in something like a chair, which seemed to grow out of the wall, facing the spiked, flashing orb. As he watched, the orb changed shape, some spikes shrinking, others growing.

"We can now converse, Zac Finn," said a clear, sexless, pleasantly urbane voice in his mind.

Zac jumped up, unnerved by the feeling of another being's voice resounding in his head. He was losing his mind. Hearing voices . . .

"Sit down," commanded the voice. Power and authority resonated in it.

Zac sat down.

"Zac Finn: I have examined your mind, your history, your sociological signposts, your interactive social mechanisms of exchange, your means of reproduction, your family units, your society's values, such as they are, your values, such as they are, your level of self-knowledge, which is microscopic, your movement through the fractal patterning reactivity of your life in all four dimensions; I have additionally been observing your race, on the planet, from time to time, as I regenerated. Your species is made up of bumbling dumbasses, on the whole. Kind of makes me ill to contemplate all the resources you have access to and the poor choices you make with them. What a bunch of knuckleheaded apes, for crying out loud."

"Wait," Zac said. "Hold on one damn minute . . ." He was determined to get at the truth no matter what happened. He was speaking aloud, because it was easier for him to concentrate that way. But the ship read his mind as he spoke. "You use the words *dumbasses,* and *knuckleheaded, crying out loud*—What's up with that? You sure you're not someone from my planet pretending to be an alien computer?"

"First of all, I'm not an alien computer or pretending to be an alien computer. Disabuse yourself of that notion. I'm not any sort of computer. Second, I am using whatever terminology from your store of word phrases that conveys my feelings best. I wish to convey irritation and disgust, and my perceptual evaluation, all at once. Dumbass knuckleheads does the job. It's your vocabulary, not mine."

"What do you know about us?" Zac said, bridling. "You haven't spent any real time with us."

"I've been observing your race since you arrived on this planet, through the occasional scan. But as I was dormant most

of the time, in regeneration mode, I was not able to see every-thing. It was enough. You seem fairly typical primate-type bipedal omnivores, predatory, astoundingly wasteful and self-deceiving. As a people you have some sociobiological altruistic instincts, as well as a capacity for elaborate societal structures and modalities of exchange. Yours is a remarkably short-lived species. Level of consciousness, averages fairly low . . ."

"Look, the big question for me, is, what do you plan to do with me? Do I even want to know? Should I beg you to kill me painlessly or what?"

"If I decide to be sensible and practical and simply put you in my samples collection, with your own bottle and label, you will be put to death quite painlessly. I see no point in cruelty to animals. But I haven't quite decided what to do yet. I'm still as-sessing the situation. Essentially, if I find the Hidden Thing of Interest in you or one others of your companions, I will be in-clined to release you, and to let you and some of the others live. That Hidden Thing of Interest is a precious thing, rare and exotic and exquisite. I thought I'd glimpsed it, before, in your people, though it was tiny, emaciated, underfed, barely alight. But I could not be sure—my senses were not fully recovered."

"What is that 'Hidden Thing of Interest' that makes someone worth preserving?"

"The spark of higher consciousness. It's usually expressed in meaningful self-sacrifice, enlightened unselfishness, mindful heroism. All that speaks of a level of inner potential, which could evolve to entelechy. I'll know it when I see it."

Zac hesitated, wondering what tack to take. He was in danger of being stuck on a pin under glass, it seemed. A dead specimen. He needed more information. "You said you'd examined others?"

"My monitor captured a few others of your kind, some years back, but they died before I was able to look deeply into their minds. Since I'm beginning to reach full regeneration, I was able to investigate your mind more thoroughly. My primary conclusion is that you personally are a flailing, bumbling loser, a chump who usually makes the wrong choices, more or less typical of a race that has allowed greed to formulate its social standards. You have only a few qualities of interest to me—and you have kept them suppressed. You are like people lost in a dark cave, wishing for light, refusing to light the candles you carry for fear of burning your fingers a little. What a lot of jackasses you people are."

"Oh and you're so much better. Probably if I had access to your memories and your history I wouldn't be all that impressed."

"Since individuals of my race, at this time, live about ten thousand of your years, at least, with our most recent civilization's history stretching for millions of years, I doubt you'd be able to follow it. You can barely count to a hundred without losing track of the process."

"Mind telling me what planet you're from?"

A collection of sounds and shapes appeared in Zac's mind, the shapes arranged in a three-dimensional lattice that seemed to intertwine meaningfully with the sounds. *"That is the name of my homeworld. The short version. The full version requires seventy-seven thousand characters to express."*

"You're not from this solar system, anyway?"

"No. Nor am I from the galaxy you so quaintly call 'the Milky Way Galaxy.' I am exploring galaxies that neighbor the one my own people are in. I'll return home soon with my

report. *In emerging from a wormhole, I was misdirected by an errant black-hole gravitational aberration, and was struck by a comet, which sent me off course, causing me to crash on this world.*

"I've lain here for hundreds of 'years' getting my strength and consciousness back. In the process I tapped the raw energy deep under this volcanic structure, with an exploratory probe, and converted it to my own uses . . ."

"Don't I get to meet you, face-to-face? Or are you inside that big round spiny thing I'm looking at?"

"'Spiny thing' . . . oh that object opposite your chair? That's a perceptual nerve cluster with sub-brain capabilities. You could not 'see me face-to-face'—my 'face' is spread over my entire person. You would have to perceive too much in three-dimensionality all at once, to see that. But look at anything around and you see part of me. Everything you see is a part of me, here. It's what you call 'the alien starship.'"

Zac felt there was something essential he was missing. "So—you *are* the spaceship? Some kind of biocomputer program talking to me? The spaceship is an unmanned drone?"

"No, I'm not a biocomputer, nor a drone, nor a transportation device except in the sense that your own body is your transportation device. I am one single organism. What you suppose to be a spaceship is a conscious organism, a creature who quite naturally is capable of flying through space, and passing through 'wormholes' to go vast distances. The creature you are addressing is not in the spaceship. What you suppose to be 'the spaceship' is itself the creature you would meet. And you, Zac Finn, are inside my body."

• • •

It was dusk before they were ready to go in search of Zac. Burying Vance took time. Marla scratched Vance's name into a shard of plains glass, which they set up as a marker. She felt strange doing it. Like she was both betraying Zac—and letting go of part of herself, at once. Vance had been a brute. She had no good reason to feel so attached to him . . .

Afterward, Marla found food and water for them in the outriders, and they rested in the shade within the hidden entrance—once Roland and Cal had dragged away the bodies of the stalkers and made sure no others were lurking around.

Then, well armed with the weapons of the fallen men, they climbed the winding stone ramp, Marla following Roland and Cal. They worked their way up the narrow canyon to the lava fields near the base of the cinder cone. Roland examined the ground closely in the failing light— and found traces where someone else had recently gone through.

"Two men, if my guess is right," he said, straightening up from the trail. "Worked their way toward that slope over there."

Marla looked doubtfully at the roseate sky, the failing light. "You think we can get through this before it gets dark? The ground's all so sharp and rugged—it'd cut us up pretty badly."

"I want to go on!" Cal insisted. "My dad is there somewhere, I know it!"

"We can't be sure that's where he is," Marla said. "He might be."

Roland smiled. "I think we'll make it if we use these."

He reached into a coat pocket and took out three small flashlights. "They were in the outriders. One each. Just move careful . . ."

They set off, treading carefully in the rugged landscape, occasionally receiving contusions on sharp volcanic rock; barking their shins on shadowy stone edges. It was awkward, carrying both the flashlights and the weapons—Cal carried Mash's shotgun, and one of Vance's pistols; Marla carried the Cobra; Roland had the Stomper in his hands, the Eridian gun strapped across his back, and pistols on his hips.

By the time they reached the slope, and the smoother lava-flow pathway, they were painfully contused and a little battered. But Cal didn't complain, Marla noticed.

It was dark, the crescent moon not giving much light. Stars offered some illumination, from this vantage; high above the dusty plain, constellations clustered like extravagant jewelry and shone out with an almost violent effulgence.

"Better switch off the flashlights," Roland said, cutting his own. "Don't know when we might run into Crannigan. I want to see him before he sees me. Last I knew we were still allies. But you never can tell. And I'm not sure how he'll feel about Marla here."

They rested a little—and then pressed on, soon coming to the deep stony gulch, and the view on the interior of the broken-open cinder cone. Here they stopped and gazed at the glowing natural amphitheater of the broken volcano. At night it was like looking into a sliced-open geode. The shadowiness of the amphitheater was interrupted by glimmers; glowing, oddly shaped objects scattered about the debris field and, farther back, a strong but fluctuating glow from an object that was difficult to identify. The curved, smooth object in the back was large—big enough to be a starship, by Marla's reckoning.

"That must be it!" Cal said excitedly. "You see it, back there? It's big as a freighter, at least!"

"Keep your voice down, kid," Roland growled softly. "Don't want Crannigan to hear us."

"I thought you were working with him . . ."

"Let's get a handle on what's up with Crannigan before we partner up with him again. There's a whole 'nother factor I've been half-expecting . . ." He glanced up at the sky.

"So much for my plan," Marla said. "I was going to start yelling for Zac."

"Not a good idea, and not just because of Crannigan. Those stalkers must have a den around here. Might be more of them. The creepy little bastards sneak up on you."

"I'm not sorry they killed that eye-patch guy," Cal said, his voice flat; his eyes cold.

Marla looked at him with concern. What had Pandora done to her son? And to her, really. Cal was in survival mode, and maybe that was good. Maybe it had gotten him through. But would she ever get her child back?

Cal was peering around. He looked disappointed. "Thought I'd see my dad here . . ."

"Your pa was here, boy," said a voice in the darkness. "Now he's back there, somewhere, I reckon. With the ship."

"Flatten down!" Roland ordered, pointing both his gun and his flashlight toward the sound of the voice. He clicked the flashlight on, and a grizzled old man with a hat made of animal skin blinked at them, put up a hand against the glare.

"Take that damn light out of my eyes!"

Roland lowered the light out of his face but kept the old man in its illumination. The old man had a combat rifle—but it wasn't pointed at anyone. "Come over here," Roland ordered. "Now. Hands up—or I'll cut you down! And I don't care how good your shield is!"

"Damn shield's not much use now," the old man grumbled. He came down the path, into a patch of light from the moon and stars. He was a weathered old man, but his eyes were bright.

"You say something about my dad, mister?" Cal asked.

"Yeah. I did. If you're Cal Finn and I figure you orta be."

"I am, yeah, and this is Roland and my mom—Marla Finn."

Berl clumsily tipped his scruffy hat to Marla. "I'm Berl. I traveled with your husband. I can tell you, he was set on getting back to you. We had our differences, Zac Finn and me. But in the end—he saved my life. Maybe sacrificed himself to do it. I'm not sure he's . . ." He shrugged. "I don't know. The monitor grabbed him, and took him in that spaceship, over there. Or whatever that thing is. I've got my doubts." He sighed. "It's a sad day. He was the closest thing I had to a friend, except for Bizzy. And I lost both of them to that space demon down there."

"Did you actually see Zac get killed?" Marla asked, her mouth suddenly so dry she could hardly get the words out.

"No, lady, I didn't. Just saw him carried off. I don't know, maybe he'll get out of there. He's a resourceful kinda guy. Went through a lot. Got away from me one time when I had him tied up. The scamp."

Cal scowled. "What'd you tie him up for?"

"Decided I didn't trust him. Guess the jury's out on that.

But he's a pretty good sort. Like I said, he came back for me when he didn't have to. Lured 'em away so I could sneak out . . . but they got him instead. Carried him off . . . You got anything to drink? Of an alcohol-based nature, I mean?"

He looked hopefully at Roland, who shook his head. "I've heard of you. Berl. The ghost of the badlands."

Berl grinned crookedly. "Might as well be one. Probably be one for real soon enough." He looked at them—his gaze weighing Cal, Roland, and Marla. "Not comfortable around so big a crowd as this . . ."

"We gotta sneak in that ship and get my dad out!" Cal declared, turning to Roland. "We can't leave him in there. He could be trapped!"

Roland shook his head. "I'm not going to put you in a trap to get him out of one. That thing, whatever it is, appears to be dangerous. I need time to think. We'll make camp behind that boulder, over there, just off the trail. And we'll figure this out . . ."

They made a cold camp, hunkered on graveled volcanic rock in the chilly shadow of a boulder, a few paces off the trail. They passed around skag jerky and water. Berl offered them Primal testicles. Marla and Cal said no; Roland cheerfully accepted one. "Like to bite one off the Primal bastard that blew up my partner . . ."

Cal suffered Marla to hold him against her, and fell asleep. She slept fitfully and woke when it was still dark, just before dawn. She thought she was dreaming, at first, when she saw the spacecraft coming down through the atmosphere, at first just a light, then taking shape as it descended, slowing its descent with pulsers. It was shaped like a step pyramid, point upward, but made of a gray-blue metal. A logo on the side of the vessel might say *Atlas* but she couldn't be sure. She recognized it as one of the larger orbital shuttles. In orbit it docked within a much larger spacecraft—which meant there was a starship up there.

She glanced over at Roland, and saw him watching it too. The shuttle descended till the top of the boulder blocked it from sight.

Roland got up and moved silently toward the trail. Marla eased Cal onto the gravel. Cal curled up, head pillowed on his arm, reluctant to fully wake.

She followed Roland out into the cool air of morning, onto the dewy lava-flow path. A gray light picked out enough of the ground so they could make their way to the edge of the cliff overlooking the deep stone gulley.

Down below they saw the orbital shuttle landing on a flattened spot in the scree, whining as it settled down, its pulsers ruffling up a cloud of dust. Nearby, apparently waiting for it to land, was a group of three men.

"That's Crannigan, Rosco, and Rans Veritas," Roland said. "Seems like Crannigan went behind my back and contacted Atlas. They told us a lander couldn't get this close. Either they were lying about that—or something's changed."

"That shuttle. Is it—?"

"Yeah, it is. Atlas Corporation. Executive Shuttle. Meaning it's got Atlas execs in it— some of the most sneaky, treacherous sons of bitches around."

TWENTY-TWO

Zac blinked, his eyes stinging as he woke. He groaned, realizing that the alien had effortlessly put him to sleep again. It made him feel completely helpless. The thing could switch him off and on like a lamp.

He looked around, feeling sick. He was *inside* the alien. Maybe the damned thing, in time, was going to digest him.

But he didn't think that it had lied to him. That voice—it was impossible to imagine that voice lying. The alien would do what it had said it would: if it decided to kill him, he'd become part of some biological sample collection, somewhere. Like the preserved animals he'd seen in natural history museums . . .

How could he be inside the creature—and in a chair?

But it wasn't organized like the animals he was familiar with. It had just as much control of its insides as its outsides. It could change the shape of its "interior storage spaces." He was sure that "the monitor" was in fact an extension, telepathically controlled, of the alien. It was as if it could send its eye out, flying around on its own, and its eye could see things for it, and pick things up, bring them back, and store them in a compartment inside it.

Now, that's pretty damn alien, Zac thought.

Maybe he could escape. Maybe the alien's attention was occupied elsewhere. It wasn't omniscient. It had limitations. Maybe he'd awakened on his own and he could slip out of this chair and find some way out . . .

He tried to stand—and was sucked back down onto the chair, by a force that was like a very specific gravitation.

"I have not yet released you," said the alien, in his mind. *"I am aware of your thoughts, your motions. You cannot surprise me."*

He felt like sobbing. But all he had left was his dignity. So, hoarsely, he said, "You going to tell me now what you're doing with me? You going to kill me? You promised me a painless death, remember . . ."

"I have not yet decided. Decisions that involve life and death, with us, are generally thought over, not decided impulsively—we are not impulsive like your jackass knucklehead people."

"Hey—you've got that sneering tone again. Listen, you creatures evolved too, didn't you, from simpler forms. Right?"

"Yes."

"Well don't you think *you* guys were jackass knuckleheads at some point? You know—in an earlier stage of evolution? Come on, fair is fair. Easy to sneer at a lower order of being. You think I bother to sneer at ants?"

To his surprise, the alien seemed to hesitate. *"You actually have a point. That's not quite enough to show you have that Hidden Thing of Interest—but it's enough to add a little bit to the scale on the side of keeping you alive longer."*

Zac felt a flicker of hope. "Look—I'm convinced I did wrong in coming here! I repent! I shouldn't have messed with you. Let me go, and I won't touch your . . . your parts. You can gather them up and you can go home, when you're finished regenerating or whatever. And I'll try to make my people better. Just . . . give me a chance."

"It's not a case of being 'better.' It's a case of being worth bothering with at all, really."

"Listen, we've got all kinds of good stuff you're not aware of. We've got art, poetry, music . . . good stuff. Even some philosophy. I've heard."

"I'm aware of some of your music through your mind. It's low-dimensional."

"I might not be the best source for appreciating our musical gifts. Listen—I can't stand this anymore. Just tell me what you plan."

"It depends on the others. You, yourself, are too ambiguous. I wish to see what those others out there will do. The ones gathered nearby. There's a woman, a young one, two men, on the cliff above; there are three others below. There is an orbit shuttlecraft I invited and which I've allowed to land, in which still other men arrive."

"You invited the shuttle?"

"I transmitted a message to it, to the effect that the previous barrier against landings nearby, from orbit, has been lifted. I want a few more of you creatures to examine. It keeps me busy while I conclude regeneration. I'll decide if I should destroy

304 | JOHN SHIRLEY

them—or permit them to go on. I don't wish them to know too much about me. Unless they have the Hidden Thing of Interest. In which case—"

"Wait—did you say a woman and a child? Do you know their names?"

"No."

Could it be them? He'd sent his wife the coordinates. Could it be really be Marla and Cal—and an orbital lander? Could it be that help was outside and it was just beyond his reach? His family might be there, close by, yet impossible to reach . . .

. . . because he was trapped by an alien who was still deciding if he would live, or die.

A sparse trail, probably left by animals, threaded down the steep slope of the gulch under the debris field. Roland descended on the animal trail, sometimes almost having to rock-climb to get down, sliding a little, ducking behind outcroppings and scrub whenever he thought he was too easily visible from the floor of the gulch. He didn't want Crannigan to know he was coming any sooner than necessary.

When he got to the bottom, Roland heard a whirring sound coming from up the gulch, near the orbital lander. He hunkered down behind a rock as something passed over, its shadow flickering by. He looked to see what it was—but it was gone. Maybe a scouter platform. Not good. Whoever was on it could be up to anything—but his first guess would be that they were on their way to scout the debris field. No way he could catch up with the platform. He hoped Marla and Berl and the kid had the sense to keep their heads down when the scouter platform floated by them.

Roland got up and jogged toward the lander, which glinted in the morning sun. A little farther and he came to the edge of the flattened bowl in the gulch, where he saw Crannigan, Rosco, and Rans talking to Gorman, the young suit from Atlas on the vehicle's ramp, about twenty meters off. The sleek young man might not be a *young* man at all, of course. Atlas execs were comped the best rejuvenation—this man could be two hundred years old.

Roland flattened in a small copse of plants, like a cane-brake that grew where a stream sometimes cut through the gulch. The streambed was now dry. He'd better keep an eye on it—it could suddenly erupt with scythids or spider-ants.

Behind Gorman stood one of the armored bodyguards. This one was in red-tinted full body armor. It wasn't impossible that he might be a robot—but more likely he was Crimson Lance elite. The bodyguard carried an Atlas AR24 Glorious Ogre combat rifle, which looked almost small in his big metal-gauntleted hands. His helmet, the face completely shuttered behind darkened glass, kept turning as he scanned the area for threats.

How many bodyguards did Gorman bring this time? Roland wondered. This bodyguard in the red-tinted armor seemed different than the other two he'd seen the last time. The elite had the best shields. Did Crannigan really have a plan for taking them down when he made his move? The armored elite wouldn't die easily.

The smart thing to do, Roland figured, would be to walk away from this whole thing right now, take Marla and Cal back to New Haven whether they wanted to or not. They should all admit they couldn't help Zac and just say the hell with Crannigan, Atlas, armored bodyguards, Rosco, and the extraterrestrial crash site. Because if he stayed and took this bull by the horns, he was caught between whatever was in that alien ship, and the armored elite.

But he'd befriended that kid. And once Roland made a friend—he was stuck. It's just the way he was.

He sighed. He wasn't going to do the smart thing. He was going to step right into the hornet's nest.

Roland waited till the red-armored elite was turned to look another way—then he stood slowly up and started walking toward the group of men, his rifle in his hands but pointed unthreateningly at the ground.

"I'm comin' in, Crannigan!" he called.

Startled, Crannigan and the others turned and stared at him. The elite raised his rifle and trained it on Roland, covering him. His amplified voice came from his helmet. "You know this one, sir?"

"Yes," Gorman said, seeming amused as Roland strolled up. "I've just been told that he was dead."

Rans, his face twitching, looked especially uncomfortable at the sight of Roland.

Roland figured the only way into that alien ship would be with enough firepower. Maybe if he got in with this bunch, he could get Zac Finn out alive. Reunite the kid with his old man.

Roland, you're a sucker, he told himself.

Aloud, as he walked up to the other men, he said, "Who told you I was dead, Mr. Gorman?"

The baby-faced exec smiled. "Crannigan here told me that."

Crannigan shrugged. "You didn't come back, Roland. Figured the stalkers got you."

"Like a man once said, the reports of my death are exaggerated. Stalkers, you said? You knew about stalkers being here, Crannigan?"

Crannigan scratched his chin. "Only after we got here. I caught a glimpse of 'em, up there on the cliff. I'd have called you—but you didn't have a communicator. Only one I've got I needed to keep."

"So you could call Gorman here?"

"Gotta brief 'em sometime." Crannigan looked at him with a small, ironic smile and a raised eyebrow—it seemed to hint, *Don't worry, I'm gonna set them up and take it all. Just like we planned.*

Roland gave him a faint nod. But he didn't trust Crannigan.

"You get close to that crash site?" Roland asked.

"Some. We got close enough to see a couple of guys in there ahead of us—one seemed like he was getting broiled by a drifter. The other one got caught by some kind of flying drone outta the alien ship. Definitely not Eridian. Whatever that thing is, it's not any alien artifact I've ever seen."

Gorman nodded. "We've established that it's the crash site of an unknown species of extraterrestrial."

"How'd you get this close?" Roland asked. "Was it bullshit about how you couldn't get here from the air?"

"No," Gorman said, looking at him coldly. Clearly he didn't like Roland's tone. "We just got a transmission that said we were clear to come down. The energy signature associated with the skybeam that knocked down our exploratory drones was gone. I thought the 'safe to land' transmission had come from Crannigan. Turns out it wasn't him. We've been puzzling that one out. I assume it wasn't you either."

"So who's that leave?" Roland wondered aloud, glancing back toward the crash site. No one had an answer for that.

"I see you haven't got the kid with you," Rosco said. "Find his body?"

"No," Roland said, glancing at Rans Veritas. "'Cause he's not dead. I . . . dug him up. Alive. Truth is, he got out of that little hole on his own. I've got him stashed somewhere safe. Don't worry about it." There was no need to tell them anything they didn't need to know—like about Berl or Marla.

He looked steadily at Rans as he asked Gorman, "This lying backstabber here—do you need him for anything, Mr. Gorman? He's not somebody you can trust. If he's at the end of his usefulness . . ."

"Do you have a problem with our dear old friend Rans?" Gorman asked coolly.

"He hit a friend of mine in the head and dropped him in a hole, is all. A hole filled with tunnel rats. And he did it for no good reason other than pure cussedness."

"The boy is lying, if that's what he told you!" Rans spat. He turned to Gorman. "You going to let this seedy road warrior threaten me? You never even hired him! You and me have a deal!"

"Yes, well—you may be of some use to us yet, Rans."

"Seems to me," Roland pointed out, "you won't need him. I saw a scouter flying in close to that crash site. They'll tell you anything this scumbag could."

Gorman nodded. "Yes, I sent two other guards to scout out the site. They may make our Rans here superfluous. We'll see."

"Now look, Mr. Gorman," Rans snarled, taking an angry step toward the exec, pointing a grimy finger at him. "You can't take that *maybe, maybe not* attitude. We got a deal—"

Gorman turned to the armored bodyguard and made a "just a little bit" sign with his thumb and forefinger. The bodyguard said, "Yes, sir."

He stepped up to Rans and backhanded him with a gauntleted hand—hitting him "just a little bit"—so that the schemer staggered backward, down the ramp, to fall flat on his back with a grunt of pain.

"He could have easily killed you, Rans, with very little additional effort," Gorman said. "Do not approach me in a threatening manner again. I'm going to tell the drones to set up camp. Keep an eye on the perimeter, Red."

"Yes, sir," said the amplified voice.

Grinning, Rosco helped Rans up. "Oughta watch your mouth, old fella."

Rans growled to himself and limped away, to sit pensively on a low boulder nearby, wiping blood from his lip and staring at the ground, face twitching.

It appeared Roland would have to put up with Rans Veritas for a while longer. Two men who had earned a reckoning. And there were a lot of others to deal with out of necessity . . .

This wasn't going to be easy. But then, on Pandora, nothing was easy for long.

Marla was trying to keep Cal contained.

He was pacing back and forth in the cold camp they'd made, under the bemused gaze of old Berl, who was leaning against a rock, meditatively chewing a Primal Beast's testicle.

"Boy, you're just burning up energy you'll need later," Berl said. "That's not gonna help your daddy."

"He's right," Marla said. "We should trust Roland. He's been reliable . . ."

Cal shook his head. "It's just that Dad is so close and we know he needs our help . . ."

"If he ain't beyond help," the old hermit muttered.

Marla glared at him.

A whining noise caught her attention. Then a whooshing sound. She looked up to see something flying over. It paused—and then moved on, out of sight beyond the top of the big boulder. Was it rescue?

Cal was already rushing out into the open and Marla was close on his heels. They stopped and stared, seeing the scouter platform descending to the path in front of them.

The platform was an open-air flying conveyance a little over two meters in diameter, with railings around the edges and grav-pulsers on its underside. Marla had seen them before in a holo, never in person. They were a new invention, used to explore unknown territory on remote planets. The platforms couldn't go very high—perhaps two hundred meters at the most—and weren't particularly fast, but they were maneuverable.

This one was occupied by two disturbingly

martial-looking figures covered head to foot in armor; each held on to the railings with one gauntleted hand, the other holding a rifle balanced on the rail, pointing generally at Marla and Cal. One's armor was tinted blue, the other silver. Both had their faces completely hidden behind helmet plasteel. They might be robots but she suspected they were corporate soldiers. On their shoulders a logo was emblazoned: ATLAS ELITE.

Marla supposed she should be pleased to see them. They might represent rescue. But somehow . . .

"Oh hey, it's those bodyguards from Atlas," Cal said. "I've seen 'em before." He sounded uncertain about what this could mean.

The platform settled to the ground, its whine subsiding. The figures on the scouter platform stared at them. Then in a deep, amplified voice, the man in blue armor said, "We were briefed about the boy. If he's the one. Who are you, lady?"

"I'm . . . Marla Finn. We've been stuck down here. We were in lifeboats from—we escaped from the *Homeworld Bound*."

"Were you authorized to use those vehicles?"

"Authorized? It was an emergency! The ship was breaking up."

"These two might be useful," said the man in blue to the man in silver. "They could have information."

"You here alone?" asked the man in silver, looking at Marla.

"We're . . . waiting for someone," Marla said. "And there's my husband too—he's . . . trapped nearby. Over in the, um . . ."

She pointed toward the crash site.

The two blank faces looked at one another. Then back at Marla. The elite in blue armor said, "You two, get onto the platform. You're coming with us."

"And—you'll take us to the Study Station, or . . . where?" Marla asked.

"I said, *get onto the platform*."

She hesitated. These men didn't behave like rescuers. And there was Zac to think of. And what about Roland?

The one in blue stepped off the platform and pointed his weapon directly at Cal. "You want me to shoot the kid?"

"Asshole," Cal said.

"What's that you said, kid?"

"You heard me."

"Cal, be quiet," Marla said. Clearly, she had no choice, she had to go with them. She decided that Berl didn't want these men to know he was here—or he'd have come out from cover already. "Come on, Cal. We're going with them. These men are . . . going to help us."

"Sure they are," Cal snorted.

But they got onto the platform, holding on to the rail between the two armored soldiers as it took off, veering into the sky.

TWENTY-THREE

have set up an additional observational mechanism," said the alien. "*It will give us a closer view.*"

"Yeah? Can I look through it too, somehow?" Zac asked.

"*That has been arranged. Try not to be a pain in the ass, however. I need to concentrate. Don't be expostulating about things too much, as you people do.*"

"Do you have to be so condescending, alien? Isn't it enough that you're probably going to stick me in a jar with a poison gas or something?"

"*Actually I don't use a poison gas; I merely switch off your nervous system with the simple expedient of—*"

"Honestly—I don't want to know, if you don't mind."

"*It's quite painless. You see I merely introduce a pulse of—*"

"I really, *really* don't want to know."

"*Suit yourself. Now, observe the space immediately in front of your chair.*"

The spiny object in front of him flared with lights, and the lights sparked from point to point, faster and faster, till they formed a matrix that extended itself into a kind of rectangle. It was as if he were watching a video that was created, over and over again, from one second to the next, with points of light in space itself. Like the image in a video without the screen. And the image quickly resolved into an exterior view of the debris field near the fallen alien's body. The point of view drifted onward, passing the monitor—which was hovering out there, keeping watch—and continuing slowly over the gulch. The image was a bit warped about the edges but quite clear in the middle.

"What if they see it and, you know, shoot at it or something?" Zac asked. "Just—out of fear that it might be an attack on them."

"It's actually quite small, not much larger than your fist. It also cloaks itself, changing its appearance to match the background as it goes. It will come quite close to them . . . and will likely remain unnoticed."

The flying point of view moved toward a metallic ziggurat shape on the basin of the gulch. A ramp was extended from the graduated pyramid, and a man in red armor stood there, with another, smaller figure wearing a spray-on suit. Nearby were several other men. Zac knew none of them except—

"Rans Veritas! There he is!"

"You know them, then?"

"I know that one—the oldest one there. The one limping around and waving his arms. He's the crook who got me started on this expedition. He must've been playing both ends against the middle . . . Wait, what's that?"

A flying platform had entered their point of view, was hovering near the ramp, settling down. Two bulky men in tinted armor rode on it—and standing between them—

"Cal! Marla!"

"Who are you referring to?"

"My wife! My son! That's them between the canned soldiers on the platform there. You've gotta let me go to them. I can't believe they're this close and I can't let them know I'm here . . ."

"Soon, they'll either know you're here—or it won't matter."

"Dammit, Crannigan, that's just dumb!"

Roland was arguing with Crannigan as the platform came in, behind him. He didn't look at it as it came in. He was focused on Crannigan. Rans Veritas and Rosco stood behind Crannigan. Gorman and his red elite were standing at the foot of the orbiter ramp to Roland's left.

Roland had the Eridian shotgun in his hand as he spoke—not threatening anyone with it, but keeping it ready. "If you blast your way into that thing you'll lose billions of dollars in retro-engineering fees! You'll wreck it, Scrap! We got to go in with those canned soldiers of Gorman's, use as little force as possible. That thing's got some kind of automated defenses—we can take those out. If there's anyone in there, we keep 'em alive that way—and we preserve all that tech."

Gorman was standing by, chewing his lip, as if not sure which course to take himself. His red-armored elite bodyguard stood still as a statue just behind him.

"Too dangerous," Crannigan insisted. "We don't know what that thing's capable of. It's glowing a little more all the time—like it's coming back online. I say we fry it from a distance, then pick up the pieces. There'll be plenty left over."

"Roland!" called someone behind him

Roland frowned, hearing Cal's voice, and turned—stared at Cal and Marla on the platform between the armored elite guards. "What the hell! What are they doing here?" His hand tightened on his gun.

"Oh no, not the kid again," Rans Veritas groaned, seeing Cal.

"We found these two gogglin' down at the crash site," said the canned soldier in silver.

"Then you did well to bring them here," Gorman said, stepping up to inspect the prisoners.

That's what they were. Prisoners. Roland knew it instantly—the canned soldiers had taken Cal and Marla prisoner. He knew that Atlas wouldn't want to deal with other claims on the crash site. No matter what Marla said, they'd be afraid she'd make a claim because she was Zac's wife. She'd told him the whole story. And that history suggested to Roland that she'd probably end up dead, in the hands of Gorman and Crannigan.

"You're Mrs. Finn, I think," Gorman said, looking her over. "Somewhat the worse for wear. What can you tell us about your husband—and the crash site. Did he get there alive? Is he there still?"

"I don't know," she said. "I lost touch with him."

Roland figured she didn't want to tell Gorman what Berl had said. She knew she couldn't trust these men.

"You are, I think, holding something back, Mrs. Finn," Gorman observed, smiling faintly. "I'm going to have to insist you tell us what that is."

She shrugged, looking at Roland. He was trying to figure out which way to jump.

"Take her in the ship, we'll interrogate her there," Gorman said, as if he were telling a mover where to put a cardboard box.

The silver-tinted canned soldier put his hand on her arm—

Cal shoved at the man's arm. "Back off my mom!"

Roland smiled. Some sand, all right.

"It's all right, Cal," Marla said, faintly. "Maybe . . . maybe they'll help us."

Roland shook his head. He knew better. "Gorman—this woman and her son are friends of mine. You need me here. Leave them alone. They're under my protection."

"You want to work for us, you let me call the shots, Roland," Gorman said, turning to him—his eyes as dead as his voice.

"Let it go, Roland," Crannigan said.

Roland shook his head. "No. She and the kid stay with me."

"You're becoming tiresome, Roland," Gorman said warningly.

"You better listen to me about that ship," Roland said, hoping to shift the conversation. "It's idiotic to blast your way into the thing."

"Don't listen to him, he's up to something!" Rans Veritas piped up. Everyone ignored him.

"You've just about convinced me to do the opposite of whatever you advise, Roland," Gorman said. "Blue, move those two into the ship . . ."

The armored elite shoved Cal and Marla off the scout platform, so they stumbled, Marla falling. Cal helped her up. He mouthed silently at Roland, *Give me a gun.*

318 | JOHN SHIRLEY

Roland shook his head. He turned to Gorman. "I'm not letting this go on. Your armored tuna cans can get me, Gorman—but not before I make you into fried executive."

Crannigan raised his own Eridian weapon. "Okay that's it, you've bucked us enough. Get out of the way or go down, Roland!"

Gorman licked his lips, clearly afraid of being caught in the cross fire. He backed toward the ramp. The red-tinted elite stepped in front of him.

"That guy won't get you up the ramp safely," Roland said. "Not when I've got this weapon. Ricochet rounds. Trust me. But I'll tell you what. I've got a score to settle with Crannigan here. You let us duke it out. You go along with whoever ends up breathing."

Gorman paused, and looked thoughtful. "That would give me some satisfaction. I'm sick of you both. But hand to hand. Knives. I don't want to have to duck stray rounds."

Roland nodded. "Works for me."

Crannigan hesitated—then nodded.

Gorman and his red armored elite took their places at Roland's left, near the ramp to the orbiter; the other two canned soldiers stood near the platform, on either side of Cal and Marla, lined up to watch the fight.

Roland figured he couldn't trust Gorman to abide by any deal. But this would win him time, get rid of Crannigan—if he came out of the fight ahead—and he knew how watching a fight could hypnotize men, for a few moments, get them to let down their guards. He might be able to grab Gorman and get him, Cal, and Marla on the platform, use it for an escape. The armored elite wouldn't shoot at him once he had Gorman. They were conditioned to protect him.

First, he had to set it up—get them off guard. Which meant taking down Crannigan.

He tossed his gun aside, trusting Crannigan would do the same thing.

Crannigan stared at him. He looked at his gun. Then pride forced the issue. Crannigan dropped his gun too.

Roland and Crannigan each drew a combat knife from their boot sheaths and crouched, facing one another. Crannigan grinned. "I guess we do have unfinished business at that, Roland. Let's do this thing."

Rosco and Rans Veritas were behind Crannigan, backed up a few strides. *Keep the fight circling,* Roland thought. He'd take down Crannigan first, then he'd rush past him, grab Gorman. With luck.

Crannigan feinted at him—the knife blade slashed at Roland's face. He evaded it easily, stepped back, then feinted in return to keep Crannigan from rushing him.

"What is this barbaric idiocy?" Marla demanded, watching with disbelief as the two men circled one another.

"You've already explained it," Gorman said, amused. "Barbaric idiocy. But it *is* entertaining . . ."

That's when Crannigan made his move, telegraphing it by snarling—Roland would have sidestepped him but he stumbled on the loose rocks. Crannigan rushed in, tried to slip past Roland's knife, his own blade hooking up toward Roland's ribs, left fist slamming into Roland's body. Roland grunted, let Crannigan's momentum carry him back—Crannigan tackling Roland, even as Roland twisted to avoid the knife. Roland fell onto his back and Crannigan struck, his blade slicing through Roland's jacket, barely cutting his side, almost burying itself in the rocky soil with a *chunk* sound. Crannigan had Roland down, the arm with Roland's knife hand pushed aside by Crannigan's shoulder, so Roland couldn't stab in at him.

Crannigan gnashed his teeth at Roland's throat. Roland could feel the merc's spittle, his hot breath, heard the clack of the teeth not quite connecting, then he got his legs under him, used all his strength to tip Crannigan over . . .

The two men were rolling, each one holding the other's knife hand. This wasn't working out as Roland had hoped. Roland found himself on the bottom again but he'd got his right knee up between them, forced Crannigan back—then shoved hard with his boot into the middle of Crannigan's chest.

"Shit!" Crannigan said, going over backward, and seeming surprised by Roland's strength.

Roland was up in a flash, feeling the killing rage in him, the warrior's energy that seemed to make the world go into slow motion around him.

Crannigan was up almost as quickly but Roland was already rushing in, grabbing Crannigan's knife hand, using his own knife to slash blur-fast up, driving the blade in under Crannigan's ribs. Roland could feel the tip push through skin, muscle, tissue—and he felt it when it pierced the hard muscle of Crannigan's heart. Crannigan screamed—and Roland whispered in his ear, "That's for McNee."

He twisted the knife, then shoved the collapsing Crannigan so that he was flung into Rans Veritas and Rosco, the two men knocked down by the spasming body.

Roland was already turning, bounding past the elite in

the red armor, grabbing the surprised Gorman around the waist. He kept going, swinging Gorman around, almost like a man with a woman in a dance move, and brought his knife blade, still bloody with Crannigan's life, up under Gorman's throat.

"I told you, Gorman, they're under my protection and they stay with me!" Roland bellowed. "Cal, get your mom on that platform!"

The three armored elites—red, blue, and silver—were swinging their weapons toward Roland.

"No, no, hold your fire, wait for your moment!" Gorman yelled. "You'll hit me with those things!"

Roland edged toward the scout platform. Cal and Marla were hurrying onto it.

And then . . . Rans Veritas grabbed Crannigan's fallen Eridian rifle . . .

"No, Rans!" Rosco shouted.

"Shut up," Rans snarled, face twitching. "He'll ruin everything; he'll bring a thousand people here and they'll take it all away from me!"

He raised the rifle to his shoulder and Rosco said, "No, dammit, you're gonna hit the boss!" Rosco tried to wrestle it away but got in the way of the muzzle. Rans pulled the trigger and Rosco was caught point-blank in the energy burst—turning to hot red ash, falling away.

Rans pointed the Eridian rifle at the platform just as Roland dragged Gorman onto it beside Marla and Cal.

"Stop him!" Gorman shrieked, staring at Rans. "Stop that idiot, he'll kill me!"

The armored red elite turned and fired his weapon at Rans—blasting him to shreds in one powerful multishot burst. But not before Rans fired again as Marla threw the switch to make the scout platform rise into the air. The flying vehicle rose up crookedly, wobbling under her inexpert control and the blast from the Eridian rifle caught the bottom of the scouter platform, but it was enough to shatter the pulsers, which gushed purple sparks and then went dark. The platform crashed down . . . then, its fuel banks exploded.

"No!" Zac shouted, inside the alien. He'd watched the entire scene from the observation node, just ten meters from the platform. "They're going to die, they're—you've got to do something! Kill me but let them go!"

"My decision is made," said the alien. *"I've seen that Hidden Thing of Interest in the man Roland, and in the boy, and to some extent in you. Observe the floor at your feet."*

Zac felt the chair let go and he stood up, staring at an irising hole in the pearly floor of the chamber. From it emerged something that looked like a transparent football; it was only slightly smaller, and the same shape. In its center was a restless light, a kind of miniature star.

"Pick it up. Then you will be picked up. You'll be carried to the scene. You can use it to destroy the three men in armor, if you pick your time. But they are powerful—they cannot be easily killed. Strike the weapon hard with both hands, onto the ground, when you are ready. I will be departing within minutes. Good luck—as you dumbasses say."

Zac picked up the transparent, football-shaped object— it felt like hard plastic under his hands, and weighed about a kilogram. It seemed filled with a translucent, iridescent liquid that rippled with energy from the miniature star at its center.

He felt something clasp him under the arms and lift him in the air. He looked up to see the monitor, flying upward toward the ceiling . . . which opened, a doorway where none had been before.

Zac said nothing as he went. He did not feel like thanking the alien.

Marla was kneeling next to Roland, on the ground next to the smoking, broken scouter platform. Roland lay on his back, eyes closed. Blood trickled from his nose. He'd stepped in front of her to catch the brunt of the explosion when the platform got hit.

She lifted Roland's heavy head into her lap. Blood trickled from his nose and the corner of his mouth. "Roland?" Was he alive? She wasn't sure. He was a magnificent man. He'd done everything he could for Cal. She found herself doing something she didn't believe in. Praying for him.

Cal knelt on the other side. "Mom? Is he dead?"

Shadows fell over them. She looked up to see Gorman brushing himself off, smoothing his hair, apparently unhurt. With him were the three men in their colored armor.

"Oh I do hope he's alive," Gorman said. "I really am not going to be happy until I have taught him a lesson about manhandling me."

"Last lesson he'll ever learn," said the elite in red armor.

Gorman turned toward his bodyguards. "You three aren't much good. You should've kept an eye on him."

"Never saw anybody move that fast before," the canned soldier in red admitted.

"What about these two, the kid and the bitch," the blue soldier said.

"Oh, we'll have to get rid of them, they're just

too problematic," Gorman said, matter-of-factly. "First, let's . . ."

"What the hell is that?" the silver soldier said, pointing.

They all looked. And saw the delta-shaped creature flying toward them, like a giant manta ray but with tentacles in front drooping down. And in its tentacles it carried a man.

"Dad!" Cal shouted, jumping up.

The monitor approached the dumbfounded onlookers, and lowered Zac to within a few steps of the armored elite and Gorman. Its tendrils released him, withdrew, and the delta-shaped creature backed away.

"Shoot that thing down!" Gorman said. "And get that artifact!"

The blue elite was aiming his rifle—he fired, an energy bullet streaked after the monitor, and glanced off it, doing no appreciable damage. It kept going—and within two seconds they lost sight of it, in the broken shell of the cinder cone.

"Cal!" Zac said as the boy started toward him. "Stay back! Marla, hold him back for his own safety!"

Marla stepped up behind Cal and dragged him back. "Cal—your dad knows what he's doing . . ." She hoped.

Zac looked at her sadly. "I'm sorry I got you into this, Marla. I'm sorry about all of it. I'm sorry we've fallen down here. I'm going to make up for it."

The elite in blue aimed his weapon at Zac. "Put that artifact down and come over here," he said.

"I'll bring it to you," Zac said. "I'll trade it for my family's safety." After a moment, as he started toward them, he added, quietly, "In a way."

He was near the three armored soldiers when Gorman suddenly said, "Wait—I don't like this. Red, Blue—all of you. Get over there and take that thing away from him. Don't damage it—it's valuable. Take it and subdue him."

The blue, the silver, and the red stepped toward him.

Zac yelled, "Cal?"

"Yeah, Dad?"

"I'm proud of you! Now you and your mother—*get down!*"

Zac's voice left no doubt. Cal grabbed Marla and both of them ducked behind the remains of the platform as Zac, with the elite soldiers closing in around him, smashed the football-shaped transparent artifact onto the stony ground, as the alien had told him . . .

The artifact shattered, and the liquid inside it instantly vaporized, exposing the miniature star to the air—Marla looked up just in time to see a bubble of intense blue light splashing outward, expanding, turning the armored men and Zac into silhouettes . . . and consuming them.

They didn't even have time to scream. The air, riven by the powerful energy pulse, shrieked for them.

Zac's body was a standing, glowing coal in the shape of a man—and then it disintegrated, blown into phosphorescent dust.

The armor on the three men was melting away—boiling the men inside as it went. But they were already dead . . .

Gnarled, blackened outlines of the armor remained standing, with the bones of the men inside like perverse sculptures. Their skulls, eye sockets smoking, staring out where their helmets had been.

Gorman was staggering, his hands over his eyes. He turned toward Marla—and she saw that his eyes had been melted from his head. "I . . . I can't see . . ."

He fell to his knees, hands over his face, and rocked there, moaning. "Help me!"

"Dad?" Cal got up and walked toward the spot, right past Gorman. Marla went after him. Smoke stunned her eyes.

Zac was gone.

"He's just . . . gone, Cal." She could hardly believe it herself. Zac—snuffed out from existence in a second. "He died. Burned up. He had some kind of explosive from the ship. He sacrificed himself to save us . . ."

Cal turned to her, weeping, and she held him close.

After a few moments, Marla heard a deep-throated groan and turned to see Roland sitting up, one hand to his head. "Feel like I was kicked in the head by Skagzilla . . ."

"Roland!" Cal blurted. He ran to him. "You're okay?"

"Wouldn't go that far. Nothing a little Dr. Zed won't fix. I'll be right as rain if I . . ." He stared at the remains of the armored elite, and the blinded Atlas exec. "What the hell happened?"

Marla shook her head. "Hard to explain. Zac was brought by . . . by something. Out of the alien crash site. He had a weapon. He got rid of the men in the armor. But we lost him. Gorman's blind . . ." She looked toward Gorman, who was groaning, muttering, hugging himself. "And maybe out of his mind."

"Yeah? Sounds like your husband found an ally. Must've impressed somebody . . ."

"He impressed me, anyhow," said Berl, as he came out

from behind a cluster of boulders on the edge of the gulch. He was shaking his shaggy head in dull amazement. "Zac and me had our differences, but he was a good man. I got here just in time to see him makin' that big flash of light and then those canned soldiers getting cooked—"

Suddenly the ground began to shake. The air shook with it; the volcanic cone, rising at the end of the gulch, quivered within itself. Then something floated out of the natural amphitheater formed by the shell. Something enormous that shone like molten silver as it came into the sunlight. It was shaped like a softly contoured hourglass, translucent and iridescent, glimmering inside with miniature stars. Sheathed in a violet energy field, it floated over the debris field . . . and suddenly the artifacts in the debris field flew upward, tumbling end over end, spinning as they went, and merged seamlessly with their gigantic progenitor.

Marla, Cal, Berl, and Roland stared. Gorman only groaned and rocked on his knees, bloody hands over his eye sockets.

Marla could make out the shape of the delta-like object that had carried Zac to them—it was limned into the side of the giant flying object, seemed to have melded with it. She could feel the regard of the creature, gazing down at her.

An insight came to her, then. The frustrated exobiologist in her spoke up. "Oh—it's not a spaceship. That's . . . an animal. I mean—an organism. A creature! An intelligent being! It's . . . its own spaceship!"

"You could be right," Roland said, getting up to stare at the thing.

"Damn right she is!" Berl said. "Look at that—it's alive!"

It moved slowly toward them, humming, whispering without words, and hovered about three hundred meters overhead. They heard a voice in their heads say, *"Try not to be such dumbasses. Have the courage to find your light."*

Then it receded, into the sky, with no visible means of acceleration. It was as if it were falling—*up*. It fell upward, into the gray-blue heavens—and vanished in the mists of the upper atmosphere, beginning its long journey home.

EPILOGUE

M arla felt strange, waiting for Roland in front of the orbiter, as dusk extended the shadows and cooled the air. She stood with her arms around Cal—who kept staring at the seared spot where his father had died. She wondered if she and Cal would ever completely get over this planet.

"The orbiter's ready, and the arrangements are made with Atlas," Roland said, coming out of the metallic step pyramid of the shuttle. Berl shuffled about with his hands in his pockets, staring at his feet, looking uncomfortable. Nearby were several fresh graves, oblong mounds of piled up gravel. The melted outlines of the elite soldiers' armor, inhabited only by bones, still stood where they'd burned, like a melancholy monument. "All you have to do is close the hatch, take your seats in the cabin, and it'll do the rest. It'll dock for you, right inside the starship's shuttle hangar— the whole thing."

"Can we . . . trust them?" Marla asked. "Atlas?"

"They made a deal with me. I'm—a former employee. I know the starship commander. Old friend of mine. I trust him. We bring them Gorman—and one of the two artifacts left, the ones Berl had. That's the deal. And they give you a ride to your next stop. Xanthus. They'll get you there."

"But they sabotaged the DropCraft," Berl said suddenly. "Zac told me about it."

Roland shook his head. "Commander says no. Says there's traces of some outside transmission. We think that was the alien—it was watching for crafts sending homing signals to its area. It transmitted over rides. Took over the security bots . . . Trying to keep people from interfering with it, when it was so close to leaving, I'd guess."

"Xanthus, huh?" Berl said. "Mostly water, that planet. Kinda pretty there, though. A lot of tropical islands on that planet and not much else. You might like it."

"Least we can do for Zac," Marla said sadly. "It was his dream to resettle there."

Cal was gazing at Roland, his eyes moist. "You could go with us. There's a lotta work there. We could be partners again."

Roland smiled sadly. "I'll see you again, partner. But . . . I'm staying, for now. I've got a lot of missions to run on this big ball of confusion for a while yet . . ."

Cal swallowed and looked toward the lander. "How's . . . the 'suit'?"

"Gorman? He's sedated. Bandaged up. I expect they'll grow him some new eyes. But he's maybe damaged in some other way they won't be able to fix."

"Screw him," Cal said, shrugging. "If he'd done things differently my dad wouldn't have had to die."

Marla nodded. Cal was going to be a handful on Xanthus.

"It's ready to go," Roland said. "Just—head on into the shuttle, take your seats."

"Hey—*Bizzy!*" Berl yelled.

They looked around to see the drifter stumping toward them down the gulch, swaying along, eyes glowing.

"What *is* that?" Cal asked, aghast and fascinated both. "It looks like a giant daddy longlegs—but . . . its body is . . . huge!"

Roland grabbed his Eridian rifle from its strap-down on his back, swung it toward Bizzy—but Berl stepped up and pushed his rifle down. "Hold your fire, there, pal. I think I might have my ol' buddy back." He strode confidently toward the drifter and whistled, chirped, murmured to it.

It clicked happily back at him and bobbed assent on its stiltlike legs.

"Ha!" Berl said, gleefully, as he turned to them. "You see that? That alien's gone and Bizzy's free now! He's back with me! We're pards again!"

Roland chuckled. "That's an, uh, imposing ally you have there . . ."

"Could be yours too, pal!" Berl said, grinning at Roland. "I've had my eye on you! I've got a place out in the country I was fixing to show Zac—a kind of oasis, it is. Safe and green and pure. Make a fine home base. I'll need a partner there. I've got a plan for finding Eridian treasure, tell you about it on the way."

Roland shrugged. "Sure. Why not. We'll talk it over."

He turned to Cal, put out his big hand—and Cal shook it gravely. Marla felt her heart wrench. It was as if Cal was losing a second father.

"I'll see you again, partner, I promise," Roland said.

"Wait—Mom, I promised him a reward!"

"Kid, forget it," Roland said.

"I was thinking about that," Marla said. "There's a lot of money, taken from Grunj—it's buried under the floorboards of a shack on the Trash Coast." She gave him directions. "It's all yours. And Berl's."

Roland nodded, looking steadily at her. "Thanks. Maybe I'll use it to visit Xanthus sometime . . ."

"Roland . . ." Marla wasn't sure exactly how to express what she wanted to ask him. "Why do you have to stay on this planet? It's so *harsh*."

Roland shrugged ruefully. "Well I'll tell you—out here, a man never has to get bored, never has to feel stuck in one place. Out here—there's always a mission. On this world"—he turned and looked at the rugged landscape— "a man is free. Really free." He smiled at them. "Gotta go. I'm burning daylight."

He nodded to Cal, and turned to walk away with Berl and Bizzy. Marla and Cal watched till they were out of sight.

Then she took her son's hand, and they went up the ramp. At the top of the ramp they stopped to look toward the place where Zac had died. "Bye, Dad," Cal said, his voice hoarse.

They went into the shuttle, found the main cabin, took their places. The seats strapped them in, they triggered takeoff, and the ramp drew into the orbiter. The hatch shut, and an impersonal robotic voice announced, "*Prepare for orbital acceleration.*"

The orbiter shuttle vibrated, whined—and lifted off. Ten minutes later they were in orbit, feeling light, and a little lost, though they were headed right for where they'd longed to be: a ship that would take them away from Pandora.

Marla and Cal looked through the viewscreen at the curve of the planet, receding below, glowing like a dying ember against the dark of space.

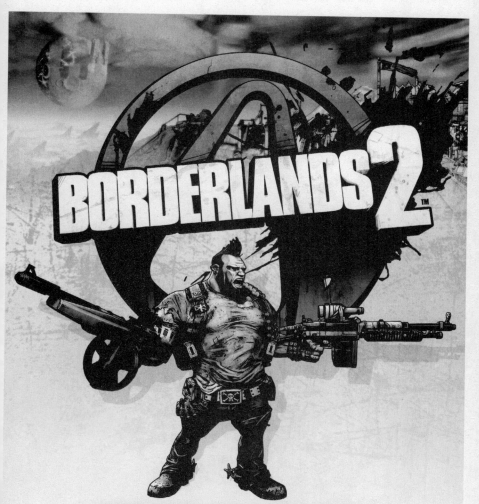

RETURN TO PANDORA
COMING SOON
WWW.BORDERLANDS2.COM